A DOSE
OF DEATH

a Helen Binney mystery

Gin Jones

This book is dedicated to Jack and Maude Perry
for all the shared holidays.

CHAPTER ONE

———

If there was anything that annoyed Helen Binney more than people who tried to help her without waiting to be asked, it was people who were cheerful and efficient while they were providing that unwanted help.

At the moment, it was Helen's nieces who were irritating her. Laura Gray, the younger one, was cheerfully fluffing the sofa's pillows, while her older sister, Lily Binney, efficiently collected the used mugs from the coffee table and carried them to the kitchen sink. The two young women puttered around the cottage's great room that encompassed both the living room and kitchen/dining areas. They tidied things that didn't need tidying, put away things that Helen preferred left out, and just generally turned the comfortable space into a sterile box.

Helen watched her nieces from the safety of her recliner. "I *like* living here all by myself. It's a nice change for me after twenty years of running the governor's mansion. Go away and leave me alone."

"You don't mean that." Laura's response was as emphatic as her pillow-fluffing and rug-straightening. "We just got here."

Lily returned from the far side of the kitchen island. "She does mean it, Laura. But it doesn't matter. It's obvious that Aunt Helen can't live here alone, so she'll have to move in with one of us, where we can take care of her."

"You're talking as if I'm old and decrepit," Helen said. "I may be retired, but it was early retirement. I don't even qualify to join AARP."

"You're old in spirit," Lily said, coming to a stop behind the sofa, where she could stare down her aunt. "You always have been, according to Dad. And you admitted you were decrepit when you started to use a cane."

It wasn't her mind that was betraying her, it was her body, ravaged by a stupid, unpredictable disease. She could still count on her clear skin, thick brown hair and sharp brown eyes, but the rest of her was falling apart. Helen automatically glanced at the front door, where her cane hung from the knob, so she wouldn't forget to take it with her whenever she went out. It was a practical solution, but she hated the constant reminder of her limitations. Ever since she'd hit forty, her lupus had been taunting her, inflaming her joints, ruining her mood and stealing her independence.

"That's no way to talk to your aunt," she said, "calling me old and decrepit."

"It's the truth." Lily was naturally slender, with model-sharp cheekbones and an equally sharp mind that never forgot anything. "You're the one who told us always to tell the truth, never to hide behind the social lies that you were so good at before you decided to become a hermit."

"I was wrong." Apparently there was something worse than receiving unsolicited and unwanted help: having her own lectures quoted back at her. "Lies are good. You should tell more of them."

Laura, as soft around the edges as the pillow she hugged to her chest, sank onto the sofa. "It would be so nice if you came to live with me and Howie. I've always wanted an extended family for my children."

"You don't have any children yet," Helen said. "And when you do, you won't want me anywhere near them. Children hate me."

"I know that's not true," Laura said, her sweet, oval face becoming even more earnest. "Lily and I always adored you when we were children."

Helen adored her nieces in return, but she wasn't foolish enough to admit it right now. If she showed the least sign of weakness, she would find herself surrounded by grand-nieces and grand-nephews, and Auntie Helen would spend the rest of her life as an unpaid babysitter. She'd worked hard for the last twenty years, coddling one bunch of babies—her ex-husband and his cronies—and she wasn't about to replace them with a new set. No, her job was done, her career as the state's first lady was over, and she had every right to enjoy her retirement. Alone.

Laura smiled encouragingly, and there were still traces of the chubby little round face she'd had as a toddler.

Despite herself, Helen said, "I might be willing to visit you and your myriad of children occasionally."

"That would be lovely." By the look in Laura's eyes, she'd forgotten she was here to browbeat her aunt, and instead was daydreaming about the dozen or more babies she planned to create with her Howie.

"Never mind the babies," Lily said. "You need to decide which of us you'll live with."

"I'll disinherit both of you if you don't stop this foolishness right now."

Lily shrugged. "You probably disinherited us years ago and willed all your money to charity."

"You'll find out eventually." Most of her substantial estate was going to charity, but the girls had also been provided for. They obviously didn't consider being disinherited much of a threat, presumably because they knew she cared about them too much to actually do it, even if they did persist in helping her against her will. Whatever little leverage the threat gave her, though, was better than nothing. She was *not* moving out of her cottage.

"We don't need your money, Aunt Helen." Laura absently re-fluffed a pillow. "We have perfectly good jobs."

"Then how do you find the time to come bother me?" Helen said, struggling to get out of the recliner. This had gone far enough. It was time to show them to the door. "You should be at work, not spending half the day coming here to bother me."

"We don't work on Sundays." Lily said. "You know, forgetting the day of the week is one of the signs of mental disorientation."

"You are not going to commit me to a mental institution just because I sometimes lose track of the days of the week now that I'm not tied to a calendar." Helen leaned against the arm of the recliner, waiting for the ache in her hip to subside enough to allow her to walk without a pronounced limp. "Especially since I know that you work plenty of weekend hours, Lily Binney, so it's perfectly logical for me to expect you to be working on a Sunday."

"Very good." Lily smiled, her face still sharp, but no longer quite as worried. Lily had never had a sweet little baby face. By the time Laura was born, Lily had already looked and acted like a miniature adult. "You're still mentally alert."

"If anyone even thinks of committing me," Helen said, "I'll get out my Rolodex. You don't want to see what happens then."

"I know what you can do with a few phone numbers," Lily said. "I'm sure it's enough to strike terror in anyone's heart."

Laura ran out of pillows to fluff. "We just want to help, Aunt Helen."

"We don't want to commit you," Lily said, letting some of her frustration show, "but we really think you should come live with one of us so you aren't alone. It isn't safe for you here."

Neither of the girls would be easy to dissuade from their current plan. Lily was single-minded and thick-skinned. Laura was easily distracted, but also easily hurt in confrontations.

"I'm perfectly fine here." Why couldn't they see how happy she was here? The cottage had always been her refuge from her public life as the governor's wife. Vacation time spent here had given her the strength to get through the rest of the year, when she'd worked long hours charming all of her husband's constituents and cronies as he worked his way up the political food chain. "I've spent a good part of every summer here alone for a dozen years. You weren't worried then."

"It's different now," Laura said. "You're older."

"I'm forty-five," Helen said, struggling not to snap at the sensitive Laura. "That doesn't make me feeble."

"No," said Lily. "Your lupus flare-ups make you feeble."

Laura, who should have been used to her sister's blunt comments, still looked shocked. Laura patted Helen's arm. "It's just that you could have been hurt badly when you fell last week, and no one would have known you were in trouble."

"I'm perfectly fine," Helen lied. Her hip still didn't feel right, even though the bruise had faded, and the x-rays had ruled out a fracture. Standing just these few minutes, even leaning against the chair, had caused it to ache again.

"That's not what Dr. Jamison said," Lily insisted. "Your hip joint is already a mess with all the inflammation, and he wants to replace it before it's too late."

"Surgeons always want to chop you up, with the least little provocation," Helen said, although she knew they were probably right about the surgery. "What ever happened to doctor-patient confidentiality, anyway?"

"Dr. Jamison is just trying to help you," Laura said.

"Heaven save me from people trying to help me," Helen muttered. "Looks like I'm going to have to get out the Rolodex after all and call my lawyer."

"You don't have a lawyer any more," Lily said. "You only threaten to call one whenever you've run out of logical arguments. I still remember when you threatened to hire a lawyer to force me to eat my dinner."

Trust Lily to remember that. She'd been all of about four at the time, and Helen had been terrified her niece would starve to death while in Helen's custody, since Lily had refused to eat anything at all for twenty-four hours. Lily had been right not to eat, even if she'd been unable to explain why at the time. It had turned out that she had a stomach virus that would have been much worse if she'd eaten even a fraction of what Helen had pushed at her.

Now was not the time to dwell on past mistakes. She couldn't lose this battle. "This time I mean it. I'm calling my lawyer."

Helen shook off Laura's hand and headed across the great room for her desk, forcing herself not to limp, despite the pain in her hip.

"You don't have to do anything desperate." Laura trailed behind her. "Come live with me and Howie. We'll feed you and drive you where you want to go and spend lots and lots of time with you."

Helen was horrified by the prospect of all that help and would have said so if she hadn't known her niece was only offering what Laura, herself, would have found appealing in the circumstances.

Helen turned to face her loving, helpful nieces. "I've got everything I need right here, thank you. Including a bunch of things neither one of you can provide."

"Like what?" Laura asked.

"Solitude, for one," Helen said. "Peace and quiet, and no one to distract me from my hobbies."

"I didn't know you had any hobbies," Laura said. "Maybe we can do them together. I was thinking about learning to knit so I can make baby clothes."

Lily would never believe Helen was taking up knitting. She needed to come up with something that at least sounded plausible. Helen glanced in the direction of the desk cabinetry that lined the side wall and thought of the boxes hidden inside there, filled with the detritus of her political career. "Scrapbooking," she said. "I'm going to do something with all the pictures and newspaper clippings from my days in the governor's mansion."

"You'll hate scrapbooking," Lily said, ignoring her sister's disapproving look. "I'm giving you one last chance to decide for yourself which one of us you want to live with."

Even if Helen didn't want to live alone, it was an impossible choice. Laura would smother her with attention, and Lily would try to dictate Helen's every move, until one of them snapped. She crossed the room to settle back into her recliner, hoping her face didn't reveal the relief she felt at getting off her feet. "I am not living with either one of you. That's final."

"Something's got to be done." Lily stared at Helen for several long moments, apparently testing their respective resolves. Helen held herself still, refusing to blink, despite the sharp pain in her hip, vaguely aware of Laura's anxious glances back and forth between her sister and her aunt.

Finally, Lily picked up her purse with a frustrated huff. "If you won't move in with one of us, how about getting someone to come live with you?"

"I'm too old for a roommate." Helen caught sight of Laura's face going from worried to dreamy. "And I'm not interested in a lover."

"Why not?" Laura said. "Howie's got an uncle who's a widower. You'd love him."

"No matchmaking," Helen said. "Either one of you tries that, and I'll move to California, and your children will never, ever meet their great-aunt."

Laura looked stricken, and Helen tried not to care.

"What about a visiting nurse, at least?" Lily said. "Someone to bring you meals and monitor your prescriptions and just check in on you, to make sure you haven't fallen again."

"I don't need a babysitter," Helen said.

Laura, whose hurt feelings always healed as quickly and easily as they were bruised, perched on the arm of the recliner and leaned in for a hug. "I'm sure we could find a nice, helpful nurse who would stop by to visit you a few times a week. As long as you're okay, she'd just say hi and then leave right away. That wouldn't be too disruptive for you."

"Forget it, Laura. She isn't going to be reasonable," Lily said, heading for the front door.

"Leaving so soon?" Helen didn't trust Lily's surrender. She was a lot tougher and more single-minded than her sister, at least when it came to any subject other than babies.

"Lily is getting her suitcase out of the car." Laura's voice sped up, the words running together the way they always did when she was trying to forestall an argument. "She's going to move in with you. See, I can't, because of Howie. He wouldn't like it if I left him alone, and we're trying to get pregnant, so of course I have to be home when he is, and Lily isn't married, and she only has her job (Okay it's a demanding one.), but she does come home for at least a few hours a night, and so she's got to be the one who moves in with you, not me, although I would if it weren't for Howie and making a baby."

Laura ran out of breath and words, and looked away guiltily, but she didn't move from her perch on the arm of the recliner, effectively trapping Helen. Through the front window, she could see Lily wrestling a suitcase out of her trunk. She had to be bluffing. Except the luggage looked heavy, far more than she'd need for a single night's stay. If it was a bluff, it was a convincing one.

Maybe it was time to compromise. It would be easier to keep Lily out now than to evict her once she'd settled in.

First, Helen needed to get away from her reluctant guard. "Why don't you go help your sister with that suitcase?"

As soon as Laura stood up, Helen grabbed the lever to drop the footrest and free herself from the recliner. She met the girls as they returned to the front door, and blocked their re-entry. "Let's talk about a compromise. How often would this nurse person have to visit in a week to make you happy?"

Laura said "three" at the same time Lily said "five."

That was what they'd wanted all along, Helen thought with relief. A visiting nurse. "I could probably live with once a week."

Lily looked at Laura and they both said "three times a week."

Lily's hand tightened on the handle of her suitcase, signaling her intent to drag it over the threshold. "That's our final offer."

"Okay. Three times a week." Helen watched to see if Lily would release her grip on the suitcase. "But the nurse just pops in her head, makes sure I'm breathing and not bleeding, and then she leaves."

"Deal," Lily said, abandoning her suitcase. "We'll find the perfect nurse for you, and I'll take care of the payments through the account I manage for you. You won't have to do anything. You can enjoy your retirement, without any stress whatsoever."

"Right," Laura said. "We're here to help you, after all."

Helen understood, however reluctantly, that they were trying to help her. She even understood that maybe, just maybe, they were right in that she needed to have someone check on her occasionally.

But they didn't have to be so damned cheerful and efficient about it.

* * *

Just three days later, Lily and Laura returned. Helen had hoped it would take weeks, maybe even months, for them to find a visiting nurse, but she had agreed to the plan, and she was prepared to make the best of it, to keep her nieces happy. It was for her own good, after all, and she was confident she could handle the three brief visits each week.

The woman with them was tall, solidly built, and the softness around the edges of her face suggested that she was in her fifties. She wore standard white nurse's clogs, but instead of a white lab jacket or pastel scrubs, she wore bright purple pants and a pink smock printed with purple teddy bears. Even Laura, when she'd been five years old and at the peak of her pink-and-purple phase, would have considered the colors too silly.

Helen stared at the bright teddy bears for another moment. They might actually be a good omen. Lily had told her the nurse specialized in geriatric patients, which, in the absence of an autoimmune disorder specialist on the local agency's staff, was a reasonable choice for someone who could handle the wide variety of symptoms that a system-wide disease like lupus could cause. If the nurse thought her scrubs were appropriate for working with adult patients, though, she was probably as silly as her shirt, and Helen would have her wrapped around her little finger in no time at all. Then she could enjoy her solitude again with minimal interruption and without hurting her nieces' feelings.

She stepped back from the door and let the three women inside, thinking that as soon as Lily and Laura left, Helen would have a nice, little chat with Nurse Goldilocks, and convince her that none of the bears in this cottage were "just right." No, the bears around here had sharp claws, huge teeth, and enough strength to tear a visiting nurse to pieces.

Once everyone was inside and the front door was closed against the chilly morning air, Laura said, "Aunt Helen, this is Melissa Shores. I'm sure you two are going to be the best of friends."

"Pleased to meet you, sweetie," Melissa said, folding Helen into a brief one-armed hug, overwhelming Helen's tense resistance. Finally, Melissa let her go and raised her six-pack of Diet Pepsi to eye level. "If you'll excuse me, though, I'll go put these in the refrigerator. Wouldn't want my soda to get warm."

No problem, Helen thought as she made her way over to the recliner. The woman wasn't going to spend enough time at the cottage to need a drink, warm or cold.

Laura took a seat at the far end of the sofa, leaving the spot closest to Helen empty. Lily remained standing behind her sister's shoulder, and said with fake nonchalance, "Melissa should have a set of keys to the cottage, in case you can't get to the door to let her in. I already gave her mine. The one you gave me a few years ago."

"I remember." Lily had wheedled it out of Helen during a weekend-long visit a couple years ago, and then had stubbornly refused to return it, using one excuse after another. "I gather the key wasn't permanently lost, after all."

"I found it in the last place I looked," Lily said with a straight face, and if Helen hadn't known her so well, she might have believed the innocent act.

"You know we're doing this because we care about you," Laura said.

Helen did know that, but it didn't change how much she hated being seen as needing help. "I suppose it's my own fault that you two turned out so bossy. I was a bad influence on you. I'll never understand why my brother ever let you visit me when you were young and impressionable."

"But we love you, Aunt Helen," Laura said.

Helen felt a brief pang of guilt, and then rallied. "Absence makes the heart grow fonder."

"Aunt Helen's trying to say she loves us too," Lily told her sister as she came around the sofa to pull her to her feet. "We should leave now, though, so she and Melissa can get to know each other."

The nurse was just returning from the kitchen, a soda can in each hand. Melissa saluted the girls with her soda, taking care not to spill the open can. She waited until the front door slammed behind them before turning her attention on her new patient.

Helen stared back. She had better things to do with her life than dealing with a babysitter. How was she going to convince the woman to leave her alone *and* not tattle on her to the girls?

Helen needed to gather more information on Melissa, just as she'd collected information on her husband's allies and enemies in her Rolodex, to find her weak spot. For now, all she was certain of was that the woman was older than herself. Her age probably explained why she was so obviously excited about a light duty assignment. She'd probably spent decades working hard at helping people. People who, unlike Helen, had wanted and needed that help.

Melissa set her two cans on the side table and sank into the sofa. "Now that your lovely nieces are gone, sweetie, we can really get to know each other. It's always hard the first day, to be without your family, dealing with someone new."

"I got over separation anxiety forty years ago," Helen said. "I don't need my nieces to make me feel secure."

"Good, good," Melissa said, sliding to the edge of the sofa, ready to get to her feet. "But I can tell you're nervous, sweetie. How can I help?"

"You can go away," Helen said. "I don't really need any help. I just agreed to hire a visiting nurse to make my nieces happy. All you have to do is pop in, confirm that I'm alive, and then leave."

"Oh, but my contract calls for a minimum one-hour visit," Melissa said. "More if needed."

"I won't tell anyone that you left early," Helen said. "You can bill the agency for your time, and I won't complain. You'll get paid, and I'll be left alone. Everyone wins."

"You want me to not do my job?" Melissa shook her head. "I can't do that. It wouldn't be right."

It figured, Helen thought. She had to get the one virtuous employee left on the planet, someone who was intent on providing an honest hour's work for an honest hour's pay. Helen would just have to make the most of it, looking for an angle to leverage the nurse out of her life.

Melissa didn't need much encouragement to spill her life's story. She had almost thirty years' nursing experience, mostly in geriatric settings, although she'd started at a children's hospital, where apparently her fashion sense had been formed and then frozen in time. Every so often, Melissa paused to chug down her Diet Pepsi. She finished the second can and retrieved a third from the refrigerator, all without ever expecting or even allowing Helen to get in a word herself.

As the mandatory hour ran out, Helen dropped increasingly blunt hints that it was time to leave. Melissa kept chattering as she emptied yet another soda can. Something more than mere words would be necessary to evict her.

Helen might not be able to wrestle the woman out the door, but Melissa had revealed her one weakness: her soda addiction. Empty the remaining cans down the sink, and Melissa would need to leave to replenish her supply. Then Helen could complain to the nursing agency that she didn't trust a nurse who demonstrated such appalling ignorance of all the health risks associated with diet soda. With luck, the new nurse might be more amenable to bribery.

Melissa was recounting a heroic rescue of an elderly patient, who probably hadn't even wanted to be rescued, when Helen decided she'd had enough. Surely, the mandatory hour was up, and if Melissa wasn't leaving, Helen was.

She pulled her cell phone out of her pocket and dialed the number of a car service.

Melissa stood and said, "Excuse me while I get another soda."

Helen waved the woman toward the refrigerator and listened impatiently for the phone call to be answered. The dispatcher picked up on the third ring, and Helen said, "I need a ride."

"Do you have a day in mind?"

"Yes. Today. Now. As soon as possible."

The dispatcher had apparently heard stranger requests, and didn't hesitate. "I'll send someone right away if you'll give me your address."

Helen gave her the information. "Tell the driver to hurry."

"Of course," the dispatcher said. "And where shall I tell him you wish to go?"

"I don't care."

"Excuse me?"

There was no time to explain. In another minute, Melissa would be refueled and watching her reluctant patient. If Helen wanted to leave, she had to go now. "Never mind. I'll tell the driver when he gets here."

"I suppose that will work," the dispatcher said. "He can call us with the itinerary. I'll just need your credit card information. We have a two-hour minimum that has to be paid up front."

Helen gave her the numbers and was hanging up when Melissa settled back on the sofa with two more cans of Diet Pepsi, one on the side table and one in her hand. "Now, where was I?"

"I don't know."

Melissa chugged down more Diet Pepsi while she thought about it, and Helen crossed the room to get her purse from the desk. Her favorite walking cane was right where it was supposed to be, hanging from the doorknob, reminding her that she should take it with her. She didn't use it often, but the last couple weeks her hip had been particularly unstable. Falling flat on her face in the front walkway, with both Melissa and the limo driver watching, would definitely ruin her dramatic exit.

Helen grabbed the cane and purse and carried them over to the window, where she could watch for the limo, while still pretending to listen to the nurse.

"Now I remember what I was talking about," Melissa said, setting down her soda for the moment. She launched another story, which Helen tuned out.

As long as Helen had a car and driver for the next two hours, she might as well do something useful. Mostly, she just needed time to think about how to get Melissa to leave her alone without upsetting her nieces unnecessarily. There had to be a way to offer her nieces some peace of mind, without having to endure Melissa.

She used to have people who could take care of this sort of thing for her, with a single phone call. A brief word with her ex-husband's security staff, or one of the lawyers he kept on retainer, and the problem would have gone away.

That was the answer, Helen thought, suddenly energized. Lawyers. She didn't need a whole fleet of them, like her ex-husband did. A single competent lawyer ought to be enough to handle one highly caffeinated, overly enthusiastic nurse.

A black Lincoln Town Car crunched along the gravel in the driveway, stopping with the passenger door directly lined up with the front path. A bald, wiry, dark-suited man emerged from the driver's side and headed for the cottage's front door.

"I'm going to see my lawyer," Helen said on her way out of the cottage. "Lock up when you leave."

* * *

"Quick, quick." Helen gestured for the driver to return to the front seat without waiting to usher her into the back. "I can close my own door. We need to get out of here before she comes after us."

"Most folks choose a less conspicuous vehicle for a getaway car, you know, but you're the boss." The driver climbed into the front. "For the next two hours, at least. They did tell you it was a two-hour minimum, didn't they?"

"No problem." Helen pulled the door shut behind her before checking over her shoulder at the door to reassure herself Melissa couldn't possibly stop them now. Melissa could call Lily to complain, but it was too late to do anything more than that. "Just start driving."

The driver put the car into gear and started down the driveway. "The dispatcher didn't tell me where we're going."

"To see my lawyer."

"Not planning on suing me, are you?" the driver said with a nervous chuckle.

"I'm not suing anyone at the moment," Helen said, "but it never hurts to be prepared."

The driver reached the end of the driveway. "Which way?"

Instead of answering him, she leaned forward to read his identification card on the dashboard, and said, "Are you from around here, Mr. Clary?"

"Call me Jack," he said. "It's too confusing otherwise. The Clary name is more common around here than Smith or Jones. You'll see, once you get to know the area."

She'd been spending summers here in Wharton for fifteen years now, and it was only now that she realized she didn't know much about the town. She'd always been delivered to the cottage by her husband's staff and then picked up a few weeks later, without ever leaving the property. It was different now. Wharton was her home, not just a vacation spot.

"Do you know any good lawyers?"

"My cousin Hank used this guy named Tate a couple years ago," Jack said. "He must be good, because he kept Hank out of jail, and if anyone deserves to be in jail, it's Hank. Along with his brothers. They'd probably be locked up, too, come to think of it, if they hadn't also hired this Tate guy."

A criminal lawyer wasn't what she'd had in mind—Melissa was a minor nuisance, not a criminal—but if the alternative was going back and being referred to as sweetie or honey or something equally saccharine, she might as well check him out. "Tate it is, then. Take me to his office, please."

Helen watched out the side window as the thick woods of the acreage around her cottage gave way to neighborhoods of large houses and only a few strategically planted saplings, and then finally to urban lots with more paving than grass. She recognized the approach to the center of town, and, while she'd never paid much attention before, it was probably where the local attorneys had their offices.

A few minutes later, Jack parked the limo in front of a weathered-looking Cape, not unlike Helen's own cottage, except that it was on a tiny lot in a more urban zone and no trees. There was a small paved parking area in front, a long handicapped ramp leading up to the main entrance, and a discreet sign on the building that read *Tate & Bancroft, PC, Attorneys At Law.*

The car door swung open, and Jack was standing there, offering Helen his hand to help her out of the back seat. He probably did the same thing for all of his customers, but it only reminded her that she wasn't the same person she'd been before the lupus had started to really act up. Before then, she'd have been out of the vehicle and halfway to the building's entrance by the time the driver could have unbuckled his seatbelt.

It didn't matter so much what Jack thought of her abilities, but lawyers worked in a world where image was everything. Their own image, their client's image, and even the judicial system's image. They knew it, but few realized how much they, themselves, were taken in by appearances and failed to see reality. Chances were that this Tate guy wasn't going to see Helen as the strong, smart, attention-grabbing person she used to be; he was going to see the decrepit, slow, and easy-to-ignore person she'd become. If that was all he saw, he might dismiss her as not worthy of his time.

Jack bent down to look inside the car. "Do you need help?"

"No." The lawyer might not have time to see her without an appointment, but if she didn't at least try to see him, she'd have to find somewhere else to go. She wanted to be sure Melissa would have left before they returned to the cottage. Being rejected by an attorney wasn't as bad as being accepted by Melissa.

Helen slid to the edge of the seat. "I can get out on my own, thank you."

Many people, especially in the service industry, would have insisted on helping, but Jack took a step back. She made a mental note to leave him an extra-large tip, as a thank you for respecting her wishes.

CHAPTER TWO

Helen left Jack to wait for her in the limo, where he was happily playing video games on his phone. She'd also left her cane behind, so her weakness wouldn't be the first thing her new attorney noticed about her.

The small reception area was unoccupied. To Helen's right were a couple leather-upholstered arm chairs that had all seen better days and a faded plaid sofa on the adjoining wall. Directly in front of her, its back to the third wall, was a heavy wood desk that was just large enough to hold the bare minimum needed for a receptionist: multi-line telephone, clunky computer monitor, keyboard, mouse, and phone-message pad.

The chair behind the desk was unoccupied, the computer wasn't humming, and the phone console didn't have a single line lit up. The surface of the desk was so tidy it looked abandoned, rather than temporarily unoccupied while the receptionist went to lunch. Helen looked closer and noticed a light coating of dust on everything.

A loud thump off to her left startled her. She turned to explain that she wasn't snooping or stealing, but had just been looking for some indication that the office was occupied, so she could arrange a consultation. There was no one to explain to, though. No one in the room except herself.

Next came the softer, more protracted sound of a box being slid along carpeting. Helen followed the noise down the hallway that led out of the reception area, hoping that no stairs would be required. Finally, she came to an open doorway. Inside the room, a tall, lean man in a dark blue t-shirt and faded jeans stood with his back to her, emptying desk drawers into moving boxes.

She knocked on his door, and he looked over his shoulder at her. "What can I do for you?"

"I'd like to talk to a lawyer."

"I was one," he said. "The name's Tate. But I'm retired now, so you want to talk to my nephew Adam Bancroft."

He didn't look old enough to be retired. There was a bit of gray in his hair, but he couldn't be any older than she was. Of course, that didn't mean anything; her career was over too. "If you're retired, why is your name still on the sign?"

"Tradition." He pulled another thick pile of papers out of a drawer and tossed them into the remaining space in the box on top of the desk.

"False advertising," Helen said.

"Whatever." He sealed the top of the box. "I'm no longer in the business of arguing, and I never did it unless I was paid. You should talk to my nephew. He's at a closing right now, but he should be back soon."

This whole thing had been a mistake. She should have taken the time to do some real research on the local legal community, instead of coming here on a whim. "It's not that important."

"Interesting." Tate stopped packing and turned to face Helen, leaning back against the desk and peering at her suspiciously. "In my experience, by the time a client gets around to talking to a lawyer, it's already a crisis, not something that can wait. Why don't you tell me what you think isn't so important? If it's that simple, I can probably answer your question right now. If not, I'll pass it on to my nephew for you. He's looking for new clients."

"I'm not ready to hire an attorney yet," Helen said. "I'm just at the point of interviewing candidates."

"One surprise after another." Tate folded his arms over his chest. "Twenty years in practice, and I've never had a client interview me before."

"Who would make an important decision like hiring a lawyer without first getting some background information?"

"Pretty much everyone," Tate said. "They just pick a name at random from the phone book."

"Not terribly businesslike." But, she had to admit, probably no worse than choosing a lawyer based on a stranger's recommendation.

"You're a businesswoman, then?" he said. "And you need a business lawyer?"

"More a general practitioner, I think."

"My nephew's the right person for that. He does corporate, real estate, and probate work." Tate reached behind him to grab a sticky note and pen, clearly no longer intrigued by her situation. "Want me to leave him a message to call you?"

"It really isn't that important."

"At least tell me your name."

Helen opened her mouth to snap at him, to let him know she didn't think that was funny. And then she realized he wasn't joking. For the last twenty years, it had seemed as if everyone had known, if not her first name, at least her last name and her status as first lady of the state. She couldn't remember the last time she'd had to introduce herself to someone who didn't already know who she was, at least in relation to her husband and his political status.

She'd wanted to stand on her own, and now she could. If a prominent local attorney didn't recognize her face, her newly official name wasn't likely to enlighten him, since only the most avid state-politics junkie would connect her maiden name with that of the governor's ex-wife.

"I'm Helen Binney."

She watched him carefully, but Tate wrote down her name with no indication he considered her anything other than the average woman on the street. It was just what she'd wanted, but not as satisfying as she'd expected it would be.

Helen checked her watch. She'd been gone less than thirty minutes so far, probably not long enough for her babysitter to run out of soda. Besides, Helen had already paid for the next ninety minutes of limousine rental. Might as well get her money's worth. "You said business law is your nephew's specialty. What's yours?"

"These days, it's woodworking," Tate said, reaching for another box and throwing things into it at random. "Before I retired, I did criminal defense work and general litigation."

"I don't need a criminal defense lawyer, and I can't imagine I ever will."

"You never know," Tate didn't pause in his packing. "I'm the best around here."

"You might have been once," Helen said. "But you're retired now."

He spared her a glance. "I'd be willing to come out of retirement for an interesting case."

"Like what?"

"The right homicide might do it." Tate closed the box and gave it a push toward the doorway. "There hasn't been an interesting murder around here in decades."

"I'll keep that in mind. If I decide to kill someone, I'll make sure it's an interesting kind of murder." Curious despite herself, Helen asked, "What is a boring murder, anyway?"

"The usual," Tate said, starting to fill another box. "Someone loses his temper over something trivial, bashes a spouse or significant other over the head, and regrets it right away, but then panics and runs away while the victim bleeds to death."

"If I killed someone, it would definitely be an interesting case," Helen said. "I don't have much of a temper, and even if I lost it, I can think of lots of other people I'd rather bash over the head than my ex-husband. At the top of the list right now is my visiting nurse."

"Let me give you some free legal advice, then." Tate turned to face her, abandoning his packing for the moment. "If you've got a hit list, don't write it down. And don't tell me your plans ahead of time. I'm still an officer of the court, and I'd be obliged to turn you in."

"You're just like everyone else I know." She shook her head in fake disappointment. "Always warning me against every little plan I make, never letting me do anything fun."

"Yeah," Tate said with as much sincerity as she'd shown. "Life's unfair like that. I'd never have gone to law school if it weren't for family pressure. I could have been a homeless drifter for the past twenty years, and instead I wasted them practicing law."

"I won't waste any more of your time, then." Helen turned to leave. "I've got a visiting nurse to dispose of. In an interesting manner."

"I appreciate the thought," he said, "but I'm still obliged to advise you not to kill anyone."

Helen retraced her steps to the front door, vaguely disappointed that she couldn't hire Tate. He wasn't like any of the lawyers at her husband's beck and call, but he seemed every bit as competent as they were. If she had him on her side, Melissa would be gone before she could drink another can of soda, and her nieces would be too amused by him to be upset. If Melissa continued to be a problem, Helen would just have to convince Tate to come out of retirement. Preferably without having to kill anyone.

* * *

Over the course of the next two weeks, Helen tried scrapbooking, like she'd told her nieces she'd planned to do. Melissa, a political junkie, helped sort the hundreds of pictures, fascinated by the candid shots of famous politicians.

Helen found them depressing, a reminder that she had nothing to show for twenty years of hard work except a box full of pictures of people she no longer cared about. Thinking she might find scrapbooking more interesting if she actually took the pictures instead of just organizing and embellishing them, she purchased a camera and figured out the basics for using it before her nieces made their regular Saturday lunchtime visit.

Helen had opened the front door to let them in, noticing that her cane wasn't hanging on the doorknob. She must have left it in Jack's Town Car when he'd taken her to the camera shop. She'd have to ask him about it later.

For now, she needed to convince her nieces that Melissa really wasn't working out. Helen snapped pictures of them while explaining how annoying the visiting nurse was. It turned out to be more difficult to put into words than she'd expected. She told them about how Melissa was showing up on days when she wasn't scheduled, letting herself into the cottage with the key that had been given to her only for emergencies. And then there was the blaring of the local talk radio station throughout her entire visit. Helen could have been lying on the floor, slowly dying from internal injuries, having fallen the night before, and she'd have been a goner before Melissa finished adjusting the radio and deigned to notice her patient. Helen had taken to hiding the radio after each visit, but the nurse managed to home in on it with the speed and precision of a GPS tracker.

Laura wavered, but Lily held fast, insisting that those were trivial nuisances, and any replacement would have similar foibles.

There was also the matter of Melissa's clumsiness, but Helen was reluctant to mention those incidents. She couldn't entirely blame the nurse for inadvertently drowning an entire bottle's worth of expensive pills. It had been an accident, after all, something that could have happened to anyone. Never mind that it had been the one drug Helen couldn't ever skip, not even a single dose, without the risk of a serious flare-up. Fortunately, she kept an extra two-week supply in an emergency bag, a habit she'd picked up from the time she'd had to evacuate the governor's mansion once, due to a bomb threat, and they hadn't been allowed back in for a week. And then there was also the time that Melissa had bumped into Helen, knocking her onto the floor. It wasn't exactly Melissa's fault, even if it had caused Helen some bruising and a strained muscle as she struggled to get back to her feet.

Melissa's clumsiness had had more serious consequences than the noisy radio, but Helen was reluctant to mention it. Her nieces might consider the fall, in particular, as proof that she needed round-the clock care. The only thing worse than Melissa's current visits was Melissa visiting even more often.

Laura and Lily had left after lunch, unconvinced of Melissa's evils, and Helen had braced herself for the next unscheduled visit from the nurse. Melissa apparently believed in a day of rest, and didn't show up at the cottage on Sunday, but by Monday morning, the return of the nurse and her soda supplies was inevitable.

Helen put her breakfast dishes into the dishwasher and then puttered around the cottage, tidying it up. Not that there was any real cleaning to do. The place was small enough that it didn't require much maintenance, and a cleaning crew came in once a month to do the things that required mobility or strength.

Finally, Helen tossed aside the dusting cloth, and headed over to her computer to view the pictures she'd taken yesterday. She opened the pictures folder to the first shot: Lily glaring into the camera.

It made her smile, but it wasn't a great picture. It wasn't even a good one. She scrolled through the other shots, and they ranged from out-of-focus to mediocre. What was she doing wrong?

She was still mulling it over when she heard a car in the driveway. A moment later, Melissa was pounding on the front door and shouting, "It's me, Melissa. Come let me in. My hands are full."

Helen pushed herself onto her feet, only then realizing how long she'd been sitting there, poring over the photographs. Her joints had stiffened, and it took a few moments before she was ready to walk across the room. When she finally opened the door, Melissa brushed past her on the way to the refrigerator with the three six-packs she was carrying. The push sent Helen off-balance, and she grabbed the door, desperate to keep herself from falling over while Melissa was there to witness her weakness and make it more difficult to stand back up. Once she had her feet under her again, she considered heading on out the open door and down the front steps, but she still hadn't found her walking cane. Besides, it was a little too chilly to sit outside for the duration of Melissa's visit.

Helen closed the door and returned to her desk. She ignored Melissa's activities in the kitchen area, and tried to concentrate on the computer screen again. Maybe if Helen ignored her, she'd give up and go away.

"Nice pictures," Melissa said, pointing at the thumbnails on the monitor. "Your nieces are very pretty."

They were pretty, but that hadn't been what Helen wanted from the pictures. She'd wanted to capture the girls' personalities, not just their superficial appearance.

"We need to talk," Melissa said. "It took you a long time to answer the door just now. Are you all right?"

"I'm fine," Helen said, keeping her focus on the screen. "I took my time, because I was hoping you'd leave if I didn't answer you."

"You know I'd never leave you," Melissa said. "That's not the problem. No, I think you had trouble opening the door. I think you need someone here for you all the time, not just during my brief visits."

Helen shook her head. Twenty years of dealing with her husband's cronies had given her the ability to keep her voice calm, even when all she wanted to do was scream. The woman who was only doing her job, after all, not trying to make Helen angry. "That's not necessary."

"I'll make the arrangements with your nieces." Melissa retrieved the radio from under the kitchen sink, and carried it over to the desk. She plugged it in and tuned it to her usual talk station.

Helen turned it off. "I need silence."

"You need life." Melissa turned the radio back on.

Helen reached down to unplug it, her hip aching with the movement. She wrapped the cord around the radio and tossed it into a desk drawer. She braced her knee against it, daring Melissa to risk causing her patient physical harm to get at it.

"I just thought you'd enjoy a little entertainment," Melissa said defensively, sitting next to her at the desk again.

"I know what I want," Helen said, maintaining eye contact again in the somewhat futile hope that Melissa could see what she refused to hear. "Right now, I don't want the radio on. I want to work on my photographs. In silence. I'm not a child, and I'm not senile, and I do not need a guardian or a friend or anything else. You can either go somewhere else in the house and leave me alone, or you can just leave completely."

"I'm only doing my job." Melissa's voice was whiney, but there was anger in her eyes.

"Not any longer," Helen said. "You're fired."

"You can't fire me," Melissa said, no longer pretending to care about her patient. "Only the person who hired me can, and that was your niece."

"They hired your agency, not you personally," Helen said. "I'll call your boss and ask for someone else."

"You didn't hire the agency, either," Melissa said smugly. "My boss won't do anything unless your nieces call him. And by then I'm sure you'll have realized that I'm only doing what's best for you."

"I can call the police and have you arrested for trespassing."

"You can try, sweetie," Melissa said, and the anger was gone from her face, replaced by the confidence that she was in control. "But the local cops all know me. Every single one of them has had a relative or two in my care. They know that sometimes patients resist their treatment. They won't get involved in a patient-caretaker dispute. Not without a court order."

Helen reached for the cell phone on the desktop, but Melissa was faster. The phone disappeared into the pocket of her unicorn-and-rainbow-printed smock. "Today isn't a good day for a car ride. Not the right weather at all."

Helen glanced at the sunshine streaming in the window. "What are you talking about? It's a lovely day."

"It's a bit chilly for someone in your condition," Melissa said. "Although, I would like to see you get more exercise. You know, the local hospital offers Tai Chi classes."

"Sounds good," Helen said. "It's got roots in the martial arts, doesn't it?"

"Don't worry, sweetie. They wouldn't expect you to fight anyone."

"That's too bad."

"I tell you what," Melissa said. "You can go outside, just a brief walk around the yard, right after your nap, sugar."

Helen was too stunned to move. Sure, her lupus caused a great deal of fatigue, but it was her choice, not someone else's, when she was tired enough to go to bed. The woman was insane, thinking she could keep Helen a captive in her own cottage. Although, she thought ruefully, it wouldn't be all that difficult to do. If Helen could have leaped out of her chair and run out of the house, she would have done it by now. With the inflammation in her joints particularly bothersome today, she couldn't outrun Melissa, and wrestling her for the phone was equally out of the question.

That didn't mean Helen had to give up. She just needed to make Melissa think she'd won, long enough to escape.

Helen got to her feet, hiding her rage and pretending to be cowed. "You may be right. I'll just go lie down for a while."

Helen was halfway across the living room, when Melissa said. "I almost forgot about your other cell phone. The one in your bedroom."

"It won't bother me while I'm resting," Helen said. "I'll turn off the ringer."

"I think it would be better if I held it for you," Melissa said.

"I don't." The phone was much more of a lifeline than the nurse was; it wouldn't drown her pills or knock her over. Helen glanced at the bedroom, considered making a run for it, or at least a fast hobble, but she was too far away. She'd never get all the way there, with the door slammed shut behind her before Melissa tackled her. Realistically speaking, she wouldn't even get halfway. At least the weakness of her body hadn't spread to her brain. She would bide her time, letting Melissa think she'd won again, until Helen had a real chance to escape.

With Melissa right behind her, Helen retrieved the back-up cell phone from her nightstand and handed it over.

Melissa pocketed it. "That's a good girl."

Now she was treating Helen like a dog, and that was exactly how Helen felt. Like a whipped dog, in fact. In her own home.

Melissa was going to regret ever taking on this assignment. Maybe even regret ever having become a visiting nurse. Helen would make sure of it. Just as soon as her "nap" was over.

Melissa left, pulling the door behind her, but leaving it slightly ajar. "I'll be right outside here if you need me."

Not in this lifetime.

Helen sat on her bed. She wasn't tired, and she didn't need a nap, and no one was going to make her take one.

Helen shook her head ruefully. She was thinking like the child Melissa thought she was.

But Helen wasn't a child. She had resources that a child didn't have.

She pushed up off the bed and crossed the room to slam the door shut and lock it. The cottage was older than it looked, with sturdy doors and locks. Melissa couldn't break in without a battering ram.

Of course, now Helen was effectively locked into her own bedroom, as unable to leave as Melissa was to enter. Once Helen got out of here, she was getting a spare phone, maybe two, to hide for emergencies like this. The basic one in her pocket at all times, another under her pillow, and perhaps one in the bathroom, hidden within the stack of towels in the linen closet. First, though, she needed to get out of here.

Melissa was between Helen and the two exterior doors of the cottage. That left the windows. Helen peered out the nearest one. Even though the bedroom was on the first floor, there was a substantial drop to the ground. Probably six feet. Not a lot, for someone who was physically fit. A few years ago, Helen wouldn't have hesitated before jumping that short distance, although, to be honest, she'd never been tempted to sneak out of her bedroom before. No one had ever dared to treat her like a child before.

Helen unlocked the window and gave the sash a tug.

"Are you all right?" Melissa said from just outside the door. "I thought I heard a noise."

"I'm fine," Helen said. "I just dropped a book."

"Put down the book and go to sleep," Melissa said.

Now wasn't the time to argue. She needed Melissa to think she'd won. "Whatever you say."

Helen sat on the bed and bounced a little to make it squeak, as if she really were lying down to nap.

Melissa's footsteps headed back to the kitchen, followed by the sound of the refrigerator opening and a soda can opening. A moment later, one of Melissa's stupid talk shows blared from the radio. For once, Helen was grateful for the noise. It was more than enough to cover the small sounds of her escape.

Helen stood up carefully and retrieved a spare walking cane from her closet. She opened the window as quietly as possible and removed the screen before tossing her cane outside. She waited a moment to make sure Melissa hadn't heard the sounds and then placed several books against the wall beneath the window to serve as steps. She climbed up them and managed to get herself seated on the window sill with her feet dangling outside. After several minutes of trying to make herself push off the safety of her perch, she finally turned over onto her stomach and, after taking a deep breath, slid down the side of the house and then to the ground.

Despite the shortness of the drop, the impact jarred her hip, and the sudden pain left her unable to move. The bit of her brain that wasn't focused on breathing through the worst of the muscle spasms was praying that Melissa hadn't heard her fall. Not only would it be embarrassing and frustrating, but if Helen was found like this, unable to breathe easily, let alone stand up, it would be persuasive evidence to convince her nieces that she couldn't be trusted to live on her own.

Eventually, though, the pain subsided and Helen was able to use her cane to maneuver herself back onto her feet. She made her way to the nearest neighbor's house, one slow, painful step at a time. Her anger at Melissa kept her going whenever she felt like giving up.

Helen knocked on the door of the nearest house, but no one was home. Helen worried that she might have to walk miles before she found someone at home, but at the second house, there was a stay-at-home mother. She was reluctant to open the door to a stranger, and insisted that Helen remain outside, but she did agree to let Helen use her phone to call Jack.

She sat on the neighbor's front porch until she saw the black luxury car approaching the driveway. She pushed herself to her feet, just in time for Jack to emerge from the Town Car and open the passenger door for her.

"What are you doing here?" he said. "You don't look so good."

"I need to go see that lawyer Tate again."

"You've got a scratch on your face," he said. "Did your nurse do that?"

"Not directly," Helen said as she settled into the car's plush seat. "Do you keep drinks in the car for passengers?"

"What did you have in mind?"

Helen couldn't actually drink anything alcoholic, because of the drugs she was taking, but she needed something bracing. "Anything except Diet Pepsi."

"There's orange juice in a cooler in the trunk."

"That'll have to do."

Jack went around to the back of the car. Helen heard the trunk open, and a moment later Jack handed her a large plastic bottle of orange juice, which he'd opened for her.

"Thanks."

"Anything for you, Ms. Binney."

"As long as I've paid up the two-hour minimum, anyway."

"You wouldn't stiff me," Jack said. "Not like some people. Just last week, I drove these sales reps to an event with their clients in a limo, and I made sure the mini-bar was stocked and the limo was immaculate, and I got them to their sports event on time, despite all sorts of construction detours and traffic back-ups, and you know what they did? They contested the bill through their credit card company. I knew they were jerks when they only left me about a one percent tip. How rude is that? One percent. Of course, I'm never going to see even that much, since it was part of the credit card charge that they contested. I mean, they musta' spent thousands on the tickets for the game, but they couldn't spare chump change for a poor working stiff."

Helen had known too many people like the passengers Jack had encountered. In fact, her ex-husband was like that, except when she'd intervened. He'd spent fortunes on sporting events and restaurants and transportation, but when it came to recognizing the people who'd made those things enjoyable, he couldn't be bothered. He wasn't a bad person, not really. In theory, he cared about people, and that was why he'd become a politician, but on a day-to-day level, he'd been oblivious to the people he was hurting. "There are a lot of jerks in this world."

"The worst thing is, there's nothing I can do when passengers are jerks," Jack said. "Not without getting fired or arrested."

"I know what you mean," Helen said. "My nurse is being a jerk, and getting rid of her is going to be complicated. It would be so much simpler if murder were legal."

"Ain't that the truth." Jack's sigh held the weight of the unfairness of the world. He closed the door and climbed into the driver's seat. "Are you sure you're all right? I could take you to the emergency room, if you want."

"It's nothing."

"I knew you were going to say that." Jack took the turn that led into the center of town, where Tate's office was located. "Some people don't complain about anything, and other people complain about every little thing. Just last week, one of my passengers bumped his head while getting out. It was his own fault—he'd gotten drunk while he was at the event I took him to—and it wasn't much of a bump, but he spent fifteen minutes yelling at me and threatening to sue the limo company."

"I hope they've got a good attorney."

"They did," Jack said. "Until Tate retired."

She'd forgotten about that little complication. "Let's hope he taught his nephew everything he knew."

* * *

With the help of Tate's nephew and a retainer that was considerably higher than what a small-town firm could reasonably command for a simple domestic matter, Helen convinced Tate to stop packing and postpone his retirement for a couple hours. He dug a battered briefcase out of one of his moving boxes and conferred with Jack before climbing into the back of the car to sit beside Helen. "Your driver knows where the courthouse is. It'll only take a couple minutes."

"The sooner you can get rid of Melissa, the better."

"Don't expect any miracles," he said. "I'm just doing my job. The job that I'm supposed to be retired from."

Jack stopped the car in front of the courthouse to let Helen and Tate out. Helen hesitated at the foot of the steep stairs into the building. She couldn't climb them, not the way her hip felt right now, at least not with any grace or confidence.

A sign with the standard wheelchair icon caught her attention. Perhaps there was another entrance she could use. The sign beneath the wheelchair icon read, "This courthouse is not wheelchair accessible," and gave a phone number to contact for more information.

Helen didn't need information; she needed an elevator.

She couldn't wait for it to be built, so she swallowed her irritation and slowly, painfully followed Tate up the stairs and into the clerk's office.

There were three people already in line at the counter, where only one clerk was working. Three other clerks sat at desks in the background, intent on their work, which apparently didn't include dealing with people at the counter.

"It may take a few minutes to arrange for the hearing. Monday mornings are usually busy with the arraignment of everyone who was arrested over the weekend, and the other scheduled matters run over to the afternoon session." Tate gestured at the battered and rusty straight-back chairs lining the wall across from the counter. "You might as well have a seat while you wait. Make yourself comfortable."

Helen looked at the battered straight-back chairs lining the wall across from the counter. No one could get comfortable in them, let alone a person with a damaged hip.

Helen feigned interest in the bulletin board beside the clerk's office doorway while she watched Tate do his job. There were three people in line before him, and while he waited, he greeted passing court officers and a few fellow lawyers, all by name and with every indication that he considered each and every one of them among his closest and dearest friends. Her ex-husband had done the same sort of thing when he was working a room. Her ex had obviously been successful with the schmoozing, since he'd been governor for a record-setting number of years, but he still wasn't half as good at it as Tate was.

Melissa didn't stand a chance against him.

Helen ignored the curious glances from the young man reading the notices on the bulletin board until he said, "Excuse me, but you're Helen Faria, aren't you? The governor's wife."

"It's Binney now. We're divorced."

"Oh, yeah," he said. "I read about it in the *Boston Globe*. I'm Geoff Loring, by the way, and I work for the *Wharton Times*. If I'd been covering your divorce, I'd have been more even-handed, given you a fair shake, showed your ex for the bastard he was."

Helen was tempted to simply ignore him, the way she'd always done with the more annoying members of the press corps surrounding her husband. The rest she'd been polite to, while still not making any on-the-record statements. She'd actually liked quite a few of the regulars, the ones who truly cared about the people they interviewed or were extraordinarily insightful. But she'd known better than to trust them with anything she didn't want plastered across the front page of a newspaper or website.

He was blond and had a nice smile in an otherwise bland face. It couldn't have been too many years—ten at the most— since he'd been writing stories for the local high school's paper instead of the grown-up edition. He didn't seem like one of the vengeful, vigilante reporters who enjoyed wallowing in human misery. It was more likely that he just had an over-sized ego, which was almost a pre-requisite for the job these days. He just wanted a story that would get him a front-page by-line, maybe picked up for syndication, to validate his opinion of himself. In a small town like Wharton, he probably didn't have that many opportunities for a story that would appeal to readers across the state. The governor's ex-wife was automatically front-page material, at least for the local paper, so she was going to have to deal with Loring as long as she lived here. There was no point in intentionally antagonizing him. At the same time, she couldn't let him think there was any chance she'd give him some sort of inside story about the governor. He'd never leave her alone if she held out the least little bit of encouragement.

"My ex-husband wasn't a bastard," she said flatly. "We just wanted different things for the remainder of our lives."

"Right." Loring's hand strayed to his smartphone, obviously tempted to take notes. "I heard you had a vacation house here. I suppose you're just staying here while you decide what to do next?"

"It's a lovely little cottage," Helen said with intentional vagueness. Where was Tate, anyway? How long did it take to fill out a few papers and ask for hearing? She glanced at the counter, where he was still chatting with the clerk.

Loring either didn't pick up on her disinterest or pretended not to. "Perhaps I could stop by the cottage sometime and have a chat."

"I don't have anything to say to the press."

"Sure you do," he said. "Just because you're not the state's first lady anymore, that doesn't mean you've got nothing interesting to say. I'm sure the local citizens would love to hear your opinions."

"I believe the weather has been unusually mild recently," she said. "Is that what you had in mind?"

"I was thinking more along the lines of discussing why you're here in the courthouse today."

She might not want to antagonize him in ways that would reflect badly on her husband, but she didn't care whether he liked her or not. "I'm trying to get people to leave me alone."

He laughed, believing, like everyone else, that she was joking. "Are you planning to get restraining orders against everyone in town?"

"If necessary," she said. "Excuse me while I go ask my lawyer to amend the paperwork."

CHAPTER THREE

───────

The reporter didn't try to stop her from joining Tate at the counter. By the time Helen had signed the application for a restraining order, and turned to leave the clerk's office, the reporter was gone. She doubted she'd scared him off permanently, so she wasn't surprised to see him waiting for her when she entered the courtroom.

Helen had attended a few high-profile hearings in Boston courthouses. They were grand high-rise buildings, with elevated benches for the judge, and extensive seating for the press and the curious public. There was nothing grand or elevated or extensive about the county courthouse. The courtroom was about the size of a high school classroom, and most of the space was taken up with rows of chairs for parties waiting for their case to be called. In front of them was a rickety, waist-high divider that separated the observers from the judge and the attorneys. The attorneys' tables were plastic veneer, and looked like they'd been purchased at the local discount store. The judge's bench was made of solid wood, but far from the weight and pomp of the city courtrooms. It was only raised a single step above the floor level, making it a little too easy for the parties to look down on the judge instead of the other way around. The judge would have to rely on the strength of his own personality, rather than the trappings of authority.

Tate led Helen past the railing and offered her a seat at one of the front tables. She heard the reporter, the only other person in the room, move so that he was sitting directly behind them. "It may be a while until we're called," Tate said. "The morning session went longer than usual, and the scheduled hearing for this afternoon was postponed to another day, so we're the only case on Judge Nolan's docket today. She may make us wait, just to see how serious we are about this."

"I'm serious."

"You don't need to convince me. I know what you're spending to be here." He pulled an issue of *Woodworker's Journal* from his briefcase, and immersed himself in it.

Helen tried to find a comfortable position on the cheap chair, a match to the ones she'd disdained in the clerk's office, without fidgeting so much that Tate would notice her discomfort. Tumbling out the window this morning really hadn't done her hip any good, but she wasn't inclined to seek any sort of medical opinion at the moment. Certainly not with Melissa on the loose. Much higher on her priority list was finding a locksmith to replace all her locks at the cottage, so Melissa couldn't just let herself in before she was served with the restraining order.

After a few minutes, Helen tried reading over Tate's shoulder. Fascinating as he obviously found the tips for lathe maintenance, she couldn't get past the second sentence without her eyes crossing.

Helen was about to give in to her hip's demand that she stand up for a few minutes, when the uniformed bailiff entered the room, admonishing everyone to rise for the entrance of Judge Samantha Nolan.

Except for her official black robe, the judge looked like Hollywood's idea of a stay-at-home grandmother: perfectly permed white hair, rounded face with a hint of jowls, and a chunky necklace offering a bit of color along the collar of the robe. She was at least ten years older than Helen, but she walked briskly and didn't hesitate at the single step up to where she presided. No one forced a visiting nurse on Judge Nolan or expected her to take a nap, Helen thought.

The judge's clerk, a chubby middle-aged blonde in clothes that were too young and too tight for her, settled at an ugly little desk next to the judge. The clerk called Helen's name and recited a case number, before saying, "You may approach the bench."

After a final glance at his copy of *Woodworker's Journal*, Tate tossed the magazine onto the table and escorted Helen up to a spot a few inches in front of the judge's bench.

Judge Nolan glanced briefly at Helen before focusing on Tate. "Don't even bother. I've read the papers. You don't have grounds for a restraining order."

The judge might look like a sweet old grandmother, but she obviously wasn't a soft touch. Helen had to admire her strength, even if it was inconvenient under the circumstances.

"I know it's unusual, judge," Tate said, "but there's more to the situation than appears on the surface. There's a power dynamic here, between nurse and patient, that's clearly being abused."

"Not a bad argument," the judge said. "I might have bought it if your client's actions hadn't made it clear that she dislikes everyone in this town, not just her nurse. She's been living here in Wharton during the summer season for as long as I've been on the bench, and she's never so much as said hello to any of the local citizens before today. I'm sure our esteemed reporter, Mr. Loring, will confirm that fact."

Helen turned around to see the reporter nodding in response to the judge's statement. He was also keying notes into his smartphone furiously, apparently trying to record every single word spoken.

The judge continued, "I seem to remember that another local reporter tried to interview her a couple years ago, and the next thing he knew, he was being called in to have a chat with his boss about being demoted to writing obituaries."

"That's not in evidence," Tate said.

"I'm taking judicial notice of a commonly known fact," Judge Nolan said. "Your client doesn't like anyone, so it's hardly surprising she dislikes this particular person she's complaining about."

"Hermit or not, Miss Binney is entitled to privacy in her own home," Tate said.

"Only from governmental intrusion. Not from other citizens, by way of a restraining order." The judge looked at Helen, adding, "Not unless she's afraid of her nurse."

Helen stiffened. She wasn't afraid of anyone. She was angry and frustrated, not scared.

After a moment, the judge focused on Tate again. "All you've shown me is that Ms. Binney is annoyed with her nurse, who may have overstepped her boundaries somewhat. You haven't offered me any evidence that the nurse offered Ms. Binney any physical harm, and I'm quite sure that Ms. Binney won't perjure herself by saying she's afraid of Ms. Shores or anyone else."

The judge turned to Helen again. "Well?"

Helen suppressed a sigh. Too bad Judge Nolan hadn't risen higher in the judiciary, leaving this job to someone who would have rubber-stamped the request for a restraining order, someone who wouldn't have put Helen in the untenable position of having to admit—in front of the note-taking reporter, and thus, indirectly, in front of the entire town—that she'd been bullied by a silly woman wearing clothes embellished with children's toys. Helen's nieces would never let her forget it.

"I'm not afraid of Melissa," Helen told the judge. "I just want her to leave me alone. That's the whole point of restraining orders, isn't it?"

"You'd think so," Judge Nolan said as she gestured for the clerk to hand her some paperwork. "But you'd be wrong. I don't even have to take this under advisement. Sorry to ruin your courtroom winning streak, Tate, but the request for a restraining order is denied."

Tate waited until the judge had left before saying, "I did warn you the odds were against you."

"So what do we do now?"

He picked up his magazine and stuffed it into his briefcase. "Now I go back to my woodworking shop, and you go stay with friends for a few days while you negotiate a termination of Melissa's contract to visit you."

"According to the judge, I don't have any friends. I hate everyone."

"That may have been a bit of an exaggeration," Tate said. "I'm sure you've got friends somewhere."

She used to, Helen thought. Back before she'd thrown herself into supporting her husband's career and hadn't had time for them. She needed to make amends or find some new friends. As soon as she got rid of Melissa.

"I won't be chased out of my own house. I'm going back there now, and she'd better be gone."

"Or what?" he said. "No, don't tell me. Just promise me you won't kill her, and you won't let your driver or one of his cousins do anything illegal."

"Don't worry," Helen said. "If I kill her, I promise not to tell you in advance, and I'll do my best to make it an interesting case for you."

* * *

Jack was leaning against the car, playing a video game, when Helen emerged from the courthouse. Tate had left her at the door, claiming he needed to return to the clerk's office on another matter, and he'd walk back to his office.

Jack tossed his smartphone into the car and ran up the courthouse steps to give her an arm to lean on if she wanted it. She considered brushing him away, but the stone steps were steep, and the railing looked shaky. She took Jack's arm with the hand not already using her cane.

After the first step, he asked, "Is it all taken care of?"

"Not exactly."

"I'm sorry," Jack said. "It's always the nice people that get taken advantage of, and the law won't do anything about it. It's just not fair."

"I probably deserved it," Helen said. "I'm not particularly nice."

Jack held the passenger door open for her. "What are you going to do now?"

Helen hated to admit it, but Tate was probably right about finding somewhere else to stay tonight. The nieces' homes weren't an option. Lily was out of town on business, and Laura's guestroom had been converted into a nursery. Helen might not have a friend she could stay with, but she could always rent a hotel room. Just until she could have the locks changed.

Jack would know the local hotels, but Helen couldn't make herself ask him. It wasn't just stubbornness. Her cottage was the only place were she felt comfortable these days. She wasn't going to be scared away from her one refuge by some crazy visiting nurse in silly pink clothes.

"First, I need a new phone and a locksmith," she told Jack. "And then I'd like to go home."

After a detour to pick up two new pre-paid cell phones that were now activated and ready for use, Jack rolled the car to a stop at the end of the driveway, headlights shining on the otherwise dark cottage.

Over his shoulder, Jack said, "Her car is gone. Doesn't look like she's still here."

"She isn't the type to give up this easily," Helen said. "She might have hidden her car out back."

"Want me to come in with you?" Jack said. "Just until you've had a chance to look around?"

She couldn't let him do her dirty work, getting rid of Melissa, but she reconsidered letting him escort her to the front door. It had been a long day, after all, what with falling out the window and all. "Would you mind?"

"For you, I'd do anything." Jack opened the back passenger door and waited patiently until she was able to emerge from the low seat.

"This job would be so much better if all the clients were like you." Jack adjusted his pace to her slow one as they made their way up the walkway. "Some of them expect the driver to wait on them hand and foot, when they're perfectly capable of taking care of themselves. There was this one guy last week: he looked like a professional boxer, and you'd think he could carry at least his puny little briefcase or his state-of-the-art-thin laptop, but no, he expected me to carry them for him, along with his three over-sized suitcases. And he had the nerve to complain that he was in a big rush, and it took me too long, because I had to make two trips to get everything into the lobby."

Jack paused while Helen unlocked the cottage's front door, before adding, "And do you think he left me a decent tip for the extra work? Not likely. Bare minimum. Not even that, really. About ten percent."

Helen flicked the wall switch to illuminate the entry area and living room, half expecting Melissa to jump out of the darkness.

All she found, though, was the sound of the talk station blaring from the radio. On the plus side, the rooms were unoccupied, just the way she liked them.

"She's definitely gone," Jack said. "You think she might come back?"

"I'm sure she will," Helen said. Probably not tonight, though.

"Want me to stick around?"

"No, I have to handle this on my own." Helen crossed the living room and unplugged the radio. "Starting with this. Would you mind taking this away until I've gotten rid of Melissa?"

"Anything for you, Ms. Binney," he said, wrapping the cord around the radio.

"I think you should call me Helen, after all you've done for me."

"You've got your new phones where you can get to them, right?"

Helen patted one of the tiny phones, safely tucked into her pocket, and shrugged her shoulders until she could feel the spare one that she'd tucked into her bra. "I have them. Melissa might confiscate one of them, but I doubt she'll think to look for a second one on me."

"Why don't you put my home phone number into the memory?" Jack said, writing it on the back of a business card. "I wouldn't mind if you called me in an emergency. If you can't get through to dispatch, just call me at home. I'll come get you, even if it's my day off. Might not be a fancy car, but at least you can get away from here if you need to."

"That's very kind." Helen withdrew the first phone from her pocket and keyed in his number to reassure him. "I'm sure it won't be necessary to call anyone except the police, though. If Melissa comes back, she's going to wish she'd never met me, even more than I wish I'd never met her."

* * *

Before Helen went to bed, she wrestled the recliner against the front door to keep Melissa out until the locks were changed.

The next morning, while waiting for the locksmith Jack had recommended, Helen settled at her desk to finish sorting through the pictures of her nieces. Her hip was less irritated than she'd expected after yesterday's escapade, but she was still grateful for the excellent lumbar support of her desk chair.

While she waited for the computer to boot, Helen glanced out the window at the overcast day and noticed something on the grass, about thirty feet away, halfway between the woods and the stairs to the back deck.

Helen pushed herself out of her chair and moved closer to the window. It wasn't some*thing*. It was some*one*. She looked again. A woman, lying face down, wearing white clogs, blue pants and a bright pink top. It had to be Melissa. The damned woman must have hidden out there last night, waiting in the shadows for Helen to return and Jack to leave. The joke was apparently on Melissa, falling asleep and missing her chance to impose her will on her patient again.

Helen shoved the window open. "Melissa! Wake up and go home."

Melissa didn't move, as oblivious to Helen's wishes as ever.

"Give it up, Melissa," Helen shouted. "You're fired, and I've barricaded the doors until the locksmith gets here to change the locks. You're not getting inside here ever again."

The sun came out from behind the clouds, and in the bright light, Melissa's hands looked deathly pale. It could have been a trick, but Helen didn't think so. No one slept that heavily.

Helen reached for the phone in her pocket and dialed 911.

"What is your emergency?" a reassuringly calm male voice said.

"I'm not sure," Helen said, "but I think there's a dead body in my yard."

"What's the address?"

She told him, and he said, "The first responders are on the way. What happened to the person?"

"I don't know. She's just lying there."

"Is she breathing?"

"I don't know." Even as she said it, Helen realized how foolish that sounded. She should have checked. "Give me a minute, and I'll go find out."

Helen pushed the recliner away from the front door and went outside, across the side yard to where Melissa was still lying, unmoving. Helen had to suppress the feeling that the nurse would, at any minute, jump up and yell, "gotcha!" Oddly enough, she almost wished that would happen.

The dispatcher said, "Are you still there?"

"Yes." Helen could hear sirens in the distance. "She's not breathing."

"What about a pulse?"

Helen knelt beside Melissa and placed two fingers on the woman's neck. She felt nothing except cold—too cold—skin. Maybe Helen had missed the artery, though. She wasn't a nurse, after all, and she couldn't exactly ask Melissa how to find a pulse.

Helen moved her fingers around the woman's neck, searching for signs of life and finding nothing. A sharp pain in her hip forced her to change position. As she straightened, she realized the material of her pants was wet where she'd been kneeling on the grass. She glanced at her knee, and it took a moment to comprehend the reason for the damp red stain.

Helen backed away from the body, absolutely convinced now that it was a body and not a person any longer.

"There's no way she has a pulse," she told the operator. "I'm not a doctor, but I think she'd need a lot more blood inside her and a lot less of it soaked into the ground in order for her heart to beat."

CHAPTER FOUR

———

Confident there was nothing more she could do for Melissa, Helen retreated to her front porch steps and waited for the emergency personnel to arrive.

All considered, it didn't take long. Her cottage was on the farthest outskirts of the town, the entrance to the private road hid among dense trees, and the narrow gravel driveway offered a challenge even to a compact car.

At the moment, there were two patrol cars and a fire truck all idling in Helen's front yard, and the ambulance was rolling to a stop. The cottage hadn't seen this many people all at once since the summer ten years ago when her ex-husband and most of his entourage had joined her here for a week. If Melissa's spirit was lingering, it was probably gloating over her posthumous success in ensuring that Helen had plenty of visitors.

Two men from the fire department still knelt beside Melissa's body, although they seemed to have reached the same conclusion Helen had, and weren't bothering with chest compressions or any other sort of first aid. When the ambulance crew arrived with a stretcher, they exchanged a few words with the firemen, punctuated by a lot of nods, a few head-shakes and several shrugs. Apparently in agreement that Melissa was beyond any help they could give, the firemen returned to their truck. The ambulance crew consulted with the police officers, presumably getting permission to remove the body.

With this confirmation that Melissa was truly gone, there was no reason for Helen to stay outside, gawking at the crime scene. No one seemed interested in what she had to say, and if they did want to talk to her, they knew where to find her.

As Helen got to her feet, she heard an additional vehicle coming up the gravel driveway. A car, not a truck.

Rubberneckers, probably. As predictable as the political groupies and busybodies she'd endured as the governor's wife. She'd come to feel sorry for them—their own lives were so empty that they had to live vicariously through other people's traumas—but now that she was retired, living on private property, she didn't have to put up with them.

Helen made her way over to the closest uniformed police officer. He stood with his arms crossed over his chest, observing the removal of the body. The officer wasn't much taller than her 5' 6" ex-husband, although he was a bit stockier. His nametag read "H. Peterson."

Helen planted herself in front of him. "Excuse me."

"You need to stand back," he said. "This is a crime scene."

"It's also my yard."

"You should still step back a ways, ma'am. I'll come with you." He took her elbow and started to lead her back toward her front path as if she didn't know where it was. "Are you all right?"

"I'm fine," Helen said, although the way he was bending over her solicitously made her feel even smaller and more fragile than usual. She pulled her arm out of his grasp. "I wasn't the one who was injured. All I did was find the body."

"Most people are traumatized by that sort of thing," Peterson said. "I can ask the paramedics to check your blood pressure if you'd like. Give you a sedative, maybe."

"I'm perfectly calm, and my blood pressure is fine." Unlike Melissa's, which was non-existent. Helen's gaze wandered back to the spot where the body had been. Would the grass look different there next year, fertilized by all that blood, becoming a sort of natural memorial to the dead woman?

"Just take it easy," Peterson said, glancing over his shoulder to watch the paramedics slam the ambulance doors shut, with the body already secured inside. "And don't hesitate to call for help if you're feeling light-headed or anything."

"I could use your help with one little thing."

He turned to face her again. "What's that, ma'am?"

She nodded at the recently arrived car. "Could you have a word with the trespassers, and ask them to leave?"

"The emergency vehicles will be gone in a minute." He'd already dismissed her from his conscious mind, and was focused instead on the taped-off scene of the crime. He looked at it as if he expected someone to leap out of the surrounding woods and confess to the murder, and he didn't want to miss the excitement.

"I don't mean the emergency vehicles." Helen pointed at the car parked across her daylily bed. "I'm talking about that vehicle."

Peterson reluctantly looked away from the scene of the murder and glanced toward the car. "Oh, that's just Geoff Loring. I know him. He's okay."

She knew that tone of voice. It meant *Don't worry your pretty little head about it.* She'd heard it far too many times from the people around her ex-husband until the message had gotten around that anyone who underestimated her would find their access to the governor cut off. She hadn't suffered a condescending attitude lightly then, and she wasn't going to start now.

"Loring's presence here is *not* okay. He's trespassing on private property, and I want him to leave. If he won't go voluntarily, I expect you to arrest him."

"No need to get all excited." Peterson stepped back with his hands in the air as if she'd physically attacked him. He might be making light of her request, but at least it had dawned on him that public relations required at least some effort, and she finally had his full attention. "Don't worry about Geoff. He's a reporter. He's just doing his job."

Which was more than she could say for this officer. "Fine. I'll go ask him to leave if you won't."

"Now, ma'am, you don't want to do that."

"Yes, I do." Helen limped across the lawn, with Peterson following. She concentrated on one step at a time, watching where she stepped on the uneven ground and leaning heavily on her cane.

"But he's a reporter," Peterson said. "You can't ask him to leave. He has First Amendment rights."

"I have some experience with both the press and First Amendment rights." Helen kept walking. "I'm quite sure that the

Constitution does not give reporters the right to trespass on private property in the pursuit of a story."

"Okay, okay," Peterson said. "I'll have a little chat with him, and you can go on inside where he can't bother you."

"I'll wait right here while you go talk to him. It shouldn't take long for you to tell him to leave." Otherwise, she knew, as soon as she was out of sight, Peterson would let the reporter do whatever he wanted. If it was just this one time, one day when there was legitimate news to cover, she wouldn't mind so much. But if she didn't put her foot down now, the reporter would return again and again, each time on a flimsier excuse than the last time. If he wouldn't leave when the police were potentially available to arrest him for trespassing, she'd never get him to leave the next time he invited himself to her property, looking for an interview. "You probably want to take my statement, anyway. As soon as Loring leaves, I'll tell you what I know about Melissa."

"We've got your name, and we know where you live," Peterson said. "That's all we need from you."

"You don't want to know where I was last night?" The police should have been grilling her by now, not verbally patting her on the head. "Don't you want to know whether Melissa and I had argued recently?"

"Not really."

Maybe they knew something she didn't. "So you know who killed her?"

"We've got a pretty good idea." Peterson looked past her, checking out the forensic team's activity at the scene of the crime again.

"A pretty good idea?" Helen felt outrage on Melissa's behalf. The nurse had been annoying, but that didn't mean she'd deserved to die, or that her killer should escape punishment. "We're talking about a murder here. Shouldn't you be considering all the possibilities until you have a beyond-reasonable-doubt certainty?"

"We will consider everything, ma'am." Peterson dragged his attention back to her.

"I must have misunderstood you, then," Helen said. "You're planning to have someone else interview me later. A lead detective, maybe."

"I'm the lead detective." He gestured at his nametag which did, indeed have a *Det.* in front of his name. "Hank Peterson. The forensics will tell us everything we need to know. There isn't anything useful that you can add."

"But I'm the one who found her. Right where I live," Helen said. "I should be the prime suspect."

"You?" Peterson smirked. "Don't worry, ma'am. You aren't even on the list."

"Why not?" Helen said, annoyed by his dismissive, condescending attitude. "Everyone knows I detested Melissa and was desperate to get rid of her. Maybe I came back from court yesterday, and she was still here, and I lost my temper and bashed her over the head."

"I don't think so."

"Why not?"

"You aren't strong enough, for one thing."

"There was a tree limb near her body," Helen said. "Something that big would do most of the damage by itself, and all I'd have to do is lift it and toss it in her direction."

"You couldn't lift it."

"Sure I could," Helen said. "I'm stronger than I look. And then there's the adrenaline factor that would make me even stronger while I was angry. She really did know how to push my buttons."

"Look," he said. "It's obvious you didn't kill her, and I've got better things to do than interview someone I'm sure didn't do it."

"Better things? Like looking for a suspect?"

"We already have one," he said. "I probably shouldn't be telling you this, but if it will set your mind at ease, we already have a solid theory of what happened. There's been a rash of late-night burglaries around here the last couple years, and I'm betting this is related. A vulnerable woman, like you, living all alone, is the perfect target for a burglar. He came here intending to rob you, Melissa surprised him, so he killed her."

Peterson sounded so certain, and it was his job to investigate these things, so maybe he was right. It still rankled that she'd been dismissed so easily. "I just want to be sure you find the culprit, officer, and lock him up."

"So you admit you didn't kill Melissa, after all," Peterson said with a self-satisfied chuckle that made Helen think someone was going to kill the homicide detective before long, if he didn't develop some better people skills.

"Don't worry," he said, in that grating, *don't worry your pretty little head* tone again. "We're going to find this guy, and we'll keep you safe. In the meantime, though, you might want to have someone come stay with you. It's not a good idea for you to be living here alone."

Helen sighed. Why did everyone insist on foisting companionship on her? "If someone moved in with me, I'd have to kill that new person, too, just like I killed Melissa."

Peterson laughed. "You're lucky I know you couldn't have done it. It's not usually a good idea to confess to murder in front of a detective."

"You sound like my lawyer," she said. "He keeps insisting I should be a good, law-abiding citizen."

Peterson didn't seem to get that she was joking. She'd better save the sarcasm for when she talked to Tate. For now, she needed to keep Peterson focused on the job at hand. He was supposed to be getting rid of the reporter. Before Helen could remind him, yet another vehicle came rumbling up the gravel driveway, going about one mile per hour and weaving to avoid the potholes. The low-slung sports car rolled to a stop behind the reporter's SUV.

A tall, skeletally thin man in his late thirties climbed out of the sports car. He wore khaki pants and a pale blue golf shirt with a darker blue ascot. Helen couldn't help staring at him; she didn't follow fashion trends, but were ascots really making a come-back?

Peterson said, "I think I'll go have a chat with Loring now."

"And then you can have the same chat with the newest trespasser."

Peterson was already halfway to Loring's vehicle and pretended not to hear her.

Meanwhile, the newcomer was avoiding Peterson while picking his way across the lawn as carefully as Helen usually did, although he didn't seem to have any particular mobility problems. She glanced down at his shoes. Standard men's loafers, as far as she could tell, although she supposed they could be an expensive brand, and he thought there might be something in her grass that would ruin them.

He finally reached her and grasped her free hand in both of his. "Is it true? Melissa's dead?"

"You should talk to the police about that," Helen said, nodding at the detective who was leaning against Loring's car now. She suspected it was more likely Detective Peterson was giving the reporter an off-the-record statement than threatening to arrest him. "Or ask the paramedics. They're trained to deal with those sorts of issues."

"I'll deal with them later." The man leaned closer to her, as if they were best friends, and they needed to speak in confidence. He kept patting her hand. "I'm more concerned about you right now."

"I'm fine," she said, taking back her hand with some difficulty. "Who are you?"

"Oh! I forgot! I've heard so much about you that it feels like we've known each other forever, and yet we've never been formally introduced." He retrieved a business card from the inner pocket of his jacket. "I'm Gordon Pierce. Owner of the home health care agency."

So this was Melissa's boss. The one who wouldn't let Helen decide just how much nursing care her patient was willing to endure.

Pierce was younger than she'd imagined him to be. Probably just as well, she thought. He would need time to recover from the havoc she was going to wreak on his career for imposing Melissa—and now the unwanted notoriety surrounding her death—on her.

Pierce placed her hand on his forearm and covered it with his own hand to escort her back to the porch. She tugged back her hand and took a step away from him, tempted to thwap him with her cane, except she needed it for balance.

"You don't need to be here," Helen said. "Melissa's family needs you more than I do."

"She doesn't have a family." Pierce placed his hand over his heart in an earnest gesture straight out of a soap opera. "Her patients were her family."

That explained a lot, Helen thought a little guiltily. Melissa might not have been as crazy as she'd seemed. She might just have been projecting her own loneliness onto Helen, looking for company for herself, more than for her patient. "What about the other nurses in the agency? They must be upset. You should go make sure they're okay."

"They're all professionals. They know our first responsibility is to our patients, and we'll deal with our personal grief later." Pierce hovered beside her as they approached her front door. "Maybe you could have a friend or family member stay with you for a few days, just until we sort this all out."

Helen was beginning to think she should start a drinking game, listing all the different ways people could find to force companionship on her. Probably not a good idea, in practice. She'd never developed the tolerance for alcohol that her ex-husband had, and if things kept going the way they were today, she'd end up in the hospital with alcohol poisoning. "I'll be fine right here."

"We'll send someone in Melissa's place, of course, but it may take a few days to work out the details." Pierce pulled out his smartphone and scrolled frantically through his contacts list. "We're pretty well booked to capacity, but I'm sure we'll find someone who's right for you."

"No rush," said Helen. "I've decided I don't really need a visiting nurse, after all. I'd been planning to cancel the contract before this happened, anyway."

"I couldn't bear the thought of putting you at risk. I *will* find you another nurse. We wouldn't want *another* tragedy."

Helen was trying to decide whether he was threatening her or simply being melodramatic, when he added, "It wouldn't take much for you to be incapacitated. I mean, look at Melissa.

She was a big, strong woman, and, well, you know what happened to her."

Not a threat, Helen decided. He was just trying to protect his stream of income by trying to convince her she needed a visiting nurse from his agency. "No one has any reason to hurt me. And I really don't need a visiting nurse. I tried it, and I didn't like it."

Pierce glanced over his shoulder in the direction of the detective, and then bent toward her, not condescendingly like the detective, but still annoying in the way it implied that she welcomed his confidences.

"The police won't admit it," he whispered, "but some of the recent unsolved burglaries have been rather violent. They started out pretty trivial, but recently a homeowner was threatened with a knife. You really shouldn't stay all the way out here alone, without someone checking in on you. I don't know how, but I'll make sure you have a new nurse by tomorrow."

Helen glanced at the detective, and judging by the way he was leaning against the SUV and laughing, he hadn't gotten around to suggesting the reporter should leave. It hardly seemed worth her time to ask Peterson to ask yet another unwanted trespasser to leave. She had a better chance of getting rid of Pierce by placating him. Much as she hated donning the old social mask she'd perfected during her stint in the governor's mansion, it was the best way to get rid of him. A little fake politeness was certainly better than bashing Pierce's head in with her cane. There'd been enough death here for one day. All she wanted was a little solitude, not solitary confinement.

"Fine," Helen said at last. "Do what you think is best for now, and we'll straighten it out later."

He left, looking relieved, while she went inside the cottage to plot his downfall.

CHAPTER FIVE

———

The interior of the cottage pulsed with the flashing blue lights of the remaining cruiser in Helen's driveway. She glanced outside to see the Geoff Loring still chatting with Detective Peterson.

It was odd that the reporter hadn't at least tried to interview her about Melissa's murder. He'd been at the court hearing yesterday and had seen for himself just how much she loathed the nurse. So why hadn't he insisted on getting a quote for his story? Peterson certainly wouldn't have stopped him, although maybe he'd convinced the reporter that they already knew who the culprit was, so Helen's observations were irrelevant.

Helen knew she should have been relieved to have avoided the interview, but it rankled that absolutely everyone had dismissed her as a witness, let alone as a suspect. She'd had the means, motive, and opportunity. She was even the one who had found the body, and the murder had happened on her land. What more would she have to do to be taken seriously?

The detective and the reporter continued chatting amicably, neither of them taking any notes or paying any attention to the forensics team. Were there really that many murders in this town that they would be so nonchalant about yet another one? Maybe she should have subscribed to the local newspaper, beginning years ago when she'd originally bought the cottage. If the town was really this dangerous, she might have to reconsider her decision to retire here.

She couldn't believe Wharton was that dangerous, though. It was more likely that the detective simply believed he'd already solved the case. A more seasoned and competent reporter would doubt his source, but Loring didn't seem likely to do that.

They both seemed happy with their theory and weren't interested in any alternatives. Least of all the theory that Helen might have been the killer.

They were making the same irritating mistake everyone else did these days: treating Helen as if she were helpless. The only way they would ever believe she was physically, if not psychologically, capable of murder was if she walked into the police station with the evidence all laid out, demonstrating not just her means, motive, and opportunity for the crime, but also exonerating every other possible suspect.

It would almost be worth doing just that, if only to prove to herself that she was still a force to be reckoned with. Besides, she needed a new hobby, since her forays into scrapbooking and photography had both been less than satisfying. Of course, there was one major stumbling block to proving that she'd killed Melissa: she hadn't done it. How could she prove something that wasn't true?

Helen fretted over the issue for a while, until it dawned on her that it might be enough to disprove their theory, rather than proving her own guilt. If she could prove that their burglar had not killed Melissa, then they'd have to start from scratch, with all the usual suspects. Including herself.

From what she'd heard, there had been dozens of previous burglaries, and it would take weeks just to contact all the victims and convince them to confide in her about the details of the crime. Investigating the burglaries might well turn out to be an interesting way to pass some time. It couldn't be worse than scrapbooking, photography, and listening to Melissa's favorite radio talk shows.

Even if she eventually came to the same conclusion as the police, that the burglar had killed Melissa, at least then she'd feel confident that the real killer had been identified. The detective didn't even need to know that she'd been poking into the case. She just needed to know for her own peace of mind that the police had a good reason—something other than their impression of her as beneath consideration—for rejecting her as the prime suspect.

First, though, she needed to let her nieces know about Melissa's death, so the news wouldn't inspire the nieces to swoop down on the cottage and kidnap Helen for her own good. Helen called Lily first, and while she was still too shocked to argue much, Helen convinced her to cooperate with cancelling the contract with the visiting-nurse agency. Then Helen called Tate's nephew and arranged to meet with Adam the next morning, so they could take care of the contract termination.

With a little luck, Helen thought, she'd be at the law office before Pierce sent out the replacement nurse, and that would be the last time anyone from the agency ever set foot on her property. Until then, there wasn't much she could do about either the visiting-nurse situation or her investigation into Melissa's murder.

Helen tried to read a recently-purchased book that she'd been anticipating for weeks, but the commotion outdoors kept her from blocking out the fact that a dead body had been found in her yard. That *she* had found a dead body. She wasn't as fragile as everyone thought she was, but neither was she impervious to the shock of an acquaintance's sudden and violent death.

She finally tossed the book aside and went to make a cup of tea. On the way, Helen noticed that her computer monitor was still on, the screen saver scrolling through some random pictures. Her camera was on the desk, still connected to the computer for the upload she'd been working on before she'd found Melissa. She might as well finish organizing the upload before she abandoned photography as a hobby.

She clicked through the thumbnails, moving the files into the appropriate folders. She doubted she'd ever look at the pictures again, because they really weren't very good, but she couldn't make herself leave them unsorted. She might not have an eye for artistic composition, but at least she was thorough and organized. Those traits had to be good for something.

Like a murder investigation, she thought.

A thorough person didn't depend on others to gather evidence for her. She didn't have all the resources of a forensics team, but she could at least take her own pictures of the crime scene.

She glanced outside at the spot where the body had lain, and realized that while she'd been going through the pictures, the rest of the emergency vehicles and all of the assorted trespassers had finally left. She disconnected her digital camera from the computer. She left her cane hanging from the doorknob, so as to leave her hands free for the photography, and went outside. She stopped at the police tape strung from the front corner of the cottage, around two trees about 30 feet apart and then back to the railing of her back deck.

Most of Helen's property was heavily wooded, opening into a small, oval clearing, with the cottage in the exact middle, and a detached garage behind and to the left of the cottage. The grass extended about 50' from the sides of the cottage and about twice that from the front and back.

Helen could still see the flattened oval area of grass where the paramedics had trampled it, all around where Melissa's body had been lying. She'd get a measuring tape to check later, but it looked to be about halfway between the deck and the first trees marking the edge of the woods. Inside the trampled area was a dark brown stain that marked where Melissa's head had lain.

Helen began photographing the area inside the police tape, taking a shot of the entire trampled area and then dividing it into an imaginary grid and photographing each one in turn, working from left to right, keeping a bit of the police tape in the shot for orientation.

When that was done, she stopped to think about what other visual clues might be important. The police had taken a tree branch, presumably because it was the murder weapon. As best she could recall, it had been about four inches in diameter and about three feet long.

She made her way along the outside of the police line to inspect the edge of the woods, looking for the source of the branch. Nothing struck her as obviously disturbed, but it wouldn't hurt to get a closer look. Nervous about crossing the uneven surface without her cane, she nevertheless made her way into the woods, keeping close to the yellow tape and following it all the way to the far end.

She didn't see any evidence that anyone else had walked out beyond the tape, either immediately before or after the murder. There were plenty of fallen branches, although most of them seemed to be in a more advanced state of decomposition than the one that had been next to Melissa. Turning back toward the spot where Melissa's body had fallen, Helen continued searching until she found another branch that was about the same size as the presumed murder weapon. She took several pictures of it, just in case they might be useful. Unlike the detective, she wasn't prepared to dismiss anything as unimportant.

In fact, she thought, it might be useful to have the actual branch for future reference, rather than just the picture. She tucked the camera into her jacket pocket and bent to inspect the branch more closely. The side that had been touching the ground was slimy and discolored, but it wasn't falling apart like most of the other similarly sized branches had been.

Assuming it was the same size as the actual murder weapon, could she have picked it up and swung it? The detective didn't think so, but Helen didn't underestimate herself the way he had. She bent to pick it up, and found it wasn't as heavy as she'd expected. It was a solid, substantial weapon, and she wouldn't want to carry it for miles, but she could definitely lift it with one hand, at least briefly. Ignoring the damp and the dirt, she placed her other hand on it, holding it like a baseball bat, and swung at an imaginary victim.

Her whole body spun with the force, and she had to release the branch to keep from falling over. Still, she felt validated. She had been able to swing it. She might not be able to do it again until she'd recovered from the jarring effect the first swing had had on her hip, but as far as she knew, one blow had been enough to kill Melissa. Helen could have done that much.

She retrieved the branch from where it had fallen, deeper in the woods, and then picked her way carefully back to the police line and onto the grass of the back yard. Even here, where it looked as smooth as a golf course, there were little hills and valleys that could trip her up if she weren't careful.

She glanced over toward the taped-off grass. The ground looked perfectly smooth there, sloping only a few consistent degrees toward the woods, so water would run away from the cottage. If it was anything like the ground under her feet, though, it wasn't as even as it appeared.

Helen placed her Exhibit A, the branch, on the back deck and returned to the blood-stained spot. She lowered herself onto her hands and knees and then lay down on the grass, getting an ant's-eye view of the ground. The area was definitely not as smooth as it had looked from a standing position.

She held the camera just high enough that the closest grass wouldn't obscure the image, and examined the area through the camera's display. From this vantage point, she could see that there was another area of trampled grass, closer to her back deck, but away from the path she'd taken with the her murder-weapon replica. They were probably just from the forensics crew or emergency personnel, but she was trying to be more thorough than the detective had been and not make any assumptions.

Struggling back to her feet, Helen contemplated the next step in her investigation. She had her photographs of the crime scene. She had her stand-in for the murder weapon. What else could she do?

Tate would know. He had to have learned about crime investigation in the course of representing criminals. She'd ask him about it if he was at the law office tomorrow morning. There had to be a way to casually slip in the question, "How can I prove I murdered someone?"

CHAPTER SIX

———

Jack arrived promptly at a quarter to ten the next morning.

"I heard about what happened to Melissa," he said as he held the door for her to enter the back of the luxury car. "Are you okay?"

"I'm fine."

He waited until they were heading down the driveway before asking, "Do the police have any leads on who did it?"

She snorted. "They think a burglar did it. They're not even considering any other options."

"A burglar?"

"Used to just steal things, but apparently he's turned violent," Helen said. "They wouldn't even consider me as a suspect."

"You?"

"Why not me?" Helen said.

Jack glanced at her in his rear-view mirror. "You probably have an alibi. When was she killed?"

"I have no idea." She hadn't thought to ask, and she didn't know enough about head wounds to make any sort of educated guess. "I doubt the police will tell me. I didn't exactly bond with the detective."

"Melissa wasn't here when we came back from the courthouse around 6:00," Jack said. "If she died before that, then you've got me and Tate and even the judge to confirm your alibi. Plus there's the log I file with the company. It would confirm when I left here."

"She could have been here, and we just didn't see her." She shivered. The body could have been lying out there all night, a few feet away from where Helen was sleeping. "It was dark when we got home, and her body was in the side yard, away from where you parked."

"We'd have noticed if her car was still here," Jack said. "I don't remember seeing it."

"You're right. It was gone then," Helen said. "She had to have been alive then to drive it away, but then how'd she get back here later? The car wasn't here when I found her body."

"The killer must have taken it, so you wouldn't notice anything was wrong," Jack said. "Give himself more time to get out of town. You'd have been suspicious if Melissa's car was here last night, and she wasn't, and you'd have gone looking for her and found the body."

Melissa really could have been dead since the previous afternoon, Helen thought. She hadn't heard a car coming or going at any time during the morning before she'd found the body, and it was hard to miss the sound of tires on her gravel driveway. The only time she might not have noticed a car arriving this morning was while she was taking a shower. But it seemed unlikely that Melissa could have arrived, been killed, and then had her car stolen by her killer, all in the ten minutes or so that Helen had been unable to hear anything outside.

"It doesn't make any sense," Helen said. "If the killer drove Melissa's car away, how did he get to my house in the first place? She's never brought anyone with her before, and it's not exactly walking distance from anywhere. I doubt anyone hires a taxi or limo to go to kill someone."

"True."

"And there were still a couple cans of her Diet Pepsi in the refrigerator this morning. She usually finishes all of them before she leaves," Helen said. "Something had to have happened to make her leave without finishing them all on Monday."

"Like realizing you'd flown the coop?"

"That's about the only thing that would tear her away from her soda and radio," Helen said. "I wonder if she told her boss. He didn't say anything about my having escaped from Melissa's care."

"She probably tried to find you first, and then got killed before she spoke to the boss."

"If Melissa did leave on Monday afternoon to look for me, and was gone when we got home, then it narrows down the time of death to somewhere between 6:00 that night, and 10:00 Tuesday morning." That was the exact time when Helen had no alibi for yesterday. She really deserved to be a suspect. "But why did Melissa stay outside in the yard, instead of letting herself into the cottage to bug me, like she normally does? She couldn't have known that I barricaded the doors against her, and I would have heard her if she'd tried to come in."

"Lost her key?"

"Maybe." Helen tried to recall if there had been keys in Melissa's hands. She didn't think so. Melissa never carried a purse, presumably because it interfered with lugging her Diet Pepsi supply into the house. The brightly-printed smocks she wore had large pockets in them, and she might have tucked the keys in there. "I wish we could see what personal effects the police found on her."

"If anyone can get that information for you," Jack said, "Tate can."

"That's what I'm counting on." That, and the fact that Tate might be tempted out of retirement by the novelty of a client trying to prove she *did* commit murder, instead of trying to prove she was innocent.

* * *

Jack parked outside Tate & Bancroft, and settled in with his video games while Helen limped into the building. The reception area was vacant, like the first time she'd been there. She heard a man's voice talking, though, so she headed down the hallway in that direction. She wasn't sure if it was Tate or his nephew. Their voices were as similar as their looks. The same height and lean build, the same dark hair, except for the gray strands that Tate had earned. The only real difference in their appearance was that Adam seemed a great deal more tense than his laid-back uncle, with tension lines already forming in his forehead.

Adam was seated behind a clutter-free desk, talking on the phone. He gestured that he'd only be a moment, and that she should come in and take a seat.

As Helen stepped forward, the ache in her hip warned that she was not ready to sit just yet, so she pretended to be fascinated by the law books lining his walls. From the sticky notes poking out from some of the books and the gaps where the occasional volume was missing, it appeared that Adam actually used his set, unlike her ex-husband who kept them for show. Her ex had always had minions with their own libraries to do the actual research for him.

Adam hung up the phone and stood to greet her. "My uncle isn't here right now."

"I didn't expect to see him. I understand that he's retired, so I came to see you. I hope you don't mind that I stopped by without an appointment, but it was something of an emergency."

"What can I do to help?"

Adam politely remained standing until Helen reluctantly folded herself into one of the client chairs. It would take too long to explain why she'd rather stand. "You know the nurse I tried to get a restraining order against?"

He nodded.

"She's dead. I found her bloody body this morning."

"That does sound serious, but not the type of legal work I do." Adam rose from his seat. "Let me see if Uncle Tate can talk to you. He's out back, in his workshop."

A few minutes later, Adam returned and sent her out back to the garage where Tate maintained a small woodworking shop. "Just follow the sound of the lathe. I can't promise he'll turn it off to talk to you, but he didn't threaten to report me to the Board of Bar Overseers if I told you where he was, so I think he's willing to listen."

The garage doors were the old-fashioned kind that swung out, rather than lifting into the ceiling. They were both propped open, but even so, the interior was poorly lit. The walls were lined with stacks of banker's boxes containing old legal files, leaving what would have been just about enough space to park one subcompact car, if it weren't filled with Tate's woodworking machinery and a rickety table cluttered with wood scraps and several elaborately detailed wood lamp stems, awaiting wiring and a shade.

Tate was standing at the lathe, patiently turning a three-foot length of wood into what appeared to be another lamp stem to match the ones on his work table. He was good at his hobby, she thought. And it was good for him. He looked peaceful. Happy, even, although he wasn't the sort to laugh out loud.

She needed a hobby like that. Something she could be good at, unlike scrapbooking and photography, and that would be so engrossing she wouldn't notice when other people were invading her space, like Melissa had done at the cottage, or, Helen thought with some guilt, like she was doing herself by entering Tate's workshop uninvited. The least she could do was wait quietly until he turned off the machinery to take a break.

Finally, Tate seemed to notice her presence and turned off the lathe. "Adam told you where I was, didn't he? Why won't anyone believe that I'm retired?"

"Probably for the same reason no one will believe me when I say I want to be left alone."

"It's too easy for clients to find me here." Tate glanced pointedly at his wrist, except there was nothing there. He jerked open a drawer in his workbench and rummaged through it. "I know I have a watch here somewhere. Don't think I won't charge you for this conversation, just because it's happening outside my office. In fact, I ought to charge double for the inconvenience."

"Go ahead. There should be something left from yesterday's retainer." Helen looked for a place to sit, but apparently Tate always worked standing up, and there wasn't room for any spare furniture. "You won't have to appeal the restraining order, at least. Melissa is dead."

He snapped around, surprise evident in his eyes. He quickly schooled his expression into its usual inscrutability, and leaned against his workbench to study her face for several seconds. "I thought we agreed you weren't going to kill her."

"I didn't, and you know it," Helen snapped. Even Tate wasn't taking her seriously. He wouldn't have joked about her guilt if he'd thought it might have been true. "I could have killed her, but I didn't."

Tate absently picked up a scrap of sandpaper and began applying it to a section of the lamp stem he'd been turning. "Then who did?"

"I don't know," Helen said. "The police think it was a burglary gone bad."

"If they change their mind and arrest you, I'm going to need a bigger retainer."

"I won't be arrested. No one believes I'm capable of murder."

He looked up from his work. "Then why are you bothering me?"

"A couple things." Helen retrieved Pierce's business card from her purse. "I need you to terminate the contract with the nursing agency. I am not going to have another visiting nurse's death on my conscience."

Tate took the card. "I thought you didn't kill the first one."

"I might kill the next nurse if I can't stop the agency from sending them out," Helen said.

"Adam can handle the contract cancellation for you," he said. "Why are you really here?"

"He doesn't do criminal cases," Helen said. "I need to know everything you can tell me about burglary."

"You running out of cash?" he said. "Considering a new career in crime so you can pay my bill?"

"I'm just wondering about Melissa's killer."

"You don't strike me as the type who indulges in pointless intellectual exercises. You've got a plan." He stared at the card in his hand for a few moments before nodding to himself. "You want to find the burglar before the police do, so you can thank him for getting rid of Melissa?"

"Not to thank him. Just to prove that he didn't do it, so the police will have a reason to keep looking and find whoever really did do it."

"You'll get arrested for interfering with a police investigation." Tate pocketed Pierce's business card. "Adam can take care of cancelling the nursing agency's contract. I've got better things to do than represent you when you haven't even been charged with a crime."

"You said you'd consider taking on an interesting homicide case," Helen said. "A patient killing her nurse isn't the routine murder."

"You didn't kill her."

"I could have."

"You aren't going to drop this, are you?" He leaned against the table where his lathe was set up. "Give me the basics. How was she killed?"

"Okay, that part was pretty standard," Helen said. "She was bashed over the head."

"Her significant other did it, then," Tate said. "Forget about the burglary angle."

"I don't think she had a significant other," Helen said. "Her boss said she didn't have any family."

"Bosses don't know everything about an employee's private life."

"I think he was right, though," Helen said. "Melissa was trying to impress me with her dedication, and told me she'd always worked such long and irregular shifts, it didn't leave any time for a personal life."

"I know how that can be," Tate said. "Do you believe the burglary theory?"

"Not particularly," Helen said. "But the police do. They think some local burglar was trying to break into my house, and Melissa got in the way."

"Sounds logical enough," Tate said.

"But shouldn't they at least consider the other options?" Helen said.

"Options like you?"

"For one," she said. "But I'm sure there are others too."

"It's not unusual for the police to jump to conclusions," Tate said. "They develop a theory, get attached to it, and then interpret the evidence in the light most favorable to the theory. It's human nature to see what they want to see and not see the inconsistencies. Makes it hard for defense counsel to convince them their case isn't as strong as they think it is."

"If I understood more about burglary, I might understand their theory better," Helen said.

"I knew it was a mistake to set up shop back here. Too damned easy for clients to find me." Tate dropped the sandpaper. "You're not going to leave until I answer all of your questions, are you?"

Helen shook her head.

"Might as well make yourself comfortable, then." Tate crossed the room to retrieve two folded director's chairs. The navy canvas was riddled with holes and coated in sawdust. He set them up across from each other, gave one a quick swipe with his hand and gestured for Helen to have a seat.

"I can't get into any specifics," Tate said as he settled into the other chair without bothering to remove even the surface layer of sawdust, "but over the years I've represented a few people charged with burglary."

"Were any of them guilty?" Helen perched on the edge of the chair.

"Let's just say none of them were convicted," Tate said. "The thing is, they're never master criminals like the ones on TV and in the movies. Most burglaries are just a matter of opportunity and desperation, not some long-planned-out heist."

"The local burglar seems pretty good at what he does," Helen said. "Apparently he's been breaking into houses around here for the last couple years, and the police don't know who he is."

"It still doesn't mean he's planning everything in advance," Tate said. "He could just be lucky. He sees a place, it's empty, figures he'll poke around and see what he can find. As long as no one sees him, and his prints aren't in the system, there's not much for the police to go on. Besides, I doubt the cops were trying too hard to find him before now."

"They don't care that houses are being broken into?"

"They're just being realistic," Tate said. "Unless it's an obvious situation of a family member stealing for drug money, break-ins are hardly ever solved. And the cops aren't going to spend too much time on a situation they're not likely to solve, especially if no one got hurt."

"I heard a knife was involved in one case."

"Not as far as I know," Tate said. "The guy they have in mind has just stolen some little stuff. No one's even caught a glimpse of him. Never seemed like much of a risk."

"Still, people feel scared after a break-in. Vulnerable."

"You don't seem to be a bundle of nerves," he said, "and you found a dead body."

"I worked in politics for twenty years. Nothing fazes me." Besides, a dead Melissa was a whole lot less scary than what the living Melissa had represented: the loss of Helen's independence.

"They'll find the burglar eventually," Tate said in what was about as close to offering compassionate reassurance as he ever came. "Probably step up the search now that they think he's turned violent."

"And then he'll hire you, and you'll get the charges dismissed."

"Not this time," Tate said. "A string of minor burglaries wouldn't tempt me out of retirement, even if the last one did escalate into murder."

"There's nothing interesting about the case at all?" Helen said. "Not even how long he's eluded the cops?"

"Not really," Tate said. "Some people are fascinated by what he steals. It's unusual from a personal point of view, but not a professional one."

"What does he steal?"

"Remote controls mostly," Tate said. "A few times he left the remote and just stole the batteries, as if he's trying to make some sort of point. People have reported that they didn't even know they'd been robbed until they used the remote to play a DVD, and nothing happened. When they checked to see if the batteries were dead, the compartment was empty."

"That's all you know?"

"About these particular burglaries, yeah." Tate said. "That's pretty much it for my expertise with burglary in general too, come to think of it. It's a pretty basic and mundane crime. No hairs to split that haven't already been split a thousand times. Now, if you want to talk about choosing the right piece of wood for a lamp stem, I could go on for hours about that."

"No, thanks." Helen struggled to her feet. "I just wanted to know about the burglaries."

"The local newspaper's archives would probably tell you more than I can." Tate stood too. "Their offices are down the street. That's where I'd start if I were investigating the case and wanted to know more about the other burglaries."

"That's where Geoff Loring works, and I'd rather not run into him."

"The guy's a twit, isn't he?" Tate said. "A lot of the paper's recent stories are available on-line if you've got internet access."

"Of course I do." Helen had always kept her indispensable contacts database in her Rolodex, where she could safeguard it against hackers and computer malfunctions, but she'd used computers for everything else while she'd worked in the governor's mansion. "Why didn't you tell me that right away?"

"You were paying for my time, and I've got expenses." Tate picked up the wood he'd been turning when she'd arrived and reached for the lathe's power switch. "Good wood, like reliable legal advice, is never cheap."

CHAPTER SEVEN

———

The newspaper's on-line archives had references to the petty burglaries going back almost three years. The earliest ones were simply entries in summaries of the police log, but about two years ago, Geoff Loring had noticed the pattern, concluded they'd all been done by one person, and coined the nickname of the Remote Control Burglar. From then on, each incident was covered in a separate article. All told, there were close to fifty of them, and it took Helen all afternoon to find them and then print them for later study.

After dinner, Helen chatted with her nieces online, reassuring them that she was fine, the police were doing their best to investigate the murder, and she'd hired an attorney to take care of cancelling the contract with the nursing agency.

"The same one who failed to get a restraining order?" Lily asked.

"That wasn't his fault," Helen said. "I have complete confidence in him."

"What was his name again?" Lily asked.

Instead of answering, Helen asked Laura if there was any news about a possible addition to the family, which was always a reliable way to change the subject. Even Lily respected her sister's fascination with all things procreational. Getting Laura involved was the only way to distract Lily.

By the time Laura ran out of newly discovered tidbits about pregnancy and infant care, Helen was able to avoid giving Lily Tate's name by claiming it was late, and she needed to get some rest.

Helen tried to go back to the newspaper articles about the Remote Control Burglar, but it turned out that she really was too tired for the sort of detailed analysis that would be necessary for any insights the police and the reporter had missed. She decided it would be best to get a good night's sleep and return to the clippings when she was refreshed.

After breakfast the next morning, Helen checked the newspaper's website to see if there was any breaking news on the investigation of either the murder or the burglaries. The only thing she found of interest was the notice of a memorial service for Melissa, scheduled for late that afternoon. She hadn't expected it to be so soon, but if there were no family members who might need to travel to get here, she supposed there was no reason to delay putting Melissa to rest.

No matter how much Helen had loathed the nurse, she felt obliged to attend the service. As her ex-husband's ambassador, she'd been to plenty of memorials for people she'd detested. She could do it one more time.

Helen called the car service and arranged for Jack to pick her up in time to arrive halfway through the service. Normally, she'd have planned to arrive early, slip in and out quickly and largely unnoticed, but it had struck her that it would be interesting to see who else was mourning Melissa. Pierce was adamant that Melissa had no family, no significant other, while Tate was confident that the killer would turn out to have been someone close to the victim. Helen hadn't thought to ask Tate whether killers routinely showed up at memorial services, the same way arsonists reportedly showed up at the fires they set. If so, someone should be checking out everyone who attended the memorial, and the police weren't likely to do it, not as long as they were convinced the Remote Control Burglar was their culprit.

After checking her closet to make sure she'd kept at least one outfit suitable for attending a funeral, and finding a plain black sweater set and black pants, Helen settled down to study the print-outs she'd made from the newspaper's archives. Even after Loring had realized the crimes had likely been committed by a single person, the articles were short, mostly just paraphrasing of the police blotter summaries, with the occasional bit of speculation about the culprit's motive for taking such inconsequential items. They verged on opinion pieces, rather than investigative journalism.

There was one longer article by Geoff Loring a few months ago, starting with a summary of the dates and locations of the burglaries, the names of the victims, and a fairly detailed list of the items stolen from each location. He'd also interviewed the police chief, eliciting only the standard response about how the police department was doing the best it could with limited resources. The article also included a few comments by random people on the street, most of whom seemed to think the burglaries were some sort of joke, not to be taken seriously.

Despite the official police stance that every crime was serious, they hadn't seemed any more concerned about the incidents than the general public was. Helen could understand why the police would work harder at catching a killer than catching a petty burglar, and even why they might have felt a little guilty when that petty burglar had become a vicious killer. But why did they think the one type of crime had morphed into the other?

As far as she could tell, there hadn't been any sort of gradual escalation that might hint at the future violence. If the police theory was correct, the burglar had made a sudden switch from one end of the crime spectrum to the other, from petty property crime to extreme personal violence. Pierce had told her that a knife had been used to threaten one of the more recent victims, which, in hindsight, might have been viewed as a warning that the burglar was about to get violent. But Helen couldn't find anything in the newspaper reports about a knife being used. Just random break-ins. Virtually the only consistent element of the crimes was the complete lack of violence. Beyond that, no one had suggested any apparent pattern, in terms of when they happened, where they happened, or even how the homes were broken into.

What was it about Melissa's murder that made the police think it had to be related to the burglaries? She read and re-read her printouts, and she still couldn't see anything in the newspaper articles that could possibly lead to that conclusion.

The police might well have evidence that she didn't know about, but she couldn't imagine why they'd have withheld information on the earlier crimes that no one was particularly interested in solving. Instead, it felt as if the police thought there was only one possible criminal in the town, so everything that happened was attributed to him. It was, perhaps, a reassuring theory for the citizens, but it didn't make any sense.

In Helen's experience, pretty much everyone was a criminal, at least in his heart of hearts. A little tax evasion here, a little office-supply theft there. Not the sort of thing that was ever caught or prosecuted, but it set the stage for bigger things. Little larcenies could easily escalate into major larcenies if the opportunity ever presented itself, but the fundamental nature of the crime—theft—would remain the same. Over the years, several of her ex-husband's acquaintances had been convicted of embezzlement or fraud, but she couldn't imagine any of them committing murder, not even to keep from being caught for the underlying crime. Perhaps the tendency to stick to one type of crime was limited to politicians, whose egos had deluded them into rejecting, right up until their sentencing, the possibility that they'd be punished. A more realistic criminal might be quicker to turn to violence to avoid being caught.

Helen glanced at the time and realized Jack would be there in a few minutes. There had to be a pattern to the burglaries, something that would help identify the criminal and show that he wouldn't have been anywhere near Melissa. Unfortunately, finding that pattern would have to wait. She needed to get ready for the wake.

Helen shoved the newspaper articles into one of her unused scrapbooks for further study and changed into the black pants and sweater set she'd found earlier. She fetched her back-up cane and headed out the front door to wait for Jack. As she reached the bottom of the porch steps, she couldn't help glancing at the far side of the yard, where the police tape still marked the scene of the crime. What had Melissa been doing over there?

She hadn't reached any conclusions by the time Jack arrived a couple minutes later. He waited for her to settle into the back seat of the luxury car and then headed back down her driveway. "Are you sure you want to go to Melissa's wake? You two weren't exactly close."

"I owe it to her anyway," Helen said. "Besides, maybe the person who killed her will be there. Tate thinks it's her significant other."

"You don't think it's the guy the police are looking for?"

"A burglary gone wrong just doesn't make sense to me."

"That's what I thought too," Jack said. "I've known some petty criminals in my time, and they're not usually violent. People steal little things all the time, but they'd never get physical about it. Like the other day, I was taking this guy home from the airport, and he seemed like a nice guy, didn't complain when we ran into some traffic, and even gave me a decent tip. But then when I was taking his luggage out of the trunk, one of the suitcases popped open, and inside was a whole linen closet's worth of hotel towels and flatware and even a cheap little iron. He could have set up his own bed and breakfast with all the stuff he'd taken. He laughed about how he didn't even want the iron, and he was going to have to pay extra because of the weight of his luggage, but he didn't care. He was just trying to get even, because he thought the hotel charged too much. He might have been irritated if he'd been caught by the hotel security guards, but he never would have even considered punching one of them."

"People can panic when they get caught. That fear can lead to anger and then violence."

"Over a few trinkets?" Jack said, shaking his head dismissively. "And not just a little shoving match, but actual murder? I don't think so. I mean, what's the worst that would have happened if Melissa had turned in a petty burglar? Whatever the penalty, it couldn't be as bad as a life sentence for murder."

She hadn't thought of that. She'd have to ask Tate about the likely sentencing for the burglaries. Until then, it was reassuring to know that Jack agreed with her about the unlikeliness of a petty burglar turning to murder. Jack certainly had plenty of time to observe human behavior, and the incentive to understand what he observed, in order to keep the passengers happy or at least reasonably satisfied.

Two people's opinions about human nature wasn't enough to completely discount the police theory, though. They might know something she didn't, something that would explain why the burglar would have been willing to kill, rather than something less drastic, like running away or even just fighting the charges in court.

Helen waited while Jack maneuvered the Town Car into the too-small space in front of the funeral home. When it came to a full stop, she said, "Maybe the burglar didn't just panic. Maybe Melissa just said the wrong thing, and he over-reacted. She was good at pushing people's buttons."

Jack got out of the Town Car and opened her door. "If Melissa was that bad, she had to have annoyed lots of other folks, and they'd have wanted to kill her more than some random burglar would."

"True." Helen slid out of the Town Car and then retrieved her cane from the back seat. "I want to see who shows up and who signed the guest book. Folks who were supposed to be her friends and coworkers could have been terminally annoyed by her."

"Does Tate know you're doing this?" Jack slammed the car door shut.

"Sort of," Helen said. "I'm counting on you to call him if they try to throw me out of the service."

* * *

Helen could hear quiet murmurs in the adjoining room, but the entry area was deserted. She stopped at the table with the guest book. She needed to sign it, but it might be best not to use her real name. Geoff Loring might see it later and become suspicious about what she'd been doing here, given her history with Melissa. But she had to write something. Even if Melissa didn't have any close family, there had to be someone who cared about her, and who deserved whatever comfort another signature would provide.

What happened to the books after the services, anyway? Helen had been to funerals as the state's first lady, and sometimes the guest books had been destined for presidential libraries, while other times they went to the grieving family members. But what happened when there was no historical value and no close family? Why even collect the signatures if they would just clutter up the home of some distant relative who would toss it onto a shelf or put it in a box in the attic until it disintegrated?

Helen flipped to the front of the guest book. Even though she'd timed her arrival toward the middle of the service, when the bulk of the visitors had already arrived, there were barely two pages worth of names. Really only one page worth in any other format, but the book had been printed with three times as much space as normal between each signature line.

It looked like the nursing agency's owner, Gordon Pierce, had been the first to arrive, followed by several people whose signatures had *RN* after them. Presumably, they were Melissa's co-workers. But that was about it for mourners. Either Melissa's past clients weren't able to visit, or they hadn't liked her any more than Helen had.

Helen turned to the next page. At the top, finally, was a signature she did recognize. She'd seen it the other day, on the paperwork denying her restraining order. Judge Samantha Nolan. She probably attended all the local funerals, at least briefly. Even though judges were appointed for life in Massachusetts, rather than being elected, they were still political appointees. Short of impeachment, judges couldn't be terminated, but if enough people complained to their representatives, a judge could find her career dead-ended, with assignments to distant, unpopular, courthouses and to the most boring of cases.

Helen felt more than heard the approach of footsteps muffled by the thick carpeting. She looked up to see a perky-faced man young enough to be in high school, wearing an oversized black suit and trying unsuccessfully to look solemn.

He stopped beside her and bent toward her solicitously. "Do you need any assistance?"

"I'm fine," Helen said. "Just needed a moment to prepare myself."

"Shall I escort you inside?"

Helen hesitated. She hated having to assume the social mask, pretending she'd had any positive feelings toward Melissa. There was no point in staying out here, though. She wasn't going to learn anything more from the guest book.

She placed her hand on the young man's arm and let him walk her into the adjoining room. It was, not surprisingly, much smaller than the places where she'd attended services on her ex-husband's behalf, and, even so, it felt far too large for the handful of people seated facing the casket and lectern. People spoke in hushed tones, and the occasional bit of laughter was quickly squelched with a guilty glance to see if anyone had heard the inappropriate sound.

Helen stood in front of the casket, paying her respects, just as she'd done for countless people she hadn't even known as well as she'd known the nurse. Melissa was no longer the muddy, bloody, contorted mess she'd been when Helen last saw her. She'd been made to look younger and more relaxed than she'd ever been in life. Helen half expected the corpse to be holding a Diet Pepsi can or two for the journey into the next world, but Melissa's empty hands were crossed over her chest.

Helen continued over to the receiving line, which consisted of just one person: Gordon Pierce. Today's ascot was a somber gray to go with his dark gray suit and white shirt. "I'm sorry for your loss," Helen said automatically.

Pierce took her free hand, the one not gripping on her cane, in his. "Thank you for coming. It would have meant a lot for Melissa to know how much you appreciated her."

Now wasn't the time or place to get into just how much Helen hadn't appreciated Melissa or anything to do with his agency. For the moment, she needed to keep Pierce mollified, long enough to pump him for information about who might have had a motive to kill Melissa. "I was hoping to meet some of her other patients. Are any of them still here?"

"It's so kind of you to ask." Without letting go of her hand, Pierce glanced at the three other people in the room, and then shook his head. "There were a few patients here earlier, but they're old and don't get out much. Besides, most patients tend to take their paid care-givers for granted and don't really think of them as human beings."

Who were those three people then? They didn't seem to be nurses, not with their frayed clothes and shaky hands. Had the funeral director dragged them in from the streets to fill the room and make it seem like more people had cared about Melissa, in the ancient tradition of hired mourners? Did anyone really do that? If not, they might be people who truly cared about Melissa. Maybe even her next of kin. Prime suspects, according to Tate. Exactly the sort of people she'd hoped to meet here.

"What about Melissa's family?" Helen said. "Are any of them here?"

"She only has one distant relative. A nephew, I think, in California," he said. "Nobody who lives around here. I felt I owed it to her to make the burial arrangements since she died on the job."

That was interesting, Helen thought. For liability reasons, she'd have expected a boss to try to establish that an employee's death had occurred at a time when she was *not* working, rather than on the job. Especially since it seemed highly unlikely that Melissa had been working at the time of her death. She'd died sometime between 6 p.m. and the following 10 a.m. Most of that time wasn't even close to her contracted late-morning/mid-day visitation hour at the cottage, and Helen certainly hadn't asked her to come out for an extra visit.

Helen pulled her hand from Pierce's grip. "I really should be going. Lots to do."

"I can save you one errand," he said. "I've found the perfect new nurse for you. Her name's Rebecca, and she has a background in physical therapy. I'm sure she'll be *perfect* for you."

Pierce had thought Melissa was perfect for her too, so she didn't have a great deal of confidence in his matchmaking skills. "I don't need a nurse any longer."

"I know we got off on the wrong foot with the first placement," he said, "but you'll like Rebecca much better."

"That's not saying much. Anyone would be less irritating than Melissa." Helen's voice must have grown sharp with her annoyance, because the three rent-a-mourners were turning to stare at her. She mollified them with a murmured, "God rest her soul."

Pierce turned so that he was between Helen and their audience, his body serving as a bit of a barrier against eavesdropping. He lowered his voice. "Melissa could be a bit strong-willed and abrasive sometimes, but she got the job done. No one died on her watch."

Except Melissa herself.

Actually, Helen thought, Pierce's claim didn't make sense. "Didn't she specialize in geriatrics? She must have lost a few patients."

"Well, sure," Pierce said. "But no more than would be expected in the circumstances. And not for any reasons she could have done anything about. That's what I meant. You can't blame her for the death of patients who were old and terminal before she was hired. It was just a coincidence that she was working with them when they died."

"Are you sure?" Helen said. "I've read about nurses giving their elderly patients lethal doses of drugs to put them out of their misery, whether they wanted it or not."

"Melissa was abrasive sometimes," he said, "but she wasn't insane, and she wasn't some sort of serial euthanizer. Ever since I took over the nursing agency, I've been doing psychological testing of prospective employees to make sure no one has that sort of inclination. We have a rigorous hiring process, and I'm sure Melissa's previous employer tested her too. She'd been at the Wharton Nursing Home for years, and it has a solid reputation."

"If it's so great, why'd she leave there?"

"Natural transition to retirement," Pierce said. "With our agency, she could work part-time, which left her free to finally have some fun. She'd always wanted to be in radio, and she was volunteering at the local station whenever she wasn't with her patients."

So that was why Melissa had been so determined to have the radio on. Helen felt a little guilty for having insisted on turning it off all the time. And a little jealous that Melissa had known exactly what she wanted to do with her retirement years; unlike Helen, Melissa had found something she really loved doing. "It's too bad she didn't have more time to enjoy the radio work."

Pierce nodded, but he was looking at the latest mourner to arrive. A real one, apparently, in a fairly new black suit. "Excuse me. That's the daughter of one of Melissa's long-term patients. She must be devastated. I'll send Rebecca out to see you tomorrow morning. You're going to love her."

"That's not necessary," Helen started to say, but he was gone, just one more person ignoring her wishes.

Helen headed for the exit. Her curiosity about Melissa's killer gave way to true empathy for the dead woman. There was a lot that Helen hadn't liked about the woman, but she had to admire the woman's sense of purpose. All Melissa had wanted was to do her job as a nurse, and to indulge her passion for radio. She could have continued to do both for at least another decade if it hadn't been for the killer. It just seemed so unfair.

Helen was silent on the ride home, and Jack, always sensitive to his passengers' preferences, didn't try to engage her in any conversation.

Helen was uncomfortably aware that if she had been the killer's victim, no one would have had the same sense of a life being cut short. Everyone had already dismissed her, because of the lupus, and she hadn't thrown herself into any new interests, the way Melissa had done with her passion for radio.

It dawned on her that she had written herself off, just like everyone else did. She'd seen her life as *over*, rather than *starting over*.

No more. Even if everyone else wrote her off, Helen knew that she was still capable of great things. All she had to do was find something she was as passionate about as she'd once been about supporting her husband's political career, or as Melissa had been about her nursing career. And even if Helen never did find an activity she cared about for her retirement, whatever she did was going to be better than getting a tree branch to the skull, followed by an employer-organized wake populated by faux mourners.

* * *

When Jack delivered Helen to her home, Lily's car was parked in front of the cottage.

Helen braced herself for Lily's sharp inquisition, but it was the softer sister, Laura, who opened the front door and greeted Helen with a hug. "We'd have been here before today, but you know how Howie is about me being away all by myself overnight, and Lily was on a business trip and didn't get home until today."

"I'm fine."

"I couldn't have done what you did," Laura said, "staying here all by yourself since the murder."

"It was no big deal." Although, really, it hadn't been easy falling asleep the first night, thinking about how Melissa had been killed right outside her bedroom, without anyone noticing until too late.

"We're here now, and that's what matters," Lily said from her spot at the kitchen island, with her laptop open in front of her. "Are you sure you want to cancel the nursing agency's contract?"

"I'm sure," Helen said as she made her way inside. "I don't need a visiting nurse, and I particularly don't need one from that agency. They're more likely to kill me than to help me."

"It's not their fault that one of their nurses was killed here."

"We don't know that." Helen propped her cane next to the door and then settled into her recliner.

"Wait," Laura said. "You think someone killed her on purpose? I thought it was a burglary gone bad."

"That's what the police say, but I'm not sure I believe it."

"You just don't want to believe it," Lily said. "It would confirm how vulnerable you are out here, all alone."

"I just want to know what happened," Helen said. "If it was a burglary gone bad, and Melissa was protecting me, I should know that for sure. I don't want to live with that kind of guilt and anxiety if it's not true, and the police can't be bothered to do their job and find the real killer."

"But if the police are right, will you finally get a security system or a medical monitor? "

"I'll consider it," Helen said. "For now, I've instructed my attorney to terminate the contract with the nursing agency. If there's evidence—persuasive evidence, I mean, not just the detective's lazy assumptions—that there's a violent burglar in the area, we can talk about my options."

"You really have an attorney?" Lily said. "When you didn't give me his name, I thought you were bluffing."

"He's real."

Lily still looked skeptical, and Helen realized it might be a little awkward explaining why she didn't have her attorney's business card, especially since if Lily called his office, she'd be told that Tate had retired. She had his number on her cell phone, at least. She scrolled through the memory until she found it, and then wrote it down for Lily. She'd talk to Adam and give him a heads-up that Lily might be calling. "Wait until tomorrow before you call. I need to let his office know that you might be calling, and that it's okay to confirm that I'm a client."

Lily took the piece of paper. "This had better not be another bluff."

"We're just concerned about you," said Laura. "Family members are supposed to care about each other."

"I appreciate that," Helen said. "I'm just tired of being treated like I'm incompetent. I understand that you do it out of love, but that doesn't explain why the cops are just as bad. They should be grilling me, not providing me with a presumed defense."

"Why would you need a defense?" Laura said.

Lily answered her sister. "Because Aunt Helen should be the prime suspect in Melissa's murder."

Laura gasped. "Aunt Helen didn't kill Melissa. She wouldn't kill anyone."

"You and I know that," Lily said, "but the police don't. They *should* suspect her."

"That's it, exactly," Helen said. "They crossed me off the list without even questioning me, as if I didn't exist."

"But why would they think you killed her?" Laura said.

"It just makes sense," Helen said. "She died on my property, which is fairly isolated. I'm the one who found her. I made it pretty clear that I disliked her. Why wouldn't I be a suspect?"

"You didn't have any reason to kill her," Laura said. "She was helping you. She was your nurse."

Lily was nodding thoughtfully. "A nurse that you didn't want. But if there was a really good reason to get rid of her, you would have told us, and we'd have cancelled the contract ourselves."

"You were out of town when things got bad," Helen said. "Canceling the contract wouldn't have stopped her, so I did what I had to do. I filed for a restraining order against her the day before she died."

"A restraining order?" Laura said. "How bad was she?"

Helen wasn't willing to admit Melissa had practically locked her in her room and Helen had been unable to stop her. It sounded so pathetic. And the smaller incidents just made her sound paranoid. She'd told the girls about them before, but even she hadn't considered them all that serious at the time. Annoying, but not enough to justify breaching a contract, let alone get a restraining order.

Helen settled for saying, "She bugged me."

"Everyone bugs you," said Lily.

"So why does everyone keep on bugging me, after I ask them to stop?" Helen said. "I obviously make it clear enough that I want to be left alone. Judge Nolan even took judicial notice of the fact that I hate everyone, for goodness sake."

"You've never gotten a restraining order in the past," Lily said. "There must have been more to the situation with Melissa than you're telling us."

Helen shrugged. "I asked her to leave, and she wouldn't, so I filed for a restraining order."

"Then you had no reason to kill Melissa," Lily said. "You had a restraining order against her, and you could have had her arrested for trespassing or breach of the court order. You didn't need to kill her."

"It wasn't that simple," Helen said. "The judge refused to issue the restraining order."

"So you decided to kill her instead," Lily said with obvious sarcasm. "I don't believe it. I don't think you even dislike people as much as you claim, and you certainly wouldn't kill someone just because she came to visit you. Otherwise, Laura and I would have been murdered in our sleep a long time ago."

"You and Laura don't play the radio at top volume when you visit," Helen said. "And when I insist, you leave."

"Is that a hint?" Lily said.

"No," Helen said. "I'm glad you're both here. I wanted to ask you about Melissa's background. I assume you checked her references."

"Of course," Lily said.

"Do you still have copies?"

"You didn't care enough to read them when she was alive. Why do you want them now?"

"I'm curious," Helen said. "I'd like to talk to some of her other patients."

"Somehow, I don't think you're feeling nostalgic," Lily said. "Talk to them about what?"

"About their motives to kill her," Helen said. "Or who else might want her dead."

"Shouldn't you leave that to the police?" Laura said. "Howie told me not to worry too much about you, that they'd take care of everything."

"The police are never going to find Melissa's killer. They're limiting their search to one specific person, and he didn't do it."

"I'm sure they'll figure it out eventually," Laura said.

Perhaps, but then Helen would never have the satisfaction of making Detective Peterson acknowledge that she was a competent human being, capable of every bit as much violence as the next person. Of course, Laura and Lily weren't likely to be sympathetic to that argument. Instead, Helen said, "The sooner we can convince them it's not the burglar, the sooner they'll find the real culprit. I won't feel safe until then."

"You could move back to Boston," Lily said.

"Or come visit Howie and me for a while," Laura said.

"That's not necessary." If Melissa hadn't driven Helen into the arms of her nieces while she was alive, then some two-bit criminal certainly wouldn't do it. "I'd just like to take a look at Melissa's references. If there's anything in there that will help the police, then I'll pass it along to them."

"You promise?" Lily said. "You won't interfere?"

Helen raised her eyebrows. "Do I ever interfere with anything?"

Lily laughed. "You've done nothing *but* interfere for the past twenty years. It was practically your job description in the governor's mansion."

"You're the only one who ever noticed, though," Helen said. "I promise no one will notice anything I do now, either."

Lily opened her laptop. "I'm emailing you the reference letters now. But don't think I've forgotten about checking up on your lawyer. I'll be calling him first thing tomorrow."

Lily would vet him far better than Helen herself had done. Fortunately, Helen was confident his credentials would hold up to scrutiny. "Just don't talk to him for too long. He's charging me by the hour, and he's not cheap."

CHAPTER EIGHT

———

Jack had the luxury car idling in Helen's driveway the next morning, as requested, a few minutes before the replacement nurse was scheduled to arrive. The doorbell rang, reminding Helen that she wanted to ask Jack if he knew any electricians who could disconnect the doorbell. Maybe create a switch so she could turn it back on if she was expecting company she actually wanted to see.

Helen peered through the windows to check on her visitor. A short, redheaded woman stood on the porch, clutching an oversized leather purse to her chest. It was big enough to hold a couple six-packs of soda, but the woman didn't look super-caffeinated, just anxious. Barely old enough to have graduated from nursing school, permanent worry lines were already forming across her forehead.

Today's anxiety was probably just because a murder had happened a few feet from where she was standing, rather than because she considered her patient a force to be reckoned with. She was about to find out how wrong she was.

Helen limped back to her desk to grab Melissa's reference letters she wanted to discuss with Tate. Returning to the front door, she glanced at the cane hanging from the front doorknob. It was the ugly back-up one, since she still hadn't found the one she'd lost. It was probably at the law office, since there weren't any other places she could recall visiting right before it disappeared. With a little luck, she'd be able to retrieve it today, and she wouldn't need to use the back-up one any longer. In fact, she could manage without any cane at all until she got to Tate's office today.

She stepped outside and quickly closed the door behind herself. On her way past the nurse, she said, "You must be Rebecca. The agency said you'd be here this morning."

"Where are you going?" Rebecca said.

"I'll be back after your shift is over," Helen said from the bottom of the stairs. "You might as well go home now, but if you want to spend your time here, you can make yourself comfortable on the back deck. It's a beautiful day, and I even left some snacks and bottles of water on the table out there for you. Just watch out for the police tape."

Helen didn't wait for an answer, but headed off to the waiting Town Car, where Jack was emerging with his usual perfect timing to open the back door for her. Once she was inside and he was behind the wheel again, Helen allowed herself to look through the back window at Rebecca. The woman was still standing on the front porch, one arm half-raised, as if uncertain whether to try to call her patient back or politely wave farewell. Rebecca needed some lessons in assertiveness, or she'd have all her patients running roughshod over her.

Not my problem, Helen thought. *Trying to be nice is what got me stuck with Melissa and if I'd gotten rid of her right away, I wouldn't have ended up with a dead body in my yard.* Helen resolutely turned away from the confused young woman on her porch and told Jack, "The print shop, please. And then the lawyer's office."

"You want me to get rid of the new nurse for you while you're meeting with Tate?" he said. "I could take care of her and be back in time to pick you up."

"No, thank you." Jack could talk like a tough guy, but as far as she could tell, he was far more likely to vanquish the virtual enemies in his smartphone's video games than any real, live unwanted people. He complained about his ungrateful passengers, but he couldn't do anything about them, any more than he could get rid of Helen's nurse. Besides, even if he could do something about Rebecca, it wasn't necessary. The nursing agency would stop sending their employees as soon as Tate convinced them there wasn't going to be any payment for their services. "I've got it under control."

"If the situation changes, you've got my number."

She patted her cell phone. "It's right here."

After a quick stop at the print shop to pick up the crime scene photographs she'd uploaded yesterday for printing in better resolution than her home printer could manage, Jack parked in front of the law firm. She declined Jack's offer of an escort into the building, and left him to his video games.

As soon as she started up the front walk, Helen heard the sound of the lathe being used in the garage behind the law offices, and decided to talk to him first, before warning Adam that Lily was going to call to check on their credentials. The garage door was open, and Tate stood with his back to it, bent over the lathe. She didn't want to startle him, so she walked around to stand in front of him and waited for him to notice her.

After a few minutes, Tate looked up, sighed, and turned off the motor. He pushed his safety goggles up to the top of his head, pulled off the ear protection, and dropped down into his director's chair. He didn't offer her a seat of her own, and she wasn't about to ask for one.

"I was wondering if you'd seen my cane?" she said. "I thought I might have left it here."

"It's not out here. I'd have noticed if I'd suddenly acquired a new piece of wood," he said. "You'd have to ask Adam if it's in the law offices."

"Because you're retired," Helen said. "That reminds me. I was wondering why you didn't quit your job before now if you found it so unfulfilling."

"Being in jail would have been more annoying than practicing law."

"They can't send you to jail for changing careers."

"No, but if I'd quit my job, I'd have ended up in jail for nonpayment of alimony."

"There are other ways to get money."

"Robbing a bank would have landed me in jail for even longer than nonpayment of alimony."

"Not if you had a good lawyer."

"And that's where it gets tricky. I'm the best defense lawyer I could afford, but you know what they say about a person having a fool for a client if he represents himself." He finally seemed to notice the papers in Helen's hand, and gave them a look that suggested he thought they were going to burst into flame and destroy his workshop. "What are those?"

She tossed the copies of Melissa's references on top of the sawdust on the workshop table. "Melissa's reference letters."

"It's a bit late now, to be inquiring into whether she was any good at her job."

"I know more than I ever wanted to know about her work skills and shortcomings," Helen said. "What I'm wondering is whether any of her previous patients had a reason to kill her."

"I doubt they'd mention it in a letter praising her."

"That's why I'm planning to go talk to them in person," Helen said. "Find out what they really thought of her. Make sure they actually wrote these letters. That sort of thing."

"Then what are you doing here interrupting my retirement again?" he said. "I'm sure I never wrote her a reference. I never even met the woman."

"You know how to talk to witnesses."

His eyebrows rose. "You expect me to go with you to the interviews?"

"I wouldn't dream of taking you away from your woodworking." She'd hoped he might have insisted on doing the interviews himself, as a knee-jerk reaction to the idea of an untrained person conducting a cross-examination, but she'd known it was a long shot, so she wasn't terribly disappointed when he didn't take the bait. "I'd like you to teach me how to examine a witness."

"It takes years of practice to get it right."

"I don't have that much time," Helen said. "I just need to know the basics. And then I'll leave you to your work here."

"Is that what it takes to get rid of you?"

"That, or murdering me."

"No more murders." Tate pulled his safety goggles off and brushed sawdust out of his hair. "For the sort of questioning you're doing, it's a little different from what you'd do in court. But you can't just go barging in there without a plan. You need to know as much as possible about the witnesses before you talk to them, so you'll notice if their answers don't sound quite right. They don't usually lie outright, just sort of re-imagine their story in ways that make them feel better about themselves. I interviewed one guy who was clocked at over a hundred miles an hour on the highway but still denied he was close to forty miles over the speed limit, because, really, everyone goes eighty on that road, and the cops allow a ten-mile-an-hour leeway, and that meant he could go ninety, so, really, he was only fifteen miles over the speed limit. His speed was a pretty simple fact, but if I hadn't already known he was clocked at a hundred-plus miles per hour, he might have led me to believe he was only going eighty. He wouldn't have been lying, exactly, just putting his own spin on it."

"I don't have time to do that kind of research. I've read the reference letters, but they don't really say anything." She'd read them carefully last night, looking for a Perry Mason moment, a tidbit that would give her an opportunity to point out inconsistencies and demand an explanation. Or a Sherlock Holmes moment, when some tiny detail would lead her to a huge epiphany. All she'd found was generic praise, too vague to pin down inconsistencies, too broad to contain any details. The same clichés showed up in at least half of the letters, although the rest of the language was varied enough that she doubted they'd all been written by the same person. Maybe that was her one insight, she thought: the letters had been dashed off, using the most obvious phrases. They were perfunctory, not passionate. None of them felt like the writer had truly cared one way or another about Melissa.

"I don't even know where to start to find out more about them," she said, "not without provoking Judge Nolan to reconsider her stance on restraining orders, with me as the one being restrained."

Tate bent forward to take the papers from the table. He flipped past Melissa's resume to the cover sheet listing the references. "This one is the father of the mayor's husband," he said, pointing to the first name. He ran his finger down the page, stopping beside each name. "She's the mother of your favorite cop, Detective Peterson. And I believe this one is somehow related to Geoff Loring. His uncle, I think."

"All pillars of the community," Helen said glumly. "The police aren't likely to be interested in arresting any of them, not when they have a perfectly good suspect who was a petty criminal. And I bet the writers of the references are all saintly role models who would never even think a violent thought, let alone act on one."

"I wouldn't go quite that far," Tate said, "but as far as I know, they're pretty clean. I've never represented any of them in a criminal case, anyway."

"*Someone* must have had a reason to kill Melissa."

"Besides the burglar," he said. "And you, of course."

Helen nodded.

"What about her other patients? The ones who didn't write reference letters for her? She must have had hundreds of patients over the years, and there are only a dozen names here."

"I haven't heard of any patients who disliked her," Helen said. "The owner of the nursing agency told me everyone was satisfied with her work, and she'd been at her previous job for decades."

"He could have lied."

"Or simply refused to hear any complaints, the way he ignored me." Helen could easily imagine Pierce being intentionally blind to Melissa's faults. "But if there were any serious problems, there would have been at least a few written complaints that he couldn't ignore. There wasn't anything in Melissa's official records. I'm sure of that much. Lily did the hiring, and she always does her homework. She would have checked out both the agency and Melissa herself."

"Melissa worked at the Wharton Nursing Home, didn't she?" Tate flipped back to the resume on top of the pile of references. "In fact, that's probably where she met her references. Lots of retired town officials there."

"More pillars of the community," Helen said. "Kind of ruins my theory that the killer might have been a prior patient."

"Some patients are actually grateful for assistance, you know."

"Not when Melissa's the one offering it," Helen said. "I may be a hermit, but I'm not usually violent, and she made me so angry that all I cared about was making her go away. She managed to get me that furious in just a few visits, working with me only part-time, in my own home. It would have been much worse if I'd been trapped in a nursing home, imprisoned with her forty hours a week, complaining about her without anyone listening. In those circumstances, murder might seem like a reasonable option."

"If a patient killed her, how'd he get out of the nursing home to do it? He couldn't have been all that stuck in his room if he could follow Melissa all the way out to the edge of town where you live."

"Probably not a patient, then," Helen said. "What about a patient's relative? Someone who realized how harmful Melissa could be, and couldn't find a more appropriate way to fix the situation, so he did what he had to do to protect his beloved, frail, old family member?"

"Except, as far as I can tell, there's no evidence that Melissa ever harmed anyone." Tate threw the papers back on the workshop table and reached for his safety goggles. "You haven't found a single person who disliked her as much as you did, and it doesn't seem likely that you will. At least not before you get yourself arrested for some misdemeanor or another."

Helen slumped back in the chair. "Maybe the police were right about the burglar also being the killer, after all."

"Much as I hate to give up all these billable minutes we've been spending together," Tate said, rising and pulling his safety goggles down over his eyes, "it sounds like you've hit a dead end. You'll just have to resign yourself to being an innocent bystander in this murder investigation, blissfully free of any threat of prison sentence."

"I wonder if the detectives are making any progress in identifying the burglar." They wouldn't be able to ignore her if she solved the case for them. "If I can't prove someone else did it, maybe I can help them find the burglar."

"You should stay out of it," he said. "You didn't even like Melissa."

"Judging from the people who attended her wake, I don't think anyone liked her all that much. They may not have hated her, but no one seems to care that she's dead. No one's putting any pressure on the police to find her killer. The detective won't listen to me, unless I do his job for him."

"Just leave me out of it. I'm retired." Tate started to pull up his ear protection, and then paused. "You know, you might be able to get some information about the past burglaries by talking to the victim witness advocate over at the district court."

"Isn't that Judge Nolan's court?" Helen said. "I didn't do too well the last time I was there."

"I didn't say it would be easy," he said. "I thought you'd appreciate the challenge."

Helen reclaimed the copies of Melissa's references. "Getting information out of a state employee is one thing I definitely know how to do."

* * *

Helen detoured into the main building to check in with Adam. He hadn't seen her cane, and he was still working on canceling the nursing agency's contract, but promised he'd call if he had any news.

A few minutes later, when Jack pulled up in front of the courthouse, Helen remembered the steep exterior stairs. Maybe she should go back to the cottage to get her back-up cane. They hadn't been gone an hour yet, and she wasn't sure if that was long enough for Rebecca to give up and leave the cottage. One confrontation with the woman was enough for today. It wasn't like Helen *enjoyed* making other people's lives more difficult.

The railing on the courthouse stairs was sturdy enough to take the place of her cane. As long as she climbed the stairs carefully, she could handle them without additional support. She slid out of the car and left Jack to his video games.

Once inside, Helen followed the signs to the victim witness advocate's cramped little office in the architecturally grand but dysfunctional building. The door, which was half-open, read *Ms. A. Jensen, Victim Witness Advocate*. Inside, behind a cheap metal desk covered with folders, legal pads, and loose papers, sat a tall blonde woman with skin so leathery it must have come from forty years of excessive sun exposure.

The woman continued tapping on her keyboard while she said, "May I help you?"

"I'm Helen Binney. I'm here about the Remote Control Burglar."

"Of course." She put down her pen and watched Helen limp into the room. "You must have had difficulty getting up here. We're still waiting for ADA-compliant improvements to be authorized."

Helen shrugged. "I'm here now."

"Other places in the state, closer to Boston, get all the luxuries, but we can't even get the necessities like wheelchair ramps," Ms. Jensen said. "None of the state politicians care about us out here. We might as well be part of New York or Connecticut for all they notice us. They come here for their vacations, to enjoy the simple life, and then they go back to the city and forget all about us."

The advocate would be even more bitter if she knew the whole truth, Helen thought. The state politicians didn't even think about the local residents when they were here on vacation. Helen had only realized recently how little she herself had mingled with the locals, and she'd been the life of the local social scene, compared to her ex-husband. He hadn't needed to leave the cottage; he'd brought all the people who'd mattered with him, either in the flesh or virtually, through phone and internet connections.

"At least we do get some basic funding for victims' reimbursement, based on the number of cases going through the courthouse. I can start a file for you and look into getting you some compensation." The woman keyed something into her computer, and then looked at Helen expectantly. "What did the burglar take from you?"

"My nurse."

The woman started to type, and then looked back at Helen. "Like a figurine? Or a doll?"

"A human being," Helen said. "The police tell me the burglar killed her."

"I read about that in the newspaper." Ms. Jensen abandoned her keyboard and leaned back in her chair. "I'm sorry for your loss, but her family is going to have to file a claim for her death. I don't think you qualify for compensation."

"I'm not looking for money," Helen said. "I just need a few questions answered."

"Good idea." Ms. Jensen brightened. "I can refer you for some counseling. The experience of losing a skilled caretaker must have traumatized you."

"Not particularly." The only trauma had come from the police, and the way they'd assumed she was incapable of doing anything whatsoever. "At least not in the way you mean. I'm fine."

The woman's sun-etched frown lines deepened in apparent disappointment that Helen wasn't traumatized. "Are you sure? Sometimes the reaction is delayed a few days. Or weeks."

"I'm sure," Helen said. "I'm fine, but Melissa isn't. And there's a killer on the loose, who might come back for me or my family."

"That's not my department. I only deal with property crimes. Most of the compensation for serious personal injuries and deaths gets handled through a civil case, rather than the token assessment that goes to victims here in the criminal court. It's usually all worked out before the paperwork comes to me. The family gets their own lawyer, and I don't get directly involved."

"As far as I know, Melissa didn't have any family," Helen said. "Just her work."

"I can't do anything about that. Are you sure there isn't anything I can do to help you?"

"There is one thing," Helen said. "You can tell me more about the burglar and what's being done to catch him. I'd feel better if I knew he was locked up."

"Everyone feels that way." Ms. Jensen said, seeming more confident, as if this was a conversation she'd had countless times before. "It's important to acknowledge that capturing the burglar is not within your control, so you can move on."

Helen tamped down her irritation. She didn't need a verbal pat on the head or assurances that everything always turned out fine in the end. Some things didn't turn out fine. She herself was living, limping proof of that fact. She didn't need false comfort; she needed answers. "I can't move on. Not until I understand why the burglar targeted my house."

"I don't know much about this particular series of crimes," Ms. Jensen said. "The police and the D.A. only tell me the information I need to steer the victims in the right direction for obtaining services. Not about the investigations themselves."

"You must know something," Helen said. "Haven't any of the burglar's other victims been in to see you?"

"All I know is that it's been happening for about five years, and there seems to be a pattern to the timing. Most of the incidents have been clustered in May, June and December, nothing the rest of the year. But they don't know why. At least, that's what I was told the last time I saw the detective in charge of the case. He didn't seem to understand how upset people were that their homes had been broken into, even if nothing valuable had been taken."

"So it's true, that the burglar only steals remote controls?"

Ms. Jensen nodded. "From what the victims tell me, he hasn't even damaged anything while he was breaking in. No broken windows, no forced locks. Nothing."

"And he's never been violent before?"

"Never," she said. "No one's seen him, so there haven't been any confrontations at all."

"Anything else you can tell me?"

"I'm afraid not. I wish there was something more I could do to make you feel safer."

"The only useful thing you could do is to convince everyone to leave me alone," Helen said. "I'd be perfectly fine if everyone would just stop bugging me."

"Sorry," Ms. Jensen said, reaching for her keyboard to erase the information she'd started to key in. "Security is too expensive. If I had a bigger budget, I might be able to help, but as it is, I can barely cover the cost of the stolen remote controls and new locks."

As Helen stood to leave she said, "I'll mention your budget limitations to the governor the next time I talk to him."

Ms. Jensen laughed. "You do that."

It was natural for a victim advocate to assume that everyone she met was weak and powerless, and Helen might have let it slide if she weren't already so irritated by the constant condescension. "Don't underestimate me. I'm going to talk to the governor, and I'm going to find Melissa's killer."

CHAPTER NINE

———

"Did you get any useful information?" Jack said as he waited for Helen to climb into the back seat of the Town Car.

"Not really."

"Shall I take you home then?"

Her new visiting nurse was probably still there, waiting out the two hours she'd been scheduled, too nervous to go tell her boss that their patient had escaped. "Not yet."

Jack closed the door behind her and buckled himself into his seat. "So where are we going?"

"I'm thinking." There had to be something Helen could do, something that might be helpful to the investigation into Melissa's murder, since no one else seemed to care about it. Tate had been right about the futility of speaking to the people who'd written references for Melissa, but maybe she could learn something from Melissa's colleagues. Starting with an explanation for why very few of them had come to her wake.

"Do you know where the Wharton Nursing Home is?"

Jack turned around to peer at her over the back of his seat. "What did that victim's advocate tell you? You don't need nursing home care. It's not a bad place, from what I've heard, but you'd hate it there."

It would probably be better if Jack didn't know exactly what she was planning. That way, he couldn't get into trouble if the police decided she was interfering with their investigation. "I don't need that kind of medical care now, but lupus is unpredictable. I need to be prepared for possible severe flare-ups in the future."

"You had me worried for a minute, there," Jack said as he turned toward the front again. He started the engine. "I'd forgotten about the waiting list to get into any decent nursing home, and this one's pretty small, so the wait is probably even longer than average. I don't even know if they'll let you tour the place without an appointment. It's just around the corner, though, so it won't take long to find out."

The nursing home was an old, three-story stone building rising out of acres of manicured lawns. It was set back at least a thousand feet from the road, and the tree-shaded driveway divided to form a circle in front of the entrance. A discreet sign next to the over-sized front doors announced that it was the Wharton Nursing Home. Otherwise, Helen would have thought it was a private residence belonging to a millionaire, like one of the Newport "cottages." Probably had been a residence in the early 1900s, before it was converted to a nursing home.

Inside, the entry area was equally impressive, with extra-high ceilings, marble floors and dark wood paneling. Only the smells gave away the building's real use; instead of wood polish, the place reeked of antiseptic, illness, and incontinence.

A reception desk had been built to match the wood paneling. The young woman behind the counter was a sharp contrast with the early 1900s style of the room. She was in her late teens, and the epitome of contemporary style, from her short spiky hair to her mini-skirt and designer shoes.

The receptionist welcomed Helen to the nursing home and pointed to a visitors' log. Helen dutifully signed her name and made a note of the time.

"You didn't indicate who you're visiting." The young receptionist pointed to the blank spot. "We need to know, for security reasons."

"I'm not here to see anyone in particular."

"So you're here to see the facilities themselves? Let me get someone to guide you around the facilities and answer any questions you may have about our services."

"That's not necessary," Helen said. "I'd really like to know more about the staff than the premises. It's the people who make or break a place."

"Oh, we have the best people here. I've seen their certificates."

"I'm sure they're all well qualified," Helen said, "but it's a matter of personalities. I'd like to meet a few of them for myself. See how we'd mesh. I knew one woman who used to work here. You might have known her. Melissa Shores."

The receptionist nodded. "I remember her. Sort of. She left a few weeks after I started working here."

"Perhaps I could talk to someone who knew her better."

"I don't know if anyone did," the receptionist said. "She kept to herself. Worked all the time. Stayed here, even when her shift was over, so she could spend more time with the patients."

"That sounds like Melissa." She wondered if the other patients had appreciated the dedication more than Helen had. "Are any of those patients still living here?"

The receptionist stared at the ornate tin ceiling for a moment. "Betty and Josie are still here. Melissa came to visit them a few weeks ago, in fact."

"Then let's say I'm here to visit Betty and Josie," Helen said, reaching for the log book. "Where will I find them?"

The receptionist typed something into her computer. "They don't have anything scheduled right now. They're ambulatory, so they're probably in the activity area. They usually sit together in front of the fireplace. There's no fire in it, of course—smoke is far too irritating for our patients—but they like to pretend it's working. They sit next to it and make hats. Betty knits and Josie crochets."

Helen followed the receptionist's directions down assorted corridors to a space that might once have been a ballroom, but was now filled with card tables and mismatched sofas. Staff members circulated among the residents, encouraging the solitary ones to engage in activities, and just generally interfering with what the patients actually wanted to do. If, as Helen had once read, there was an infinite variety of hells, each one designed to maximize the soul's misery, this place was her own hell. Before she agreed to live in a place like this, she'd move in with Laura and Howie and a hundred grand-nieces and grand-nephews.

Just as the receptionist had predicted, two women were seated in wingback chairs in front of the cold fireplace. Judging by the piles of yarn in their laps, they had to be Betty and Josie. One woman was in her late seventies, still sturdy-looking, wearing an ankle-length black skirt topped by a black sweater sprinkled with brightly colored snips of yarn. Leaning against the feet of her chair was a tapestry bag, presumably filled with supplies, and in each lap was a pile of yarn. Her bag was made out of a tapestry fabric. The other woman was thinner and wore a pastel tunic over baggy jeans. She was a few years older, physically, but the neon green highlights in her blonde hair and the hot-pink Hello Kitty backpack holding her supplies suggested she was younger in spirit.

Helen ignored the staff members converging on her, and went over to the fireplace, trying to look like the women there were long-time acquaintances.

"What are you making?"

"Chemo caps," the woman to the left of the fireplace said, holding up a multi-colored band hanging from a circular needle. She had to be Betty, the knitter. "They're for people who've lost their hair or the ability to keep warm, due to chemo treatments."

"Want to join us?" the other woman, Josie, said. "We've got extra yarn and needles."

"I don't know how to knit," Helen said. "Or crochet."

"We could teach you," Betty said.

That wasn't a bad idea, actually. If Helen was going to stay in Wharton for the rest of her life, she ought to know more people than her driver and a retired lawyer. These two women would be a good start. If the residents in the nursing home were as connected to the local political scene as Tate had suggested, then Betty and Josie could probably introduce Helen to everyone else in town.

For all Helen knew, making hats might even turn out to be a hobby she could enjoy as much as Tate enjoyed his woodworking. "Maybe I can come back for a lesson some other time. I can't stay long today."

Josie nudged Betty. "He's here again."

Betty glanced toward the doorway, and Helen turned to see Geoff Loring standing there.

Helen turned a nearby wingback chair so it would hide her, unless he looked too closely, and dropped into the faded upholstery. "Does he have family staying here?"

"A cousin with MS. But today he's here for work," Josie said. "Comes out here every Wednesday, like clockwork. Does some fluff piece on one of the residents."

Betty laughed. "If he only knew…"

"Knew what?"

"Hello, ladies." Geoff stopped behind Helen. "Mind if I join you?"

"Have you figured out that we're the cool kids yet?" Josie said. "Are you going to interview us finally?"

"Not this week," Geoff said. "I'm saving you for a slow news cycle."

"Then you're here about Melissa's murder?" Helen said.

He shook his head. "That's old news. I'm on the trail of something bigger than that."

"Something bigger than murder?" Helen said. "Something to do with the nursing home?"

"I can't say," he said, although the smug look on his face did all the talking for him.

"I know," Josie said excitedly. "You solved the mystery of the missing teddy bear."

"What missing teddy bear?" he asked.

Betty and Josie shared another glance that suggested Geoff didn't have a clue about anything that went on at the nursing home.

"Never mind," Betty said. "We were just telling Helen about the nice little stories you do on the residents here. She's going to join our knitting circle."

"Maybe you'll convince her to let me interview her next."

"I'm not a nursing home resident," Helen said. "Just wanted to meet some of the people who knew Melissa. She used to work here, you know."

"Most of her career, I think," Geoff said. "I'd been meaning to interview her, but I waited too long. A lot of the city leaders and their family members have ended up here, and Melissa probably worked with most of them. She must have had some great experiences with them, and they'd have made great stories."

"Melissa wouldn't have told you anything," Josie said, jerking a length of yarn from its skein. "She wasn't a gossip."

That was true enough, Helen thought. Melissa had talked non-stop, but it hadn't been gossip. She'd never mentioned anyone by name, except for the day they'd been sorting pictures from the governor's mansion, and Melissa had been able to identify most of the politicians in them, some of whom Helen couldn't even remember. Until now, she hadn't stopped to think that Melissa could have known even more than just the names and job descriptions when it came to local public figures.

"Melissa would have talked to me." Geoff smiled at Helen. "Everyone does, eventually."

It sounded a bit like a threat, Helen thought, not that there was anything he could do to her if she refused to talk to him, on or off the record. He wasn't really interested in her life, anyway. He was after bigger fish, just as he'd been hoping to pump Melissa for information about her better-known patients. Melissa wouldn't have told him anything, but her patients might not have known that. One of them might have had a reason to take drastic measures to keep her quiet.

Helen asked, "Did anyone know you were planning to interview Melissa?"

"I don't share my story leads with anyone," he said. "When are you going to sit down with me for an interview?"

Never. But he wouldn't accept that. Better to give him an excuse he had to accept. "It's too soon after Melissa's death."

"I understand." Geoff patted her on the shoulder. "What happened to Melissa would have upset even a seasoned reporter like me. When you're up to it, though, call me, and we'll talk."

Not without my lawyer present. Helen shrugged his hand off her shoulder. When had everyone decided they could touch her without her permission? She'd have to ask Tate later about the definition of assault. Not that she could do much about Geoff's and Pierce's annoying little familiarities. The local judge wouldn't be any more sympathetic to criminal charges against them than she'd been to the request for a restraining order against Melissa.

Anxious to leave, now that it was obvious Geoff's presence would keep the women from saying anything useful,

Helen stood. She nodded at Betty and Josie. "I'm sorry I can't stay and learn to make hats. I've got someone waiting for me outside."

"Stop by any time," Josie said. "We've always got spare supplies for anyone who wants to join in."

"I'll do that." It would have to be a time when Geoff wasn't around, so Helen could find out what the women knew that the reporter had missed. It might not have anything to do with Melissa, but she didn't have any better leads.

"I'll walk out with you," Geoff said.

"No need," Helen said. "You've got a much better chance at getting a scoop if you stay here and learn to knit."

* * *

Geoff walked Helen out of the nursing home anyway, holding doors and offering the assistance she hadn't requested and didn't need or appreciate. If he thought that holding a few doors would convince her to give him an exclusive interview, he had another think coming.

As they approached the luxury car, Jack looked up from his video game. He glared at Geoff, who either didn't notice or didn't see any reason why he should care about the driver's disapproval. Geoff was still talking about how much she'd enjoy reading the story he wrote about her when Jack slammed the Town Car door behind Helen, cutting off the reporter's wheedling.

Jack waited until they reached the end of the long driveway before asking, "Where to?"

It was safe to go back to the cottage now, she thought. Rebecca should be long gone, and, thanks to Geoff's untimely interference, she didn't have any leads to follow. "Home, please."

"Why is that reporter bothering you?" Jack said as they headed toward the center of the town.

"It's his job."

As they drove past Tate's office, Helen noticed that the garage doors were closed, suggesting he'd closed up shop early. She wondered if he'd found that retirement wasn't quite what he'd expected it to be, and even his beloved woodworking wasn't enough to keep him occupied, or if he'd given in to the demands of his clients and gone into the law office itself.

"But why does Geoff keep harassing you?" Jack said. "Shouldn't he be writing about Melissa's murder?"

"If he were a real investigative reporter, he would be looking into the murder," Helen said. "But he doesn't seem to have the right skills for the job. I've known some great reporters, and they question everything, and then mull over everything they're told, deciding for themselves what makes sense, what doesn't. Geoff Loring doesn't do anything more than write up basic summaries of what people tell him, like a first-grader writing a book report. It's what he did with the information the police gave him on Melissa's murder. It's what he does with the human interest stories on the nursing home residents. And it's what he wants to do with a story about me—summarize whatever I say, and hope that people find it interesting, just because I'm the governor's ex-wife."

"You probably got that a lot before you moved here," Jack said. "I'll make sure to keep an eye out for him the future, so we can avoid him."

"Don't worry about it," Helen said. "I can take care of myself."

"How did he know you were at the nursing home?"

Helen was startled by the idea that Geoff might have been following her. She'd encountered a couple minor stalkers in her days in the governor's mansion, but she hadn't expected that sort of thing now that she was retired. Then she realized that Jack was giving Geoff far more credit than he deserved.

"I'm sure he wasn't following me. It's a small town, after all. Nothing more than a coincidence, running into me there. Apparently he visits there at least once a week."

"He shouldn't be bothering the people who live there, either."

"I don't think they mind. It breaks up the monotony of their days," she said. "There's no harm in it. It's not like he's doing any real investigating. He seems to think there's a big story just out of reach somewhere, but he'd be better off if he actually dug into some of the stuff he's already written about, and got to the bottom of it."

"Like Melissa's death?"

"That would be a good start," Helen said. "The burglaries, too. They've been going on for so long that someone should have had some idea of who was doing them before Melissa was killed. I've read all the newspaper accounts, and no one seems to know anything at all about the perpetrator."

"What's to know?" Jack said. "Someone's stealing stuff. Happens all the time. I had a limo passenger two weeks ago who stole the towel that was wrapped around the champagne bottle. I mean, the guy could afford a thousand-dollar bottle of champagne, and he's too cheap to buy his own kitchen towels."

"That's different," Helen said. "Your passenger didn't break into someone's house to steal anything. It didn't require any planning or skills. Just see something and grab it."

"Maybe the other burglaries happened the same way," Jack said. "Spur of the moment sort of things."

"They're certainly random enough for that to be true," Helen said. "Random enough that you'd expect the thefts to be unconnected, but the police are sure they're all connected, because of the oddity of what was taken and not taken. Beyond that, no one's been able to see any clear pattern in the timing or motivation or geography. The victim advocate said that most of them happened in May, June and December, but that doesn't narrow things down too much. I thought there was supposed to be more of a pattern to crimes."

"You can't believe everything you read." Jack turned the Town Car onto her street. "Especially in the local paper."

"That's certainly true." Geoff Loring wouldn't recognize a pattern if she drew it on his notepad. And the police hadn't been taking the burglaries seriously until now. They hadn't collected any fingerprints or checked for other forensic evidence at those crime scenes, so there was nothing to compare to the items confiscated from the vicinity of where Melissa was killed. "Until the burglar strikes again, there really isn't much that anyone can do to identify him."

"If he knows what's good for him," Jack said, "he's lying low until the killer's caught."

Jack ought to know how a criminal would think, what with all the family members who'd hired Tate to represent them. "What were your cousins arrested for, anyway?"

"You don't think they'd try to rob you, do you?" Jack braked more sharply than usual at the last stop sign before her driveway. "I wouldn't let them do that to someone nice like you."

"They might not have bothered to ask for your permission."

"They're not burglars," Jack said firmly, easing off the brake and rolling the Town Car forward. "Their arrests were always for assault. They'd get drunk and then start fistfights. They've got good jobs, and they don't have any reason to steal from anyone, least of all from someone who'd never done anything bad to them. They work hard and they play hard, that's all."

Interesting, Helen thought. In the governor's mansion, financial skirmishes among colleagues were the norm, but physical assaults were largely unheard of. In Jack's world, assault was practically respectable, while theft was considered bad form.

"If you trust your cousins," she said, "then so do I."

"Good." Jack parked in front of her cottage. "I like you, Miss Binney, but I couldn't work with someone who didn't trust me and my family."

CHAPTER TEN

———

Jack delivered Helen back home at noon, two hours after they'd left, which should have been plenty of time for Rebecca to leave. The nurse apparently had a deeply buried stubborn streak, though, judging by the fact that she was still waiting on the front porch, sitting on the uncomfortably hard brick, looking anxious and apologetic.

"I know you don't want me here, but I can't charge for time when you're not here," Rebecca said as she rose to her feet. "I don't have any other appointments for today, and I really need the money. I won't be a bother, I promise. You'll hardly even know I'm here."

Helen could feel herself succumbing to guilt at the thought of sending the nurse home without her billable time. Helen didn't need a nurse, but she could use some help.

"As long as you're here," Helen said, "you might as well come in and help me organize some papers."

"Papers?" Rebecca said. "But I'm from the nursing agency, not the secretarial one. You don't expect me to type, do you? I've never been very good at it. It takes me forever to key my notes into the new electronic patient files."

Helen unlocked the front door. "No typing, I promise. But if you come into my house, I expect you to provide the help I actually need, not the help I don't want."

She clutched her bag uncertainly. "I'm supposed to take your blood pressure. I'm not sure I'll get paid if I don't do it."

"If they won't pay you for the visit because of that, I will," Helen said. "Or you can leave. I don't need anything other than the help with my papers."

The nurse took a tentative step into the cottage, without closing the door behind her. "Maybe I should call someone to find out what I should do."

"That's up to you." Helen limped over to her built-in desk space. Her hip still hadn't settled down after the tumble out the bedroom window. She should have taken the spare cane with her on this morning's trip, but she'd been counting on finding the other one at Tate's office, and she hated the way the spare one's ugliness drew attention to her mobility issues even more than the one she'd lost. Next time she went out, though, she wasn't going to be so vain. It was more important to get her hip stabilized. If her nieces saw her hobbling like she was now, they'd have her committed, for sure.

Rebecca looked at her cell phone uncertainly, while Helen checked her answering machine. Lily had called to let her know that a security consultant would be visiting the cottage to design a system for her.

Oh, goodie. More visitors.

Helen looked at the stack of scrapbooks filled with newspaper articles about the burglar and then looked at the dithering Rebecca. "Make up your mind," Helen snapped, "If you're going to stay, then you can help me carry these scrapbooks over to the kitchen island. After that, I could use something to eat to keep up my strength. We both could. There's plenty of food in the fridge. Or do I need to hire a caterer?"

"No, no," Rebecca said, dropping her cell phone back into the pocket of her pastel pink scrubs top. At least there were no sickeningly cute animals on it. "I can make lunch for you. I've been taking nutrition classes, you know."

"I don't want nutrition lectures." She didn't need another person telling her what she could and couldn't eat, on top of everyone already telling her what she could and couldn't do. "I just want lunch."

Rebecca let the door shut behind her and scurried across the room to retrieve the scrapbooks and carry them over to the kitchen island. She then went to investigate the contents of Helen's refrigerator. Fortunately, Helen had chosen the food in there herself, so whatever Rebecca came up with couldn't be too bad. Helen could afford to be nice to her, this once. After all, it was going to be Rebecca's last day here. If Tate's nephew was even half as good as Tate claimed he was, he'd have the agency's contract cancelled by tomorrow.

Rebecca was putting the final touches on a salad and mumbling about the high-fat content of the available dressings, when there was a knock at the front door.

"I'll get it," Rebecca said, pushing aside some of the papers on the island to make room for the salad bowl next to Helen's right hand.

Helen's first impulse was to tell Rebecca to ignore the visitor, but then she realized it was probably the security system guy, so she didn't object.

When Gordon Pierce walked in, though, Helen regretted not insisting on answering the door herself. This was what she got for letting other people help her: a visitor wearing a lime green and pink plaid seersucker jacket with a matching green cravat.

He bent to whisper to Rebecca. "How's she doing today?"

"I can hear you," Helen said.

Rebecca looked back over her shoulder at Helen, as if asking for permission to answer her boss.

Helen took pity on Rebecca and said, "I'm fine. I'm always fine, or I would be if everyone would just leave me alone. That's what I keep telling everyone, and no one ever listens to me."

Pierce nodded, and confided to Rebecca in the same, perfectly audible whisper, "I see she's in one of her moods again. Don't worry. It's not your fault. You can head on out now. I'll stay with the patient for a while."

"But I haven't taken her blood pressure yet, and you can't do it." Rebecca's hand came up to cover her mouth, as if belatedly realizing she'd criticized her boss.

Helen silently cheered her on. *You tell him, girl. Damn right Pierce wasn't taking my blood pressure. Not unless he wanted to have assault charges filed against him.*

Pierce took Rebecca's hand and patted it. "I think we can skip the blood pressure reading, just this once."

Rebecca turned to Helen, pleading for understanding.

"Stay or leave, it's up to you," Helen told her before turning to Pierce. "My blood pressure is fine. Or it was until you showed up. What do you want?"

"Nothing worth your getting all worked up about," he said.

Rebecca scurried across the room to grab her bag and leave. She shut the door behind her, so carefully that Helen didn't even hear the door latch click into place, having already turned back to the pile of scrapbooks on the island in front of her.

"I was just wondering," Pierce said as he took the seat across from Helen. "Did Melissa leave any of her paperwork here? You know how the medical insurance companies are, I'm sure. If we want to get paid, we have to dot every "i," cross every "t." In triplicate."

"Melissa didn't leave anything inside the cottage." Except a couple cans of Diet Pepsi, but Helen had poured them out already. "The police confiscated everything she had on her."

"They don't have what I'm looking for." Pierce helped himself to a cucumber slice from Helen's salad, and she slapped his hand away before he could take another one.

"Maybe they're in her car."

"I've already checked there."

"I didn't know they'd found it," Helen said. "Where was it?"

"At the repair shop," Pierce said. "Apparently it broke down on the way to your cottage that morning. Something to do with the alternator, I'm told. Such a dedicated nurse, Melissa was. She called for a tow, and then hitched a ride here, so you wouldn't be here all alone."

"I like being alone," Helen said automatically. She would have been more irritated with Pierce if it weren't for the fact at least now she knew that Melissa had been killed in the morning, not the night before. If she could find out exactly when the tow truck had been called, it would help to narrow down the time of death even more. "Melissa wasn't supposed to be here that morning. It would have been better if she'd gone with her car to the repair shop."

"I understand. You don't want to feel responsible for her being surprised by the burglar." He reached for another cucumber slice, and Helen pushed the whole salad toward him. She certainly wasn't going to eat it now.

"I'm not responsible for Melissa's being here that morning," Helen said. "Especially if it was before 9:00. I never do anything before then, and she knew it. If she was driving somewhere at that hour, it wasn't to come see me."

"Where else would she have been going?" he said, picking up her salad bowl. "She called for the tow a little after 7:30 that morning. It wouldn't have taken more than ten or fifteen minutes for her to get here from where her car was picked up. Even if she had to wait a few minutes to catch a ride, she'd have been here by 8:00. There wasn't enough time to go see another patient before coming back to check on you, especially without her own car. She must have come straight here, planning to wait outside until you woke up, but instead she ran into the burglar."

He was probably right, up to the point where it was the burglar doing the murder. Helen usually got out of bed around 8:30, and that morning had been pretty routine up until the discovery of Melissa's body. Certainly no fatal scuffle had been going on outside. Helen would have noticed.

The call to the tow company put Melissa's time of death between 8:00 and 8:30. It also meant that Helen didn't have much of an alibi. Being at home, alone and asleep, was even more worthless than usual when the murder occurred a few feet away from the suspect's bedroom window. The police really should have been investigating Helen instead of assuming that a petty burglar had suddenly graduated to murder.

Pierce set down the empty salad bowl. "So, how do you like Rebecca?"

"I'm sure she's a very nice person and is very skilled," Helen said, "but I don't need a nurse."

"We could try someone else." He pulled out his smartphone. "What about…"

"No," Helen said. "I'm not agreeing to anything without my lawyer present. If you haven't talked to him already, he'll be calling you. It's the firm of Tate and Bancroft."

Pierce stopped scrolling through his database. "You don't need a lawyer to talk to me. I'm here for you, whatever you need."

"That's the whole problem," Helen said. "I don't need anything, and I don't want you or anyone else here."

"I understand," he said, putting away the smartphone and taking Helen's hand to pat it.

She was so startled by his easy capitulation that she didn't pull her hand away.

"You miss Melissa," he said. "We all do. She was so beloved by her patients. It's why I hired her, you know—her dedication to her work. It wasn't easy to steal her away from the nursing home."

Now that he mentioned it, she did wonder why Melissa would have agreed to give up the job she supposedly loved so much. "How did you get her to leave the nursing home?"

"I wouldn't have been able to, without the budget cuts there," Pierce said. "You know how it is with government-run entities these days, and the nursing home is owned by the town. It's been hit with budget issues like every other department."

That was the sort of thing Helen could understand. It had been hard enough running the governor's mansion before all the recent state budget cuts. She couldn't imagine how her successor, her ex's cousin, was managing in the current economy.

Pierce continued, "Melissa loved her work, didn't ever want to retire completely. And they were cutting hours at the nursing home. She couldn't bear to see what it did to her patients, and she couldn't live on what they were paying her, not without a second job, and if she did that, she wouldn't have time to volunteer at the radio station. I could offer her enough to live on, even working part-time."

"So the money was the only reason she left?"

"What else is there, really?" Pierce said.

"Job satisfaction." Even when Helen's duties in the governor's mansion had been overwhelming, she'd always known that she was doing something worthwhile, and that she was appreciated. Leaving the work behind had, in many ways, been harder than leaving her marriage behind. "What about her patients? Didn't she feel like she was abandoning them?"

"Of course. And they loved her. All of them. But she didn't have any choice. She needed a living wage. It's not like she had any family who could help her out."

Or friends, as far as Helen had been able to tell from the attendance at Melissa's wake. The woman really had been all alone in the world. There was no one with any strong emotional ties to Melissa, the sort where love might turn to hate or murderous rage. But if the murder wasn't personal to Melissa, it really did mean the burglar was the most likely suspect in her murder. Other than Helen, of course. She knew she hadn't done it, and the burglar theory still didn't feel right. That left only one other possibility: that the murder had been completely random.

She had to force herself to consider the possibility. A random killer meant that, in all likelihood, he would never be identified and charged with the crime. Notwithstanding all the advances in forensics, there was no way to find a random killer, no way to stop him, no way to feel secure from him. Just thinking about it made her feel more helpless than everyone already believed she was.

Helen was relieved to hear a vehicle's tires crunching to a stop in her gravel driveway. Even the prospect of more visitors was better than dwelling on helplessness. It was probably the security company, but Pierce didn't need to know that. Better to let him think it was something he wanted to avoid.

"It sounds like my lawyer is here," she told Pierce. "He said he might stop by this afternoon. As long as you're still here, you might as well make yourself useful, and let him in, so you can discuss cancellation of the contract."

"Actually, I was just leaving," Pierce said, jogging toward the back door. "I'll talk to him later."

She was relieved to see him go, and amused by how much of a rush he'd been in, as if he'd thought she might try to stop him. There was no chance of that. She couldn't have caught up with his long-legged pace on a good day, and today definitely wasn't a good one.

* * *

The arriving vehicle actually belonged to Lily. Laura got out of the passenger side and raced over to the front porch to hug Helen.

A moment later, Lily joined them and said, "Pierce from the nursing agency called me first thing this morning. He's not happy."

"Too bad," Helen said. "Come see my latest scrapbook."

"I'm sure it's beautiful." Laura let herself into the cottage and headed over to the kitchen island, where she dutifully turned the pages filled with newspaper clippings. Even Laura couldn't bring herself to consider the unembellished text esthetically pleasing, so she settled for saying, "Interesting."

"I thought you gave up scrapbooking," Lily said. "Didn't you switch to photography?"

"That's the beauty of retirement. I can do both." Helen pushed aside an empty scrapbook and found the packet of pictures she'd picked up from the local print shop earlier. "Want to see my latest prints?"

"Not unless they're a lot better than the ones you emailed us," Lily said. "If you hadn't told me they were from your visit with us, I wouldn't have recognized anything in them."

"She's bound to get better with practice," Laura said, pulling the pictures out of the packet. "Or not."

Lily glanced at the top one. "That's a picture of grass. Not bad, if that's what you're aiming for, but why would you want a picture of grass?"

"I like grass." Helen reached for the pictures. "It's a classic subject for art. Walt Whitman wrote a whole book of poems about grass. Why can't I photograph it?"

"Wait." Lily tugged the packet out of her sister's hands and flipped through the pictures. "I know what these are. They're pictures of the crime scene in your yard. You're still trying to prove you killed Melissa."

Helen took the pictures back. "Someone has to do it."

"The police," Lily said firmly. "Not you. You're supposed to stay safely inside your nice little cottage, scrapbooking or doing whatever else you enjoy, not wandering around outside taking pictures of grass and police tape."

Laura said, "They're very nice pictures of grass and police tape, actually. I do think you're getting better at photography. Maybe you're just better at landscapes than portraits."

"That's a kind thought," Helen said. "I may have a better hobby lined up, anyway. I met someone who offered to teach me to knit. Or crochet. Something that involves yarn, anyway."

"I'm not buying it," Lily said. "You wouldn't give up your murder investigation that easily. At least promise me you won't interfere with the official investigation."

"There's nothing to interfere with," Helen said. "The police are investigating the wrong suspect."

"What if they're right?" Laura said. "What if the burglar really was here, and he comes back, and he finds you here, all alone?"

"I'm getting an alarm system."

"That's a good start," Lily said. "But it's not enough. By the time the police could respond—assuming you haven't totally alienated them, so that they dally on the way—you could be seriously hurt."

"I'll get a dog," Helen said. "Burglars are supposed to be afraid of them. More than they worry about alarm systems."

"I'd like a dog," Laura said. "Howie says we have to wait until the children are older, though."

"Aunt Helen won't get a dog," Lily said. "The only creature that irritates her more than *homo sapiens* is *canis lupus familiaris*."

"I'll get an attack cat."

"Cats are nice too," Laura said. "Maybe we'll get a dog *and* a cat for the kids. But a cat might be dangerous for you. They can get underfoot. What if you tripped over it?"

"Besides, a pet can't really help if someone's here to kill you," Lily said. "A vicious enough dog might protect you, but you wouldn't be able to handle him by yourself. And a pet can't dial 911 for real help. You need someone here with you, at least part-time, and you know it."

"I don't need anyone," Helen said. "Look what happened to the last person who was here, and she wasn't even full-time. I don't want another death on my conscience."

"You don't feel the least bit guilty about Melissa's death," Lily said.

She was wrong, but Helen didn't want to give her nieces yet another reason to worry. "You and Laura are feeling enough guilt for the three of us."

"We did hire her," Laura said. "It's natural that we'd feel responsible for her, since she died protecting you."

"That's not what happened," Helen said, even though she knew it was futile.

"You just don't want to believe it's what happened," Lily said. "I'd like to not believe it too, but it's the only thing that makes sense."

"It was *not* the Remote Control Burglar who killed her," Helen said. "If you read the newspaper articles about him, you'd know it. In fact, if you actually want to be helpful, you *would* read these articles about him. There has to be a clue to his identity or at least his MO here somewhere, and I just can't see it. Maybe a fresh pair of eyes will help."

"If that's what you really want—" Laura began, only to be cut off by her sister.

Lily said, "Don't encourage her."

Maybe establishing a timeline for the burglaries would help establish some sort of pattern to them, Helen thought, tuning out the girls' chatter. The victim advocate had mentioned that virtually all of the burglaries had happened in May, June, and December. So, if the burglar really was the killer, what had he been doing at her house in March? Unless the pattern wasn't as clear as the victim advocate had suggested. It might be worth double-checking. Now that the newspaper articles were organized in the scrapbooks, she could make a spreadsheet. Date, location, stolen items. That sort of thing. The police had probably done something similar, but it wouldn't hurt if she went over it again.

Helen searched through the clutter on the kitchen island for a blank piece of paper, and realized that there was pause in the girls' conversation. They were waiting for her to say something. "Right, right. Whatever."

"Really?" Laura said, her excited tone warning Helen that it was time to pay attention again. She'd work on the burglar's timeline after the nieces left.

"Don't give her the chance to change her mind," Lily said.

"Change my mind about what?"

"Agreeing to hire a big, strong, scary person to stay here until the killer is caught," Laura said.

"I never agreed to that."

Lily shook her head. "Short-term memory is a tricky thing. They say it's the first part of the brain to fail, and before you know it, Dr. Jamison is signing the paperwork to have you committed involuntarily to a nursing home."

"It's up to you," Laura said. "But it's a good idea. If the burglar knew there was a big, strong person living here, he would think twice about coming back."

"What about your driver?" Laura said. "Would he be interested in a part-time security job?"

"You haven't met Jack yet, have you?" Helen said. "He's not what you'd call big or strong. Unless, of course, the threat comes from an animated villain in one of his video games. Then, he's lethal."

"We can find someone for you," Lily said.

"Give me a minute to think." A live-in bodyguard would be even more irritating than a visiting nurse. She needed to come up with an alternative, someone who would satisfy the nieces, while also staying out of her way. There were a number of people back in Boston who would have been happy to do whatever she asked, stopping by whenever the nieces were visiting, but staying out of her way the rest of the time. Here, though, she couldn't think of anyone who might help, and it was too far to expect someone to come out from Boston.

Besides Jack, the only person she knew reasonably well around here was Tate. He met the criteria of big and strong, and if she had to have someone around, he had the additional virtue of not talking much. Besides, most of the criminals in town either were indebted to him for keeping them out of jail in the past, or were keeping open the option of hiring him in the future, so they wouldn't bother anyone he was connected with.

"I've got someone in mind," Helen said. "Before you two do anything drastic, give me a couple days to see if he's interested."

CHAPTER ELEVEN

―――――

After the nieces left, Helen called Jack to take her to Tate's office. She found the lawyer in his cluttered, dark garage workshop, making what she assumed was another lamp stem.

"Don't tell me," Tate said as he turned off the lathe. "You've killed someone else. Probably the reporter. Geoff Loring."

"Not yet, although he's fairly high on my list," Helen said. "I promise to make it both unpredictable and unusual when I kill my next victim, though."

"I appreciate it." Tate took off his goggles. "My clients so seldom consider my boredom quotient when they're contemplating a crime."

"I would never be that gauche," Helen said. "In fact, I'm here because I've been thinking about how you deserve something better than this sorry excuse for a woodworking shop."

He shrugged. "The price is right. I'd have to convince my nephew to hire me full-time if I wanted to rent a real workshop, and then I wouldn't have time to use it."

"There's another option," Helen said. "I have an unused garage on my property. It has much better lighting and more space, and potential clients wouldn't be able to find you out there."

"*You* could still find me."

"A small price to pay for a nice, private workshop," she said, skimming over the additional commitment she needed from him: convincing her nieces that he was watching over her on a regular basis. He couldn't be all that averse to a white lie or two; it was practically a prerequisite for his work as a lawyer, after all. And she only needed him to agree not to contradict her when she claimed he was staying in the guest suite on the second floor of the cottage.

"With you, there are always hidden costs." Tate paused, clearly weighing whether he could afford her offer. "You're right about how cramped this space is, though. No promises, but I'll stop by later to take a look at your garage. If it's better than this, I'll consider it."

"You won't regret it." Her garage was infinitely better than this place. "I'll be home all afternoon. Stop by whenever you'd like."

"I will. Now, go away so I can get some work done."

She turned to leave and then remembered her favorite cane, which she still hadn't found. "Do you know if Adam has had a chance to look for my other cane? I still haven't found it, and I can't think of where else I might have left it.

He shook his head. "I haven't seen it, and Adam hasn't said anything to me about it. You know, I could make you a new one, if you want. I made several of them as practice pieces when I first took up wood-turning."

"I'd rather find the old one," Helen said. "Its disappearance is going to bug me until I do."

Adam appeared in the doorway. "Uncle Tate? One of your old clients is asking for you. Said no one else can help him. He won't believe me when I say you've retired, and he refuses to leave until he hears it from you. You'll have to explain it to him."

Helen couldn't have timed the ex-client's arrival better if she'd planned it. She hid her grin with a scowl. "Some clients are just so demanding. You'll never get a moment to yourself as long as you're working so close to the law office."

Tate shook his head at her, and told his nephew, "I'll be there in a minute."

"Don't bother to see me out," Helen said. "Go take care of your client. I'm sure he won't take up too much of your valuable woodworking time."

* * *

The next time there was a knock on the cottage's front door, Helen took the precaution of peering out the window beside the front door to confirm that it was indeed Tate standing on the porch.

"Give me a minute to get the keys," she told him, "and I'll show you the garage."

Tate nodded. "I'll meet you over there. I want to take a look at the windows from the outside."

Helen snagged the keys from the kitchen island and her ugly spare cane from beside the front door and then headed out of the cottage. Halfway to the garage, she heard another vehicle arriving. This time, it was the security company's van. She tossed the garage keys to Tate, and went to greet the latest arrival.

A muscle-bound, redheaded man was climbing out of the driver's side door. He introduced himself as Marty Reed, the owner of the security company, and launched into an earnest spiel about the urgent need for security in an increasingly unsafe world.

Helen was vaguely aware of another person getting out of the far side of the vehicle, but it wasn't until he came around the front of the van and said, "Afternoon, Miss Binney," that she realized it was Jack. Instead of his traditional dark suit, he wore a uniform that matched the one the company's owner wore: blue work pants with a matching shirt emblazoned with the security company's logo on its back.

"If the front door's open," Jack said, "I'll let myself in. I need to take some measurements for our records, while the boss is discussing all the options with you."

Jack was inside the cottage by the time Tate emerged from the garage and strolled over to greet Marty by name. After the two men shook hands, Marty excused himself to go check on his assistant.

"Well?" said Helen. "Would the garage be suitable for your workshop?"

"I'm considering it." Tate returned the keys to her. "What's up with the security system? I thought you didn't believe the interrupted-burglary theory."

"I don't," she said. "My nieces were worried, and I didn't want them upset, so I let them hire the security company."

"They made a good choice," Tate said, leaning against the van. "Marty's the best in town."

"It's not particularly reassuring to know that my security expert is on a first-name basis with a criminal defense lawyer."

"I never represented him," Tate said. "He installed the system at my office."

The cottage's front door opened. Jack came down the steps and jogged toward the van.

"Jack." Tate acknowledged the man without any of the warmness he'd shown when greeting Marty.

Jack pulled open the back door of the van. "It's okay, Tate. Ms. Binney knows about my family's disreputable past, and that you represented my cousins. I was the one who recommended you to her."

"Thanks," Tate said. "But I wasn't worried about the effect of your reputation on her. I was more concerned about the effect of her reputation on you. Has she gotten you fired from your driving job already?"

"Nah," Jack said. "I just help Marty out whenever he needs an extra hand, if I'm not scheduled to drive. You know how it is. This time of year, things can be a little slow in the transportation industry."

"See?" Helen said. "Not everything is my fault."

"Just Melissa's murder," Tate said dryly.

"Ms. Binney had nothing to do with that," Jack said earnestly. "She's a good person. I should know. I see all kinds in my business."

"It's okay," Helen told Jack, with a quelling glance at Tate. She really didn't need yet another person helping her unnecessarily. Especially if he was going to be visiting the garage on a daily basis.

"But he called you a murderer," Jack said. "What if someone believed him?"

"No one really believes I can do anything," Helen reassured him. "No one's going to arrest me. And if someone does, I've already got Tate on retainer. He'd have to represent me for free if he's the one who gets me into trouble, and he'd really hate that."

Tate shrugged. "I don't know. Might be nice to have my landlord in jail. No one to bother me in my new workshop."

"Workshop?" Jack looked confused.

"Tate's going to be using the garage for his woodworking," Helen said.

Jack perked up. "That's wonderful, Ms. Binney. Then you won't be alone any more."

Oh, yeah, just what she'd always wanted.

Tate grinned and told the well-meaning Jack, "I'm sure Ms. Binney appreciates having visitors here as much as I enjoyed them in my old workshop."

* * *

Tate took the garage keys with him to have duplicates made, Marty and Jack roamed around the cottage taking measurements, and Helen settled down at the kitchen island to study the newspaper clippings about the burglaries.

There had to be a pattern to the crimes, she thought, even if no one had seen it yet. A spreadsheet, that was what she needed. If she collected all the data she had in one spot, then she'd be able to see the missing link. Sort of like when she'd used computerized charts to arrange the seating for her husband's sit-down events. She'd always found it helpful to have all the information about the guests in one organized spot. That way, she could see who was feuding with whom, so she could keep them apart, while still accommodating all the protocols for seniority and other statuses.

Eventually, Marty and Jack left with a promise to have a quote ready for Lily's approval by Monday. Helen moved her clippings and notes back to the computer desk to begin filling in the cells of a spreadsheet. Dates, addresses, times of day, items taken, anything at all that she could learn about the victims from the newspaper clippings. She added columns for types of residence, size of family, presence of dogs and other security measures. There were houses, condos, apartments; big families, small families and individuals; dogs and no dogs; alarm systems and no alarm systems.

Hours later, when she was done, she had to admit that as far as she could tell, the police were right. There was absolutely no pattern to the burglaries. If not for the one thing that linked them—the fact that the only stolen items were remote controls—the variety in the data would have suggested that the crimes were unrelated, and there were several thieves instead of just one.

She couldn't believe that there was a whole gang of thieves interested in nothing but remote controls. It *had* to be the work of a single criminal.

Something about the data was niggling at her, though. She was missing some connection, and she knew it. She just couldn't seem to put her finger—or her cursor—on it.

Helen retrieved some left-over salad from the refrigerator and nibbled on it at her desk. She studied the spreadsheet for another hour, and the only thing that came close to being a pattern was the time of day when the crimes occurred. She couldn't come up with a specific time for some of the thefts, but at least for those cases where the time could be pinpointed, they had all taken place in the late afternoon, between 2 p.m. and 4 p.m. The story was the same each time: the victim went to run an errand or pick up the kids at school, and the remote that they remembered tossing on a table or counter on the way out the door was missing when they returned home. But that only accounted for about half of the thefts. The other half of the victims were unable to say when the remote had gone missing. Most couldn't even say for sure which day it had happened, let alone pinpoint a two-hour timeframe.

Still, Helen thought it was interesting that no one had mentioned a theft happening while they were out delivering the kids to school in the morning, rather than picking them up in the afternoon. Not one of the thefts had been reported to have happened anywhere close to the time when Melissa had purportedly encountered the burglar.

Helen couldn't point to any concrete reason, but studying the newspaper articles had left her more convinced than ever that Melissa hadn't been killed by the Remote Control Burglar. Not that anyone cared about what Helen believed. Detective Peterson wouldn't listen to anything she might tell him, and she had to admit that there probably wasn't much he could do with the fact that half of the crimes had happened at approximately the same time of day. It didn't provide anyone with an alibi, it didn't offer any insights into the burglar's motivation, and it didn't narrow down the possible suspects for either Melissa's killer or the Remote Control Burglar.

Helen had to acknowledge that she'd hit a dead end, at least until she could get more information to key into her spreadsheet. The police weren't going to tell her anything more, but she might be able to get something out of Geoff Loring. At least he pretended to listen to her. It was risky, because she didn't want to lead him on, giving him a reason to believe she might grant him an on-the-record interview. But she needed to know what he might have left out of the newspaper articles. She'd just have to make it clear that she only wanted to talk about one story—Melissa's—and not her own.

It was too late to talk to Geoff tonight, but she could call him first thing tomorrow to arrange a meeting.

CHAPTER TWELVE

———

The next morning, before Helen had a chance to call Geoff Loring, Lily and Laura were knocking at the cottage's front door. Laura was carrying a canvas bag, presumably containing brunch, as an apology for their unannounced visit. Except, with Laura's hit-or-miss baking, she might need to follow up later with an apology for the food.

Helen let them in, and Laura bustled over to the kitchen island with her canvas bag. Helen watched long enough to see that Laura had brought what appeared to be a mountain of irregularly shaped home-made bagels, before settling at the kitchen island with Lily. "Are you two going to show up every day from now on?"

Lily shook her head. "We're just following up on the security arrangements."

"The alarm company was out here yesterday, and the owner's planning to send you the proposal on Monday," Helen said. "As far as I can tell, he's planning to make this cottage safer than the governor's mansion."

"What about the human component?" Lily said. "You were supposed to find someone to stay with you until the killer is caught."

"It's all been arranged," Helen said.

Laura paused halfway through pulling the foil off the top of the cream cheese tub. "You found a roommate? Already?"

"Are the bagels ready to eat?" Helen said. "I'm starved."

"I know they look a little funny, but I think they taste good," Laura said. "Considering this was my first time with any kind of yeast breads."

"I'm sure the bagels will be fine," Lily said, from long experience with placating her sister about her cooking. "I'm more interested in hearing about the roommate. Who is he? When's he moving in?"

"You don't know him," Helen said. "He's a woodworker. Needed a better workshop space."

"An artist?" Lily said, radiating suspicion. "Maybe I should check him out before he actually moves in. What's his full name?"

"I told you I'd handle this," Helen said, except then she heard a vehicle coming up her gravel driveway and realized it was probably Tate. Too late to warn him off until her nieces left. If people were so intent on visiting her, was it too much to ask that they call ahead? "That's probably him now."

"Do you think he'd like a bagel?" Laura said.

Lily could learn a lot—too much, maybe—from a stranger's reaction to a bagel, especially if this was one of Laura's misses instead of one of the hits. "I think he'd like to be left alone."

"I'll take him a bagel," Lily said. "Everyone likes bagels."

Helen glanced out the window. Tate had backed a big black pick-up truck to the garage, and was getting out of the driver's side while Adam was getting out of the passenger side. "Better make it two. He brought a helper."

Helen snagged her ugly spare cane on the way out to the garage, resigned to the fact that there was no way she would be able to get to Tate and warn him off before the determined, more mobile, bagel-bearing Lily pounced on him. Helen had to trust that Tate would be as unencouraging with Lily as he was with everyone else who interfered with his woodworking.

When Helen reached the pick-up, Tate and Adam were already rolling a large, metal work table down a ramp from the truck bed and into the empty garage. Lily was waiting for them inside with two bagels wrapped in paper napkins.

"Hi. I'm Helen's niece, Lily," she said, handing Tate a bagel.

"Thanks." Tate placed his untasted bagel on the just-moved table before heading back up the ramp.

Lily, still clutching the second bagel, followed him to the truck, although she had enough sense to stay off the ramp and out of the way. At least for the moment.

"I hear you're an artist," Lily said.

Tate picked up a toolbox and carried it down the ramp. "Woodworker."

Lily stayed beside him. "Have you been doing that kind of thing for long?"

"Decades." Tate returned to the truck with Lily shadowing him.

"You must be really good, then. Where do you sell your products?"

Tate carried a milk crate full of assorted tools to the garage. "I can afford the rent here, if that's what you want to know."

"Did you give Aunt Helen your financial information?"

"Your aunt's satisfied with the deal. That's good enough for me." He tapped Adam on the shoulder. "This isn't a spectator sport. You're supposed to be helping, so you can be rid of me, at last."

"I don't want to be rid of you," Adam said as he joined his uncle on the truck's bed to help maneuver the tool cabinet onto a hand truck. "I keep asking you to stick around, in fact. Nobody wants you to leave, except for you, so I have to accept it."

"See?" Helen said to Lily. "Some people defer to their elders' wishes."

"Some people aren't me." Lily turned her sights on Adam, making Helen think she'd made a mistake in bringing him to her niece's attention. Despite Adam's legal training, he just didn't have the extensive experience that his uncle had with deflecting difficult questions.

Lily sauntered over to the hapless Adam. "This bagel's for you."

"Thanks," he said, and unlike his uncle, he immediately unwrapped the napkin to check it out. "What kind is it?"

"Home-made kind," Lily said. "Just eat it, and tell me what you think of it."

"You made it?" Adam broke off a bite-sized piece and studied it carefully.

"My sister did." Lily pointed at Laura, who was arranging five place settings on the table of the back deck. "She likes to cook."

Adam still hesitated. "Is she any good at it?"

"You'll find out as soon as you taste it," Lily said.

"Have you tried it yet?" Adam said.

"She's my sister," Lily said. "I eat her food all the time."

"But you haven't tried the bagels yet." He looked down at the bite-sized piece in his hand warily. Then he broke off a second piece. "Here. You go first."

Helen relaxed and leaned against the back of the truck. Adam might not have as much experience as his uncle, but he wasn't the soft touch he appeared to be.

Lily took the offered chunk of bagel and cream cheese, and popped it into her mouth. She chewed determinedly for several seconds and then swallowed, sticking her tongue out, as if she were a reality-show contestant who had to prove she'd really eaten some disgusting thing. "Good stuff. Sticks to your ribs."

Helen couldn't tell if the bagel had actually been good or not. Lily had a lot of practice eating and praising Laura's food, even when it was horrible.

Adam had automatically looked down at Lily's ribs, except that his gaze never got much farther down than her breasts before it darted back up to her face. He popped the bagel bite into his mouth and chewed. And chewed. And chewed.

It took him longer than it had taken Lily, but eventually he swallowed it. "Good flavor," he said, with obvious diplomacy.

Lily smiled and leaned in to whisper conspiratorially. "You don't have to eat the whole thing. Just put it next to Tate's, and I'll inadvertently knock them both into the trash bin when I go past the table."

"I wouldn't want to hurt your sister's feelings," Adam said, before popping another bite into his mouth and heading off to grab some of the wood stock from the piles in the truck.

If he believed that as long as his mouth was full, Lily couldn't interrogate him about Tate, he'd seriously underestimated her.

Lily shadowed him the way she'd done with his uncle. "What kind of work do *you* do?"

"I'm a lawyer." Adam laid the armful of wood onto a pallet in the far corner of the garage and returned to the truck with Lily at his heels. "I took over my uncle's practice when he retired."

Uh-oh. Dangerous territory there. No need for Lily to know that the woodworker and the lawyer uncle were the same person. Helen needed a distraction. She grabbed one of the lengths of wood stock from the truck, propped it up on her shoulder with her non-cane hand, and began carrying it over to the garage.

"Aunt Helen!" Lily said. "What do you think you're doing?"

"I'm making up for the nuisance you're being," Helen said. "This stuff won't move itself."

"You can't carry that and still use your cane properly," Lily said, taking the wood from her and carrying it into the garage.

"That reminds me." Adam paused halfway between the truck and the garage. "I've looked everywhere at the offices for your other cane. It's definitely not there."

"Thanks for looking," Helen said, watching Lily collect several pieces of wood stock from the truck.

Without Lily's interrogation efforts, it didn't take long for them to empty out the truck bed. The two-car garage still looked cavernous, with nothing but the worktable, lathe, tool boxes, and wood stock in it. Tate hadn't even brought the two directors' chairs, probably to discourage her from visiting him.

Lily brushed her hands against her jeans, and said, "So. When are you bringing the rest of your stuff?"

Tate gave Helen a questioning look, before answering. "I don't need a whole lot of equipment. Most of what I had in my old studio was junk, nothing to do with my current work. When I started wood turning, one of the things that appealed to me was how little equipment it required. Makes it easy to move too. Now that I have the space, I may invest in some other table tools, though."

"I'm not talking about your work stuff," Lily said. "I mean your other things."

"I live pretty simply." Tate tossed a set of keys to Adam. "Do me a favor, would you, and take the truck back to your cousin, and pick up my car? I'll be here, working out some details with my landlord."

Lily said, "I've got my laptop in the cottage, if you need to draw up a rental contract."

"That won't be necessary," Helen said. "Why don't you go see how Laura's doing? I need to talk to my new tenant for a minute."

Lily looked like she wanted to argue, but she'd always known when it was time to retreat until a better opportunity arose. For the moment, she was willing to leave Helen and Tate alone in the garage. Lily joined Laura on the back deck, far enough away that she couldn't hear the conversation inside the garage.

"Lily hasn't given up interrogating you," Helen said. "She can be a bit stubborn."

"Like aunt, like niece," Tate said. "Why does she think I need to move more things over here?"

"She doesn't want me to be alone," Helen said. "No one does. It's very annoying."

"You're easily annoyed." He wandered over to the tool cabinet, unlocked it, and began checking the contents.

"What did you want to talk to me about in private?"

"I figured you wouldn't want your nieces to hear that there's been another remote control burglary," he said. "Maybe it will give the cops some more information to go on, now that they've got a reason to pay attention."

Helen leaned against the work table. "Tell me about it."

"It probably happened a few days ago, before the murder, but no one noticed anything was missing until yesterday."

"Are they sure it's the same guy?" Helen said. "Most of the other burglaries happened in the spring and fall, not in the summer."

"Definitely the same guy," Tate said. "The only thing that was stolen was fourteen remote controls."

"Not likely to be anyone else, then." Helen thought for a moment. "Who has fourteen remote controls lying around to be stolen, anyway? According to the newspaper accounts, the average for these burglaries has been around three."

"The average number of things operated by remote in each household is probably escalating too," Tate said. "In this case, several were for advanced equipment, like HVAC controls and security cameras that the homeowner could adjust from anywhere in the house. The cops weren't saying if they'd gotten any useful images. I'm guessing they didn't, or they'd have been crowing about it. All they said was that there were actually fifteen remotes in the victim's house, and the burglar missed one."

"Still, fourteen is a lot," Helen said. "And the homeowner didn't notice the minute they were stolen, which suggests they weren't actually used much."

"Some guys like to have the latest tech, even if they don't actually use it."

Helen's ex-husband had been like that, replacing his cell phone with the newest technology every few months, without having learned to use even a small percentage of the features in the older cell phone. She suspected Tate either had a simple phone or at least knew how to use every single feature it had. He would have noticed if one of his remotes was stolen, within a few hours.

"I suppose knowing the exact number of remotes taken isn't very helpful," Helen said. "After all, the burglar must have a couple hundred of them by now, far more than he could possibly use, and yet he keeps on stealing them."

"It may not be a clue that could be used to narrow down the suspects," Tate said, "but if he's ever arrested, the specialized ones for the security system is solid evidence connecting him with the most recent theft. The generic remotes that you could buy anywhere would be easy to explain away if I were defending the burglar, but I'd have a hard time coming up with an innocent explanation for having the remote for an expensive security system."

"What else did you hear about the latest incident?" Helen said. "Do they have any idea what time the theft happened?"

"Not really."

"What about a time it could *not* have happened?" Helen said. "I was reading up on the previous burglaries, and it looks like the burglar isn't much of a morning person."

"I didn't get many details."

"Never mind," Helen said. "I'll ask Geoff Loring about it. I was planning to talk to him today, anyway."

"Just promise me you won't tell him that you're the most likely suspect for having killed Melissa," he said. "He might believe you, and he'd be able to testify against you at trial. I wouldn't be able to exclude it as hearsay, because a confession is admissible as a statement against interest."

"I'll let him do all the talking," Helen promised. "I just want to see if he knows anything else about the burglaries. If we can figure out who the burglar is, the police can arrest him, and if we're lucky, he'll have an airtight alibi for when Melissa was killed. Then they'll have to take me seriously."

"And I'll have to defend you against murder charges." Tate glanced at his piles and piles of wood stock. "I suppose it would be worth my time. I could use some more wood, and it's not cheap. A murder-defense retainer would just about cover the additional stock I've been considering."

"Before you start spending that imaginary retainer, you'll have to help me identify the burglar."

"Oh, no," Tate said. "I just get people out of trouble, not into it. Better that I not know you're planning to meddle in a police investigation."

"Just tell me something," Helen said. "Is there always a pattern to crimes? An MO, like they say in the movies and on TV?"

"I suppose. But most of the time, it's not some master plan. It's not a purple feather left at the crime scene or some special method of entry into the building. Usually it's just that the person is a thief or an addict. He happens to see something he wants and he takes it. He doesn't stop to work out all the details. The pattern has more to do with geography than anything else. At least, that was always the case with my clients."

"The difference is," Helen said, "your clients got caught, and the Remote Control Burglar didn't. I'm guessing he's smarter than your clients, and maybe smart criminals have real MO's."

"How smart can he be when he's risking a jail sentence over a pile of worthless hunks of plastic?"

"You're the one who's supposed to understand the criminal mind," Helen said. "It's your job. It's why I'm allowing you to use my garage, after all—so I have access to your insights."

"The way you see it, then, the use of the garage covers the cost of the legal advice you're asking for?" he said. "Maybe your niece is right, and we should have a lease written up."

"I don't expect you to answer my questions forever," she said. "Just until I figure out who the burglar is, and he's arrested, so my nieces will leave me alone."

"I see," Tate said. "Does that mean that if I help you identify the burglar, you won't need me any longer, and you'll kick me out of the garage, firing me and evicting me, all in one? Somehow, that doesn't seem like much of an incentive for me to help you."

"I really hate a man who knows the rules of formal logic and isn't afraid to use them."

"You hate everyone."

"I try," Helen said. "But I won't kick you out of your new studio when we find the burglar. You can stay as long as you'd like. I'm not worried about you pestering me the way everyone else does."

Tate nodded. "We'd better get out to the deck before Lily gets suspicious."

"She's always suspicious," Helen said as she reached for her cane. "It's when she starts getting helpful that you need to worry."

CHAPTER THIRTEEN

———

Tate deflected Lily's questions and managed to eat an entire bagel, to Laura's delight, before Adam returned with Tate's car, and then the two men left. Helen convinced the nieces to leave shortly afterwards, telling them she'd promised to visit some friends at the nursing home. It wasn't a lie, as such. She had promised Betty and Josie she'd come back sometime, and the common room of the nursing home would be a good, neutral place to meet Geoff Loring. She sent him an email, asking him to meet her there at 2:00, and received a confirmation a few minutes later. If she got there early, before the reporter arrived, she might be able to ask Betty and Josie about the story they'd hinted at before, the one that Geoff was missing. It probably had nothing to do with Melissa's murder, but it wasn't much more of a long shot than expecting to get any more information from the reporter.

Jack delivered Helen to the nursing home at 1:30. She signed the guest ledger and headed for the common room. Betty and Josie weren't in their usual seats near the unlit fireplace, and one of the nursing staff explained that the women had been signed out of the nursing home for a few hours with Betty's daughter.

As it turned out, Helen wouldn't have been able to have a private moment with them, anyway. Geoff was already there, his youthful blond hair a contrast to the white and silver heads around him. He was wandering from patient to patient, seemingly at random, pumping them for information on his elusive big story.

Helen settled in what she thought of as Betty's chair near the fireplace and waited for Geoff to notice her. He had stopped his wanderings to lean over a frail, old man who was almost completely deaf. Despite the old man's attempt at conversation, Geoff was looking around the room. Helen could tell when he noticed her. He stood up, tugged on the tails of his faded, moss-green polo shirt, without actually removing any of the wrinkles, and abandoned the old man to race over to perch on the edge of Josie's chair.

"What's this all about?" he said. "Do you have a story for me?"

"If I do, you'll be the first reporter I'll call," Helen said. "But first I need some information."

"From me?"

"You're the best investigative reporter in the area." The *only* investigative reporter, actually. "If you don't have the answers, no one does."

He settled deeper into the upholstered chair, adjusting the pillows behind him before leaning back. "What do you want to know?"

"Melissa's killer," Helen said. "What are you doing to find him?"

He waved his hand dismissively. "That story isn't worth pursuing. Not for someone of my caliber. Everyone knows who killed her. It was the Remote Control Burglar."

"But what if it's not?" Helen said. "And why does everyone assume it's him?"

"Who else could it be?"

"That's what you're supposed to be investigating."

"I've got a bigger story to pursue." He peered around the room before leaning forward and lowering his voice, which only served to catch the attention of the nearest residents, some of whom had much better hearing than the old man Geoff had abandoned so readily. "I'm working on something that's going to shock the whole town. Starting with all the town officials who have relatives here at the nursing home."

The two women and one man who'd been blatantly eavesdropping, all shook their heads dismissively and went back to chatting with each other.

"I'm sure it will be an excellent story," Helen said, "but I'm new to town, so it won't really affect me. Not the way

Melissa's murder and the Remote Control Burglaries do. Are you sure there isn't anything you know about either one that you haven't included in your printed stories? Maybe something that an editor cut?"

"Most of my pieces run exactly as I write them," Geoff said. "There was this one story about the burglaries, though, that hit right around the time when the schools were finishing up for the year last spring, and the paper needed to run a lot of fluff pieces about the high school seniors, and we ran out of space, so a couple of my paragraphs got cut."

"Anything interesting in those paragraphs?"

"If it's not interesting, I don't write it," Geoff said. "Usually, anyway. In that case, I'd added a few paragraphs to recap the previous burglaries. There'd been a whole spate of them that spring, but it had been a few weeks since they'd happened, so I summarized the earlier ones. There'd been five victims, I think, over the course of two weeks in May."

"Doesn't sound terribly riveting." Helen said. "I can see why the editor cut it."

"It was plenty interesting, and I could have written even more if they'd let me. But editors never get it right. The reporter on the ground knows what the real story is. But they never listen to us." Geoff acknowledged a passing resident before adding, "You know, I'd forgotten, but there was one interesting fact that I noticed when I did the summary. All of the incidents were reported to the police within a couple days of each other, but it seemed likely that the actual burglaries had happened over a much longer stretch of time. A couple weeks, maybe a month. Some of the victims said they'd been too busy to watch television, so it could have been a while since the remotes were taken. One told me she might not have noticed for weeks longer, except she'd needed to play some sample DVDs from the videographers she was considering for her daughter's wedding."

"How did you explain it?" Helen said. "The delay in reporting the thefts, I mean."

"I didn't. It's not my job to explain anything. I just lay out the facts. The readers get to make up their own minds, come to their own conclusions."

"But weren't you curious?"

"Not really." He watched as an attendant pushed an old woman in a wheelchair into the common area. Nodding toward the newcomer, he whispered, "Do you know who she is?"

Helen shook her head. She'd never met the woman, although there was something vaguely familiar about her.

"That's Judge Nolan's mother," he said. "The judge is going to be shocked when she reads my story about what's been going on here."

Helen peered at the old woman: white-haired, obviously frail, but cheerful in her greetings of the fellow patients. She didn't use anyone's name, so perhaps she had a bit of dementia, but she didn't seem scared or unhappy or anything else that would suggest she'd been mistreated. "She seems fine to me."

"Everything always looks fine on the surface," he said smugly. "Dig a little deeper, though, and everything's dirty."

"How dirty?"

"I can't say." He looked into the mirror over the fireplace to adjust the collar of his polo shirt, removing a few of the creases on one side and pulling the other side out of alignment. "Not yet. Gotta protect my scoop until it's ready to go to print."

There was something about the way he said it, or perhaps it was just the way he didn't give in to his enthusiasm for showing off what he knew, that made Helen think that, as Betty and Josie had claimed, Geoff didn't actually have any inside information whatsoever about problems here at the nursing home. He was just fishing, hoping that if he spent enough time here, he'd stumble across something interesting. His claim to be onto something big was just bait, a form of encouragement for people to tell him their side of a situation he was pretending to have already uncovered. Meanwhile, he was missing out on a real story: Melissa's murder, and the police mishandling of the investigation.

Despite her misgivings, Helen said, "Good luck with the scoop."

"You could give me your own scoop," he said. "Just give me an hour's time, and I'll write the best piece you've ever read. Hey, I could even write your official biography."

"No, thanks," Helen said. "My life isn't over yet."

"Volume one, then."

"I'm really not interested in talking about my past. You'll have to wait until I'm as old as..." Helen caught sight of the white-haired old woman being pushed around the room in her wheelchair. "As old as Judge Nolan's mother."

"No one will care then," Geoff said.

"Good." Helen pushed herself to her feet.

Geoff stood too. "I get it. You've signed some sort of non-disclosure agreement as part of your divorce."

"Believe whatever you want," Helen said, "but make sure you have impeccable sources before you print anything about me. I've got a good lawyer, and I'm not afraid to use him."

* * *

On the ride home, Helen was starting to think she was as ill-suited for crime investigation as she was for scrapbooking and photography. She'd thought talking to Geoff was worth the risk, but he hadn't known anything useful.

"Marty called while you were in the nursing home," Jack said. "He's got the design of your security system all worked out with your niece already, and he's ordered a few parts he doesn't have in stock. Should be ready to install by the middle of the week."

"My nieces will be relieved," Helen said. "I'm still not convinced I need anything more than my cell phones. No matter how fancy it is, the security system can't do much more than dial 911 for me."

"If you use it properly, it can do a lot more than that," Jack said, earnest in the defense of his part-time boss. "Marty doesn't throw in extras, just for the sake of driving up the fee. Not unless people want those extras, of course. Some people like bells and whistles. They don't care about using them; they just want to be able to say they've got the latest thing in technology. Like, there was this guy who rented the vehicle a couple weeks ago for a business trip with some colleagues. He made sure everyone knew that he had the newest, most expensive phone on the market, but then when we got to the airport, and he wanted to check to make sure his flight was on time, he couldn't even figure out how to turn on the phone. He had to borrow mine."

"I hope he appreciated it."

"Ha!" Jack said. "They never do. I wish someone would teach them how it feels to be taken advantage of and then tossed aside."

That was it, Helen thought. *Teaching people a lesson.* That was what the Remote Control Burglar was all about. He wasn't stealing for a profit; he was doing it to teach the victims a lesson. He was showing them what it was like to lose control over their lives.

Interesting, that the burglar was making the exact point that Jack longed to make. The latest victim even sounded a lot like Jack's recent passenger, the one with the high-tech phone he didn't know how to use. The most recently burglarized homeowner had had a plethora of high-tech equipment, judging by the number of remotes involved, and he didn't use the technology much, considering how long it had taken for him to notice the remotes were missing or to check his security camera's images.

What if it was more than a coincidence? What if Jack was the Remote Control Burglar?

Helen forced herself to watch the scenery instead of staring at Jack's reflection in the rear-view mirror, where he might notice her dawning suspicion.

It all fit, from the pettiness of it, to the time of day, and even the most active months. The crimes never occurred in the morning, and Jack worked an evening schedule, often out driving until 2 in the morning, so he would likely sleep in later than most people and not leave the house before noon unless he had a scheduled driving gig. Most of the thefts had occurred between 2 and 4 in the afternoon, which would be prime recreation time for him, with most of his work shifts scheduled for after dinner time. Plus, there was the fact that the victim advocate had noticed, that most of the crimes occurring in the spring and late fall. They were busy seasons for limo drivers, with proms and weddings and holiday parties, when the sheer numbers of passengers meant that there were bound to be more of them who annoyed Jack into taking his revenge. The rest of the year, when there were fewer passengers, there'd still be occasional causes for irritation, which would explain the burglaries outside the peak months.

It all made sense. Jack was the Remote Control Burglar, getting even with his worst passengers for their petty cruelties.

Helen was fairly certain she was right, but she didn't have enough to bring it to the police's attention. It was just a theory, after all. Probably not even enough, if the police believed her, to justify their questioning Jack. Besides, the police wouldn't pay any attention to her ideas.

For once, it worked to her benefit that no one ever listened to her. She might suspect Jack of some minor thefts, but if the police ever connected Jack to the burglaries, they'd be charging him with Melissa's murder. It was one thing to think that Jack had done some foolish and regrettable crimes, but quite another to suspect him of committing murder in the course of a theft gone wrong.

The police had to be wrong that the Remote Control Burglar had killed Melissa. Jack hadn't had any reason to hurt Melissa or even target her for one of his retribution raids. Melissa hadn't treated him badly, hadn't even talked to him as far as Helen knew.

Unless...

Melissa hadn't treated Jack badly, but she'd treated Helen badly, and Jack had taken on the role of Helen's protector. He might have targeted Melissa's remote controls, not for upsetting him, but for upsetting Helen. She still couldn't imagine him killing anyone. Surely, he wouldn't have killed Melissa on Helen's behalf.

Could he? He'd once asked if she wanted him to take care of Melissa, but...no, that was ridiculous. Jack wasn't a killer. Even if he'd taken it on himself to scare Melissa off, he wouldn't have killed her. He knew Helen had wanted the nurse to leave her alone, not to die.

No, Jack would never have done anything violent. He was a talker and a passive-aggressive type, not a murderer.

Unless the death had been an accident. Helen—and apparently the police—had been assuming the killer had picked up the bloody branch that forensics had taken away, and intentionally hit Melissa with it. But what if she'd been pushed and fell, hitting her head on the branch? Tragic, of course, but not intentional. Not murder. Anyone, even Jack or Helen herself, could have been involved in that kind of an accident.

The only problem with that theory is that there wasn't any reason why either of them—Melissa or Jack—would have been at her house before 9:30, engaging in some sort of physical confrontation. It was possible, though. Melissa could have been staking out the cottage, to make sure Helen didn't leave, and Jack could have been keeping an eye on the cottage to make sure Helen wasn't bothered by Melissa.

Helen became aware that Jack was still talking without noticing her distraction. He was describing a more recent passenger who'd annoyed him. Probably the Remote Control Burglar's next victim.

It was one thing for her to remain silent about his past burglaries, but she couldn't be complicit in his future crimes. Now that she knew what he was doing, she had to convince him to stop before he did hurt someone. Or before he was caught and charged with a crime he hadn't committed.

While Helen resented help that was foisted on her when she didn't need it, she also knew when she was in over her head and had to ask for assistance. She didn't know what to do about Jack, and the police wouldn't be any help.

Tate would know what to do.

CHAPTER FOURTEEN

———

Jack continued to chat through the rest of the trip to the cottage, oblivious to Helen's distraction. He left with a cheerful wave, and a promise to return with Marty on Monday to begin installation of her security system.

Helen toasted one of the left-over bagels, and melted cheese on top of it for dinner. She ate at her desk, studying the spreadsheet of burglary data, searching for a flaw in her theory that Jack was the Remote Control Burglar. After a while, too tired to look at the screen any longer, she had to conclude that there just wasn't anything to exonerate Jack.

The next morning, when she was more alert, she tried again, but everything still pointed to Jack as the burglar. She paced the great room, waiting for Tate to appear at his new workshop, unable to stay away from his passion, even on a Sunday. If there was a flaw in her theory, he would find it.

Helen stopped her pacing long enough to check in with her nieces by email, to confirm she was still alive and well and didn't need them to come check on her again. When she finished and looked out the window, she was surprised to see that Tate's car was parked outside the garage. She'd been so engrossed in her email that she hadn't heard the crunch of its arrival on her gravel driveway. Now, though, she could hear some thumping inside the garage. She grabbed her cane and headed over to the garage, where she let herself in through the half-open door.

Tate looked up from the box he'd been emptying. "For someone who wants to be left alone, you sure do like to socialize."

"I talked to Geoff Loring yesterday, and I know who the Remote Control Burglar is."

Tate's eyebrows rose. "So Geoff had the missing piece of the puzzle, after all, and didn't even know it? He must be thrilled that he's finally got a real scoop."

"He doesn't know," she said. "I only figured it out on the way home from seeing him. Jack is the Remote Control Burglar."

"Jack who?" Understanding dawned on his face. "You mean Jack Clary? Your driver?"

Helen nodded and waited for Tate to convince her she was wrong.

"Hunh." Tate leaned against his worktable and crossed his arms over his chest. "I suppose you could make a case against him. What's your evidence?"

She told him about the long list of passengers who'd annoyed him, and his desire for a little payback, and the way his schedule coincided with the timing of the thefts.

"It fits," Tate said, "but it's pretty circumstantial."

"But if I'm right?" Helen said. "I don't want to get him into trouble, but we need to convince him not to commit any more crimes."

"Good luck with that."

"I think he'd listen to me, especially since he's got to know how risky it is, now that the police are paying more attention to the burglaries," Helen said. "But what if I'm wrong about him? What if he isn't the burglar?"

"He'll be outraged by your accusation, and he'll never let you forget that you thought he was a criminal," Tate said. "The Clarys do tend to hold grudges. He'd probably decide to become your own personal burglar, stealing your remotes. He'd come back, again and again, every time you replaced them. You'd have to turn on your television manually for the rest of your life."

"That does sound like him. I'd deserve it too. If I were wrong. I don't think I am." After a moment of silence, Helen said, "He'd take the intervention better if it came from you."

Tate shook his head. "Not my job. I'm retired."

"What if you knew he was going to commit another crime?" she said. "Don't you have an obligation, as an officer of the court, to do something to stop him?"

"Not as long as he doesn't use me to help him commit the crimes."

"If we caught him in the act, we'd know for sure that he was the burglar," Helen said.

"Are you planning to stalk him? Follow him everywhere he goes until he strikes again?" Jack said. "It could take weeks. Months, even, before he decides to steal another remote. Especially given his most recent collection of fourteen of them."

"He's going to act soon. He was talking about someone today, and it sounded like he'd chosen a new victim. If we knew who his recent passengers were, we might be able to figure out who he was targeting, and catch him at it. Then we'd know for sure that he's the burglar."

"You're going to do this with or without my help, aren't you?"

"Jack's in over his head," Helen said. "If he goes ahead with another burglary, and the police catch him, they're going to charge him with murder, and they might make it stick. He's not a killer, and we both know it. You can't let it get that far."

"I know the owner of the limo company," Tate said reluctantly. "I might be able to get some information from him. Not until sometime tomorrow, though, if you don't want him to be overly suspicious that I called him on a Sunday."

"I don't want Jack to lose his job. You can't tell his boss why you need the information."

"He knows better than to ask," Tate said. "If Jack's past becomes public knowledge, it will hurt the limo company's reputation too. It's better for everyone if it stays a mystery. As long as you can convince Jack not to steal again."

"I'll convince him," Helen said. "I've had years of experience with convincing people to do what's in their best interest."

"Interesting," Tate said. "You've never learned to take that kind of advice yourself."

"I don't need people telling me what to do."

"I bet that's what your victims thought too," Tate said. "Just stay out of trouble while I work on getting the passenger list. Don't make me miss out on my retirement for nothing."

"I'll be at the nursing home, visiting some friends," Helen said. "How much trouble can I get into there?"

* * *

Late on Monday morning, Jack drove Helen back to the nursing home. She'd been a little worried that she might betray her suspicion of him, but he was preoccupied with telling her about his latest run-in with inconsiderate passengers.

Helen left him waiting in the Town Car, already immersed in a game on his smartphone, and went to find Betty and Josie. The receptionist referred her to the common room, where the two women were seated in their favorite places in front of the fireplace, busy with their yarns and needles and hooks.

Betty raised her knitting and waved it at Helen. "Come join us."

"I didn't mean to interrupt."

"Don't be silly," Josie said. "We're old, but we can still multi-task."

The two women did, indeed, continue making perfectly even little stitches without even watching what they were doing. "How long have you been knitting and crocheting?"

"Forever," Betty said. "I started when I was a teen, and Josie started in college. We both tried to give it up at various times over the years, but it's an addiction, and we kept coming back to it."

That was what Helen needed for her retirement: something she enjoyed so much that she couldn't give it up, even if she wanted to. "You mentioned teaching me to make hats, and I was going to stop at the crafts store on the way here, but I didn't know what I'd need."

"Not a problem." Josie tucked the hat she was working on into the space between her hip and the chair, and dove into the Hello Kitty backpack that was on her lap. "We've got more yarn in our stashes than we'd be able to use in the combined lifetimes of everyone in the nursing home, and I always carry a few extra hooks. I like having options for new projects. Besides,

I'm always dropping them, and sometimes it's easier to just use another one until I can find someone to pick it up for me."

Betty nodded. "Crochet is easier for a beginner. Josie will set you up, and once you're comfortable working with one hook, we'll show you how to knit with two needles, so you can decide which you prefer."

Helen pulled up a third chair and leaned her cane against the armrest. At least here she wasn't the only one carrying such an ugly thing.

Within minutes, Helen was pulling loops through each other, forming first a long chain and then something that looked vaguely like the very wobbly edge of a cap.

"This yarn is pretty," she said, trying not to feel that she was doing it a disservice.

"You missed a stitch." Josie pointed to a gap in the fabric. "It takes some practice before you can talk and work at the same time."

"I can listen and work, though," Helen said. "I'm curious about what Geoff Loring has been up to here, and I bet you two know."

Betty and Josie shared a glance, before Betty confided, "We hate to speak ill of anyone who's down and out, but Geoff doesn't have any idea what's going on here. Not the people, not the politics, not the finances. Or the ways that all three intersect."

"But you two know."

"Mind your stitches," Josie said amiably. "You made two in one hole right there, and for now we're working on keeping the cap the same size, not increasing or decreasing."

"It's ironic, really," Betty said. "Geoff didn't have a lead on anything more exciting than the memoirs of some old has-beens, but someone thought he did. We heard that he was in the emergency room this morning, getting a cast on his arm. It seems he was jumped by a bunch of thugs who told him he'd better stay out of the nursing home, or else. And then they broke his wrist, so he couldn't type up his story."

"Geoff was attacked?"

"By Neanderthals." Josie rolled her eyes. "Even the oldest resident here knows that computers can take dictation these days, with the proper software. Breaking arms just isn't as effective as it used to be."

Helen realized she couldn't concentrate on both her stitching and her listening, after all. She showed the yarn mercy and let it fall into her lap. "So Geoff's going to write his story, after all?"

"That's the irony," Betty said. "He didn't have a story that anyone would be upset about. Still doesn't. No one here has told him about anything that's happened in the last ten years."

"You know," Josie said, picking up the abandoned mess in Helen's lap and pulling out the last dozen stitches. "He might have had a lead without realizing it. He interviewed Melissa a few weeks ago, and now she's dead. Maybe she told him something she shouldn't have, and it got her killed and him assaulted."

"You don't think the Remote Control Burglar killed Melissa?"

"Please," Josie said, sounding more like a teenager than an octogenarian. "He's been stealing remote controls for at least five years without going on a murderous rampage, or even escalating to stealing something valuable, like the televisions that are operated by the remote controls. Why would he suddenly escalate to murder?"

"Melissa's death could have been an accident," Helen said. "The police think she might have surprised him, and she got killed in the course of the burglar's escaping."

"Her death could have been a lot of things, but I don't think it had anything to do with burglary," Betty said, agreeing with her friend. "I think it started out as a romantic rendezvous and something went wrong. Melissa was meeting her lover in your lovely woods, and…I don't know. Maybe there was another lover, and he saw Melissa kissing the other man, and in a fit of jealousy, he tried to kill them both, but the lover got away and only Melissa died. Her killer probably hovered over her dying body, weeping and going insane with regret."

Helen had a hard time picturing any scenario in which Melissa was the heroine, and this one seemed even less likely than the theory that Melissa had tried to stop the Remote Control

Burglar. "Did Melissa even have a lover? Her boss said she didn't even have any family or close friends."

"It's possible," Josie said eagerly. "No one talks about their romantic triangles, after all. The whole point is to keep them secret. Not that anyone is very good at hiding things from us. You wouldn't believe the things we see while we're just sitting here, quietly making hats."

"Anything that might explain why Melissa was killed?"

The two women looked at each other and shrugged. Betty answered for them. "Not really. Everyone's been talking about it, but no one here really knows anything about what goes on outside our walls. Mostly, what we hear is just gossip about the residents and the staff. Melissa's been gone long enough that half the people here have forgotten they ever knew her."

Josie snorted. "The residents here aren't exactly reliable witnesses. Half the time, I forget what I'm crocheting until Betty reminds me. It's a good thing I learned to crochet when I was a kid, because I'd hate to forget that."

Another dead end, Helen thought. Maybe Tate had had better luck with the owner of the limo company.

"I'd better get going." She tried to return the tangled pile of yarn, with the hook buried in its depths, but Josie insisted that she keep it to practice on at home.

"I wish I could stay longer," Helen said, "but I'm expecting a visit from a friend at my cottage this afternoon."

"A friend or a lover?" Josie said.

"Sorry to disappoint you," Helen said. "He's just a friend. He saves all his passion for chunks of exotic wood."

CHAPTER FIFTEEN

———

Tate had, indeed, had more success than Helen had. With the cooperation of the limo company's owner, he'd identified a recent passenger in Jack's car, who, if Helen's theory was right, might well be the next victim of his remote control thefts.

Tate and Helen were now sitting in his car, half a block away and around the corner, where they could keep the house in sight, without being obvious about it.

"This is a waste of time." Tate tossed aside the woodworking catalogue he'd been reading for the last two hours.

Since most of the burglaries had occurred between 2:00 and 4:00, they'd arrived around 1:30. Since then, while Tate read, Helen had been dutifully stabbing her crochet hook into what she hoped was the right spot for each of the subsequent stitches.

"We've got half an hour left until 4:00," Helen said. "Jack will show up by then. Unless you picked the wrong victim from his passenger list. I'm sure he's driven more than one inconsiderate person in the last couple weeks."

"Most of them were regulars, business people he's worked with dozens of times before, and who haven't been hit by the burglar," Tate said. "I'm going on the theory that this is someone he hasn't driven before, or he would have already robbed them. There were only two new people on his schedule for the last two weeks, and only one was male. If you're right about Jack, it's got to be this one."

"I'm right," Helen said. "He'll be here. If not today, then tomorrow or the next day."

"Easy for you to say," Tate said. "I can't exactly bring my lathe with me, but you've got your knitting."

"Crochet." She showed him the metal crochet hook. "See? One hook instead of two needles."

He took the hook from her and turned it around, peering at it closely. "I could make one of those out of wood."

She reclaimed it from him. "How long did it take before you knew woodworking was what you wanted to do with your time?"

"I knew it the first time I turned on the lathe in shop class and saw a block of wood spinning," he said. "I've still got the piece I turned that day. I saved it to look at whenever I'm struggling with a difficult new piece. I certainly didn't do a great job with that first one, but I could feel the potential, and it inspires me every time I look at it."

Helen looked down at the tangle in her lap. Maybe this crocheting thing wasn't the right retirement hobby for her, after all. She certainly hadn't felt any potential when she'd taken the crochet hook from Josie, or even as the stitches had started to pile up. Looking at it now certainly didn't inspire her. She'd managed to make a beautiful, multicolored skein of yarn into an incredibly ugly lump. Still, there was always knitting to try. She might feel different about that, and she liked Betty and Josie, who seemed to enjoy sharing their love of textiles as much as they enjoyed sharing the local gossip.

"Hey," Tate said, straightening in his seat. "That looks like Jack's truck."

A twenty-year-old beige pick-up in mint condition had parked a few houses down from the one they were watching. A moment later, Jack hopped out of the driver's side. Relief that she hadn't accused an innocent man mingled with concern for Jack.

"How about that?" Tate said. "You were right. Can we leave now?"

"We can't let him commit another crime," Helen said. "You need to talk to him."

"Me?" Tate said. "Not my job. I'm retired, and I've got a workshop that I've barely had a chance to use, thanks to you."

"Then why did you come with me?"

"I was curious," he said, grudgingly. "The Remote Control Burglar's been a long-standing joke in this town."

"It won't be a joke if Jack is arrested for Melissa's murder."

"It looks like Jack's about done with his surreptitious scoping-out of the neighborhood," Tate said. "I can't believe he hasn't been caught by now. He couldn't look more conspicuous if he tried. If you're going to hold an intervention, now's the time to do it."

"You'll at least wait for me in the car, won't you?" Helen said. "I'm not sure Jack will give me a ride home, after this."

"You're running out of time to reach him before he gets inside the house." Tate turned on the car and drove the few yards to the front of the victim's house.

As they approached, Jack, who had started up the driveway of his next victim, turned to check on them. Guilt was written all over his face.

Tate got out of the car, leaving Helen to grab her cane and scramble after him.

"Helen's been looking for you, Jack."

"Did you need a ride somewhere, Ms. Binney?" Tate dug in his pocket for his cell phone. "The limo company didn't page me."

"I don't need a ride," Helen said. "We know why you're here."

"What?" Jack said. "I'm just—"

"Don't bother," Tate said. "I expect my clients to lie to me, but Helen trusts you. Don't lie to her."

Jack looked at his feet. "I didn't mean to get you involved, Ms. Binney."

Maybe not consciously, Helen thought, but he'd known she was trying to identify the Remote Control Burglar, and yet he'd continued to feed her the information that had enabled her to identify him. If he'd really wanted to keep his secret, he wouldn't have mentioned his latest victim. "You were ready to stop doing the burglaries, though. And that's why we're here. To insist that you not do it any longer. It's too risky. If the police figure it out, they'll arrest you, and not just for burglary."

"I didn't kill Melissa," Jack said. "I wouldn't do that."

"I'm going to take a walk," Tate said. "I don't want to hear this. There's no client confidentiality since I'm not representing Jack."

"Come on," Helen said. "We'll go back to your truck, and you can tell me everything."

Jack hesitated, glancing at the house he'd been targeting.

"Let it go, Jack," she said. "Getting some revenge isn't worth going to jail. I didn't specifically ask Tate for any advice for you, but I bet he'd tell you that 'the victim deserved it' isn't a legal defense to burglary."

"This was going to be my last time," Jack said. "I was going to stop after this one."

"And now you're going to stop *before* this one." Helen tugged him in the direction of his truck.

He started walking with her. "You know I didn't kill Melissa, right?"

"I believe you, but that's because I know you, and I'm not desperate to find a scapegoat. The police need to arrest someone, to make everyone else feels safe."

"I'm not a violent person. You can ask anyone. I didn't even vandalize any property during the burglaries. I planned to, the first time I broke into a passenger's house. I brought a can of spray paint, and I was going to mess up his garage. But then I found an open window, and I went into the house itself, and I was going to paint in there instead, because I was really angry. But I just couldn't do it. The guy had been a jerk, but even he didn't deserve weeks and weeks of repairs. So I figured I'd steal something valuable. I started to disconnect the wires to his TV, and then realized I had a perfectly good TV at home, and I had no idea how to fence a stolen one, so there was no real point to stealing it. I noticed the remote, lying there on the coffee table, and this was before I got a smartphone, and I thought, 'hey, I could use some batteries for my videogames, and wouldn't the guy be irritated when he went to use the remote and the batteries were missing?' I figured that was enough payback. So I picked up the remote and turned it over, and then I realized I'd gotten my fingerprints all over it, so I might as well take the whole thing. That was even better, in a way, because he'd waste a bunch of time looking for it, the way he'd wasted my time."

"It's got to stop now," Helen said as they reached his pick-up.

"I know," he said. "It's hard, though. Doing this makes me feel like a sort of low-level superhero, teaching jerks a lesson, taking care of the little bad guys who aren't big enough problems for real heroes to deal with. I don't even have a use for the batteries any more, now that I have games on my smartphone, but it's a habit. Like an addiction."

"Maybe there's a twelve-step program for theft," Helen said. "Or you can find a new, more legally acceptable volunteer activity to replace the jerk-punishing activity. I'll help you."

"I've seen your scrapbooks and photography," he said. "No offense, but I'm not sure you're the best mentor when it comes to recreational activities."

"Tate, then. He can introduce you to woodworking."

"You think he'd do it?"

"He's even more addicted to woodworking than you are to remote controls. He loves to talk about his work." Of course, both Tate and Jack obviously preferred to work alone, so that could be a problem. "If he won't help, Betty and Josie will. They're always looking for someone new to teach. Just promise me you won't come back here, and you won't break into any other houses."

"I promise," Jack said, but Helen caught him glancing longingly at the house they'd just left.

"Listen to me, Jack," she said. "Tate thinks we should turn you in to the cops, but I'm not going to do that. Not as long as I don't hear about another break-in. But I will turn you in if it happens again."

Jack turned away from the house. He stared at her for a long moment. "It's over. I promise. I'll find a new hobby."

Helen waited until he climbed into his truck and drove away. Then she headed over to Tate's car. Jack was wrong. It wasn't over. Not until Melissa's killer was arrested.

Unfortunately, there was no one other than Jack, in his guise as the remote control burglar, with any apparent motive. Melissa didn't have any of the usual suspects: family members, or a lover, let alone the two jealous lovers that Betty and Josie had dreamed up. Melissa didn't have any co-workers or rivals with a grudge. Everyone loved her. Or at least didn't hate her.

Except for Helen.

Why couldn't the police see that she was the prime suspect?

"Well?" Tate said as she climbed into the seat beside him. "Is he going to turn himself in?"

"No. But he is going to stop stealing remote controls."

"And start stealing televisions?"

"He's giving up burglary completely."

Tate didn't say anything, but she could feel his skepticism for the duration of the silent trip home. At the cottage, he let her out at the front path and then parked in his usual spot, intent on returning to his beloved tools and chunks of wood.

She'd pushed him far enough for today, she decided, so she left him alone in the garage and went into the cottage. She still had plenty of questions she would have liked to ask. What would happen to Jack if the police did arrest him? Would Tate come out of retirement to defend him? Actually, if it came to it, would Tate come out of retirement to defend her, if the police finally realized that their theory about the Remote Control Burglar was wrong?

Helen tried to relax with Josie's crochet hook and skein of yarn, but the stitches only grew tighter and more malformed. She couldn't help thinking that there had to be someone else with a motive to kill Melissa. She just needed to find that person.

Helen abandoned her yarn, and started a new spreadsheet, like the one she'd made for the remote control burglaries, only this time, she focused on Melissa, and all the people the nurse had had any contact with. She didn't have much information, though, not like all the newspaper articles she'd had for the burglaries, so it didn't take long before she realized she needed to talk to Betty and Josie again, to see if they had any facts to support their jealous-lover scenario.

* * *

The next morning, Helen's planned trip to the nursing home was delayed by the arrival of Detective Peterson and his forensics team. Helen hadn't had a chance to call the car service company to schedule a ride before they arrived, and an hour later, the police were on their way out of her driveway just as Tate was entering it.

She was never going to have a moment to herself, ever again.

At least Tate's arrival saved her having to call him. He wasn't going to like the latest news any more than she did.

She started over to the garage while Tate parked his car and got out of it.

He nodded toward where the police cars had just turned out of her driveway. "Do I need to increase my retainer from you in anticipation of a murder charge?"

"They still don't suspect decrepit, old me," Helen said. "They've arrested Jack. They got a tip that he's the Remote Control Burglar."

"And they came all the way out here, just to tell you that?" he said. "They don't usually go door to door, announcing every arrest."

"No, they came with a search warrant."

He frowned. "You should have called me the minute they showed it to you."

"I did," she said. "You didn't answer."

"I'm retired. I don't turn my phone on unless I'm using it." He sighed. "I'll keep it on for the duration of the investigation into Melissa's murder. But just until then. After that, I'm definitely retired."

"Thank you."

"Don't thank me," he said, turning toward the garage entrance. "Just tell your niece—the one who handles your money—to expect an invoice from the firm."

"She already knows," Helen said, following him into his work space. "I'm half expecting a visit from both girls any minute now. I had to tell them about Jack, and they didn't like it."

"How did the cops finger Jack for the burglaries, anyway?"

"I wondered about that myself," Helen said. "Detective Peterson told me they got an anonymous tip. They didn't have any leads, as far as I could tell, and they never would have figured it out on their own. I'm afraid Jack's going to think one of us turned him in."

"Not me." Tate crossed the room to consider his pile of wood stock. "I haven't given up my license to practice, so I've got to abide by the ethics rules. It wouldn't look good for me to be turning in potential clients."

"Who else knew?"

"You'd have to ask Jack that."

"He's going to think I turned him in." She leaned against the work table. "At least they haven't charged him with murder yet, just the burglaries. They did a search of his apartment before they came here, and they found a bunch of the stolen remote controls. They didn't find any real evidence tying him to Melissa, though. That's what they were searching for here."

Tate turned away from the length of wood he'd been examining for flaws. "What did they think they'd find?"

"The murder weapon."

"I thought you said they took it away with them the day she was killed."

"I thought so," Helen said. "They did too, originally, but it turns out the bloody branch wasn't the murder weapon. It just had some spatter."

"Do they know what did kill Melissa?"

"Now, they do."

"They found the murder weapon?"

"They found something, and it's not good news for Jack," Helen said. "They didn't know what they were looking for initially. Detective Peterson told me they were looking for something about the same size as the branch, but with a smoother surface."

He glanced at the collection of lamp stems lined up on a shelf along the back wall. "That could describe a lot of things."

"But they only found one thing that matched the description." Helen raised her ugly, back-up cane. "They found my other walking cane. The one I thought I'd left at your office.

It was in the woods, and it had a lot of blood on it. I think they got the right weapon this time."

"Are you sure it's your cane?" Tate said. "Lots of people use them."

"I'm pretty sure it was mine," Helen said. "It wasn't a standard drugstore style, and the last time I saw it was before Melissa was killed."

"That's not good." Tate stared at the garage doors, as if he could see through them.

Helen followed his gaze, imagining Detective Peterson returning, blue lights blazing, to arrest her, having confirmed that it was indeed her cane, the blood was Melissa's, and Jack had an alibi.

"We don't know for sure that the cane was yours," Tate said. "Maybe you just left yours somewhere. If we can find yours that would help."

"I'd already looked everywhere," Helen said. "Adam checked your offices, and it's not there. The only other place I can remember seeing it was in the Town Car, and it isn't there any longer. No, the cane the forensics team found is mine."

"Which means that the murder weapon is covered with your fingerprints. That could be a challenge to explain to a jury."

"It's not my fingerprints I'm worried about," she said. "It's Jack's. I'm pretty sure he held it for me a few times while I was getting in and out of the Town Car. As long as the police refuse to consider me a suspect, if they find Jack's prints on the cane, they're going to assume Jack is the only possibility."

"And if the police do consider you a suspect, I'll be so busy with your defense that it'll be months before I can use my new workshop again. I'm beginning to think I should have stayed in the old place. All of my other clients put together were less trouble than you are all by yourself. "

"I did promise to make the case interesting if you had to represent me for murder."

"From now on, just promise me you won't find any more dead bodies." Tate picked up a length of wood that he apparently deemed satisfactory, and carried it over to the lathe. "I really do want to retire before I'm eighty."

"Don't worry," Helen said. "They're not going to arrest me. But Jack's in trouble if we can't figure out who the real murderer is. The police aren't going to be looking, not if they've got his fingerprints on the murder weapon. That would be enough to convict him, wouldn't it?"

"There's still some room for reasonable doubt." Tate picked up his safety goggles and absently put them on top of his head. "He'd need a good lawyer, though."

"Like you."

Tate shook his head. "Even if I weren't retired, I couldn't do it. Conflict of interest. I'm already committed to representing you, and the best way to defend him is to throw you under the bus, as an alternative suspect to create reasonable doubt. I can't do that if I'm representing you too."

"Then we need to make sure it doesn't come to that," Helen said. "We've got to find another suspect."

Tate shook his head even more emphatically. "Not me. I'm staying out of it. You can do it if you want. It'll save me the trouble of having to defend you in court."

The sound of a car entering the gravel driveway saved Helen the trouble of having to argue with him. She limped over to look out the windows of the garage door. Her latest unannounced visitors were Tate's smarter-than-he-looked nephew, who should have known better than to come out here, and Lily, who had apparently overcome Adam's better inclinations.

CHAPTER SIXTEEN

———

Helen was inclined to shut the doors and lock them up, but Tate convinced her they wouldn't leave, so they might as well get it over with. Helen followed him out to the driveway.

Lily was out of the car before Adam could even turn off the engine. ""We heard about the arrest of your driver, and you weren't answering your phone, so I came to make sure you were okay. Laura wanted to be here, but Howie needed her at home."

"Doesn't someone need you for anything?" Helen asked. "You've wasted a two-hour trip."

"I was here in town, talking to Adam already."

Grilling him, more likely.

"I didn't tell her anything," Adam assured Helen and his uncle.

Lily turned on Tate. "You didn't tell me you're a lawyer."

"I'm retired," Tate said. "I prefer to call myself a woodworker now. Saves me from having to listen to a lot of bad jokes. No one ever says, 'first, kill all the woodworkers.' "

"Once a lawyer, always a lawyer," Lily said. "What's your angle? Why are you living out here? You'd better not be trying to take advantage of my aunt."

Tate snorted. "I'd be crazy to try. She kills anyone who annoys her."

This time, Lily turned on her aunt. "You didn't really tell him that you killed Melissa, did you?" Lily didn't wait for an answer before turning to Adam. "You need to do something about this. Whatever my aunt said, it's covered by attorney-client privilege, right? Give me your bank account information, and I'll have the retainer in there before you get back to the office."

"There's no rush," Helen said. "Tate's already agreed to represent me if I'm arrested."

Lily narrowed her eyes at Tate. "I thought you were retired."

"I figured I'd go out on a high note. One last, sensational murder trial: governor's ex-wife on trial for brutally killing a helpless servant." Tate gestured at the garage doors. "Plus, I get a free studio out of the deal, all set up for when the trial's over."

"Unless Aunt Helen is found guilty," Lily said. "Then the cottage, with the garage, will be sold, and you'll be evicted."

Tate shrugged. "Just one more incentive to win. I've never had a personal stake in the outcome before."

Lily tensed, and Adam put his arm around her. "Don't. He's just teasing you. He really is a very good lawyer. He won't let anything happen to your aunt."

"And who's going to protect her from him?"

"We will," Adam said. "You and me. We'll go back to my office and talk about it some more. They'll behave like rational adults if we leave them alone."

"I don't know if we can trust them on their own," Lily said. "Neither of them noticed that Aunt Helen's been riding around town with a burglar who's probably a killer too."

"Actually, we did notice," Helen said. "We figured out what Jack had been doing before the police did. But Jack didn't kill anyone. And he certainly wouldn't hurt me."

"You've only known the man for a few days," Lily said. "You're a good judge of character, but even you can make mistakes. Remember that guy who applied to be your assistant, and you were all set to offer him the job until I uncovered his alias? Multiple aliases, as I recall."

"I'm sure you also checked into the car service and Jack," Helen said. "Did you find anything worrisome?"

"No," Lily said. "But that doesn't mean anything. He eluded the police for five years too."

Tate spoke up, finally. "Much as it pains me to admit it, Helen's right about one thing. Jack is harmless."

"Then the real killer is still out there," Lily said, never one to let go of a perceived problem. "What if you were the target, Aunt Helen, and he killed the nurse by mistake? He might come back and try again."

"The security system will be up and running in the next couple days," Helen said. "And I really don't think anyone wants to kill me. Your uncle has all the enemies, not me. Once, people might have wanted to use me to get at him, but it wouldn't make sense to try that now."

"Hunh," Tate said. "I hadn't thought about the possibility that someone from your days in the governor's mansion might have wanted to kill you. Are you sure you didn't make any enemies there? We should definitely talk about the possibilities. Without any third parties listening in. Wouldn't want to undermine the attorney-client privilege."

Tate was brilliant, Helen thought. He'd made it appear that the best way for Lily to help was by leaving. "There are comfortable chairs on the back deck. We can go there and chat in private."

"Come on," Adam said, tugging Lily toward the car. "They have things to discuss."

"Have you had lunch yet?" she asked Tate as they headed for the back deck. "I'm sure I've got some cold cuts in the fridge."

Tate looked longingly at the garage doors before following her. "I could eat."

Helen went inside and threw together a pile of ham and cheese sandwiches. She tossed them onto a plate, along with a bag of paper napkins. Tate met her at the back door and took everything from her. She went back for a couple bottles of lemonade. By then Adam's car had disappeared down the driveway, and they no longer had to pretend to be talking about lawyer-client material.

Helen decided she ought to let Tate finish his sandwich before she grilled him for ideas about how to save Jack.

Tate had only finished half of his sandwich before he said, "Well? Who might have wanted to kill you?"

"No one. I just wanted Lily and Adam to leave, so we could do something more useful, like figure out why someone would kill Melissa."

"That's not my job," Tate said. "If we're not going to talk about the risk to you, I'm going back to the garage."

Helen set down her lemonade bottle with an irritated thud. "There's no risk to me."

"I'm not so sure Lily's wrong," Tate said. "There must be at least a few people who are still harboring a grudge against you for decisions you made in the governor's mansion. Invitations that weren't issued, events that weren't attended, dresses that weren't complimented."

He wasn't going to give up. She picked up her lemonade again and picked at the paper label while she considered the people she might have slighted. They did exist; it wasn't possible to please everyone at every event for twenty years. She knew she'd been called a few names and been trashed behind her back. On the occasions when she'd heard about the complaints, she'd been upset, and she'd lost quite a few nights' sleep. But that was back when it happened. Now, though? She couldn't remember any of the specific incidents, and the trash-talkers probably couldn't either. "I wasn't involved in anything that was worth killing for."

"You might be surprised at what people will kill over," Tate said. "Your supposed motive for killing Melissa is that she asked you to take a nap. Compared to that, just about anything that happened at the governor's mansion is a more persuasive motive."

"Okay, so maybe there were a few hurt feelings back then," Helen said. "But I've been gone from public life for almost two years now. If anyone had wanted to kill me, they'd have done it before I moved here instead of waiting until I left the city."

"Maybe they couldn't get to you there," Tate said. "You probably had all sorts of security in place before you moved here."

"Your theory is that someone's been obsessing for years, because I didn't invite him to a boring chicken dinner, where he'd have the chance to contribute his money to my husband's campaign? And he's been waiting all this time for his chance to kill me? And then he botched it so badly that he killed someone else?"

Tate shrugged. "Reasonable doubt. That's all we'd need at trial."

"No one is trying to kill me," she said, not bothering to hide her irritation.

"Then who killed Melissa?" Tate said. "If it wasn't you, and it wasn't someone trying to kill you, then you've got to admit that Jack really is the most likely culprit."

"Jack didn't do it." Helen took out her frustration on her lemonade bottle again, thumping it down on the table. Maybe if she repeated herself often enough, someone would listen to her. "Jack didn't do it. He doesn't have any motive. He believes in revenge, but only at a tit for tat level. He never did anything to his passengers that was worse than what they'd done to him. If he'd gone after Melissa, it would have been on the nuisance level, not something as disproportionate as murder."

Tate frowned suddenly. "Is that what you're worried about? That Jack did, in fact, kill Melissa, not for himself but for you? You think he was trying to protect you, and you feel responsible?"

"I *am* responsible," Helen said. "I should have made a bigger fuss the first day, and gotten rid of Melissa then, before she'd really settled in. Or I could have gotten over my pride in my independence and lied to the judge about being afraid, so she'd grant the restraining order. Then no one would have been hurt."

Tate shook his head. "Never, ever tell your lawyer you're willing to commit perjury."

"It wouldn't have been a total lie," Helen confessed. "Toward the end, Melissa really did scare me."

"I know."

"Well, then," Helen said briskly. "You'll understand why I feel responsible for Jack getting the best defense possible. That means you'll have to do it."

"Sorry, still a conflict of interest." He picked up the second half of his sandwich and set about finishing it as if their conversation was done.

"I could waive the conflict, couldn't I?" Helen said. "At least temporarily. You just have to keep him out of trouble until we figure out who really killed Melissa. Then there won't be a trial involving either one of us."

Tate finished the rest of his sandwich before answering. "The waiver would only work if it's absolutely clear that you've both considered all the possible risks. What if I managed to get Jack out on bail, and it turns out he really did kill Melissa? He might come after you next."

"Jack wouldn't hurt me," Helen said. "He had no reason even to steal my remote controls and no reason to be here the morning Melissa was killed. He didn't drop by unless I scheduled a ride, and I hadn't done that. Besides, he told me he didn't kill her, and I believe him. You should ask him for yourself."

"You don't really expect him to confess to me, do you?" Tate said. "I've never, ever had a client, no matter how blatantly guilty, confess to me. And if Jack turned out to be the exception, you'd never know, because I couldn't tell you. Attorney-client confidentiality."

"You could if he agreed."

"But then you'd have to testify to his confession, and I'd have blown any chance at a defense," Tate said. "I'm too good an attorney to do that, even if my client were foolish enough to let me."

"I need to do something," Helen said. "I can't let Jack get railroaded. None of this would have happened to him if he hadn't been working for me."

"Why not leave the investigation to the police?"

"They're too slow," Helen said. "I want to settle into a nice, peaceful retirement, and that won't happen until the right person is arrested for Melissa's murder. I've got to find that person. Betty and Josie think Melissa might have had a boyfriend that her boss didn't know about, but I thought they were just making it up. I didn't realize it then, but I was as bad as the police in assuming they didn't know anything. If you won't help me find Melissa's killer, maybe they will."

"Good luck," Tate said, picking up his empty plate and her abandoned one to take them into the kitchen for her. "I'll be in the workshop if you need me to get you out of jail. Just remember, if you get arrested for interfering in the investigation, don't say anything except that you want to talk to your lawyer."

It figured, Helen thought. Whenever she actually wanted some help, there were no volunteers.

* * *

Helen automatically speed-dialed the number to arrange for Jack to come pick her up, and the line was ringing before she realized that Jack wouldn't be available. He was still being questioned about Melissa's murder.

She cut off the call. She didn't need a fancy vehicle, and it wasn't worth the price without Jack as the driver. A regular cab would do until she could get Jack out of jail.

A cab driver would expect a specific destination, though, and would be less inclined to wait around for her to make up her mind about where to go. She'd better make sure Betty and Josie were back at the nursing home before she arranged her ride.

The receptionist at the nursing home told her that Betty and Josie had been confined to their rooms until late afternoon, to make sure they'd rest after their exhausting day out with family. She left a message for them to call her when they were able to have a visitor.

With Jack in custody, she couldn't waste the hours until then. She needed to do something to help him.

Helen settled at her desk to review her spreadsheets on suspects for Melissa's murder. She, herself, was the first entry, but of course she hadn't done it. Jack was next, just for the sake of thoroughness, but she was equally certain that he wasn't guilty either.

Then there was Melissa's employer, Gordon Pierce, who annoyed her, but she couldn't see what motive he'd have had for killing one of his own employees.

Beyond that, there were mostly just generic possibilities: family, significant other, co-workers, patients, friends. Who could put names to them, other than Betty and Josie? The reporter, Geoff Loring, perhaps, but he was out of commission and probably too scared to talk to anyone about Melissa. There was Gordon Pierce too, but she'd rather not talk to him again until the contract with his agency had been terminated. Besides, she wasn't entirely sure she believed anything he said. He kept pretending he cared about Helen's well-being, while making it clear he only cared about her money. That wasn't unusual for a business owner, and providing nursing services was a business after all. She wouldn't normally consider his puffery to be dishonesty, but he'd made other comments that made her doubt him. He'd claimed that Melissa had no family or significant other, but Betty and Josie seemed to think otherwise.

What else had Gordon Pierce told her that she could check on?

Helen pulled out a pad with random notes she'd made before starting the spreadsheets. She scanned it until she found a summary of Pierce's visit when he'd scared Rebecca off. Most of it was just a rant about how annoying he was and how sorry she felt for Rebecca. At least Helen could look forward to an end to her dealings with Pierce, but Rebecca would continue to be bullied by him, probably for her entire career, too meek to look for a better job. What if Adam could rescue Rebecca at the same time he was getting Helen out of the nursing agency's contract?

Helen sighed. She didn't have the time to save Rebecca right now. Maybe later, after Jack was absolved of Melissa's murder.

She read her notes on Pierce's visit again. He'd said something about Melissa interning at the local radio station on her days off. Maybe she'd managed to upset someone there. The people there would make better suspects anyway, since they weren't confined to the nursing home and could easily follow Melissa to Helen's cottage.

The cab driver dropped her off in front of a downtown bank building. The place had been built around the same time as the local courthouse, but at least this landlord had heard of the Americans with Disabilities Act and had installed an elevator, which took her to the second floor where the radio station was located.

Across from the elevator glass doors opened into a bland reception area that could have belonged to an insurance agency or dentist's office or just about any other sort of small business. There was a cheap, built-in counter between the lobby where Helen stood and the three work desks. Two of them were unoccupied, although there was enough personal clutter and piles of paper to suggest that they were used regularly. The third desk held a cheap, plastic-encased sign indicating that its occupant was the sales manager for the station, and the tense-looking woman perched on the edge of her chair and stared intently at her computer monitor without ever looking up. Helen wondered if the woman was as uninterested in visitors as she seemed, or was she merely pretending to be too busy to care about a potential advertiser. Helen wasn't sure if she should take the woman's lack of interest personally, as yet another example of being ignored. The woman might act like this all the time, as some sort of ploy to convince advertisers of the scarcity of the service he was buying.

Helen had more important things to worry about, so she concentrated on the receptionist, an elderly woman wearing an earbud and wrapping up a conversation on it. Apparently having disconnected the call, the receptionist greeted Helen with a nod. "If you're looking for the Chamber of Commerce, they moved three buildings down the street."

"I'm in the right place," Helen said, glancing at the only decoration on the wall, which was a three-foot high version of the station's logo. "I'd like to speak to whoever coordinates your volunteers."

"Volunteers?"

"Maybe you call them interns."

"We don't have any interns. Not anymore."

"I know," Helen said. "That's why you need me. I'm looking for some volunteer opportunities, and I heard that Melissa Shores interned here, and now that she's unavailable, I thought you might be looking for someone to take her place."

"Were you a friend of Melissa's?"

The sales manager had torn herself away from her studied lack of interest and was staring at Helen, intent on hearing her answer. Was it guilt or mere curiosity? Could she have had some sort of personal relationship with Melissa, either positive or negative?

Helen watched the sales manager while answering the receptionist. "We were just acquaintances."

The sales manager sighed and turned back to her computer. It looked more like disappointed curiosity than any real anxiety about the situation. Nothing personal there.

Helen focused on the receptionist. "What about you? Did you know Melissa well?"

"We never really had the chance to get to know her well," the receptionist said, and the sound of a stifled snort came from the sales manager. "Okay, so no one really wanted to get to know her well."

Helen wondered if Melissa had even noticed that no one liked her here. "She was a difficult person to get along with. But she'd been coming here for a long time, and this is a pretty small space. There must have been someone who dealt with her regularly."

"She worked in a back room most of the time. It was make-work mostly. She had some sort of local political connections, I think, so the manager had to find something for her to do. It wasn't anything that really needed doing." There was no animosity in her voice, not even true irritation. Nothing that might give rise to murder.

The receptionist smiled apologetically. "It's not likely that we'll need an intern again, but I can take your name and number, and keep it on file."

Even if none of the rank and file employees had anything against Melissa, there was still the station manager. He could have resented the way Melissa had been foisted on him by someone with political connections. Or he might have spent enough time with Melissa for her to have pushed him into the same sort of unreasonable anger Helen herself had felt toward the nurse. She needed to talk to him before she wrote off the station's employees as potential suspects.

"Maybe the station's manager could find me something to do," Helen said. "Could I talk to him?"

"It's not a good time."

The place wasn't exactly hopping with activity, as far as Helen could see. The sales manager was dutifully staring at her monitor, but she'd relaxed, dropping the pretense of being in high demand by other advertisers.

In other circumstances Helen might have accepted the polite brush-off, but with Jack on the verge of arrest, she couldn't afford to give up so easily. She hated to do it, but there was one way to guarantee that someone would talk to her. She wouldn't do it for herself, but Jack didn't have many other options. Whatever connections Melissa might have had to get this job, Helen was certain her own connections were even better.

"It's just that Governor Faria—he's my ex-husband, you know, but we're still on good terms—always said that I'd be an asset to any news organization if I weren't already working for him. Now that I'm on my own, I figured I'd see if he was right."

"You know the governor?" the receptionist said, her hand hovering over a button on her telephone console.

"We're just friends these days," Helen said. "We don't see each other much, but we do talk."

"Let me see if Sam's back from lunch."

A minute later, a short, thin man in his sixties, came through an unmarked door to the left of the reception counter and stood in the opening. "Mrs. Faria," he said, in a booming radio-announcer voice completely at odds with his small size. "It's an honor to meet you."

"It's Binney now," she said. "Call me Helen."

"I'm Sam Johnson, the station manager." He backed through the door he'd just come through, holding it for Helen. "Let me show you around."

"I've heard so much about this place." Most of the time Helen hadn't been listening to Melissa's constant chatter, but some of it must have been about the radio station. "Where did Melissa work when she was here?"

"Melissa?" he said. "Oh, you mean the woman who got killed the other day. We had her doing transcripts of shows, in case someone might request a copy. Not that anyone ever does, but it kept her busy and out of our way."

"I had the impression she wanted to work in the studio booth itself."

"Everyone does," he said with a smile that, like his voice, was bigger than seemed physically possible. "But we start them out in a safe location. After a while, everyone in radio develops a sort of extra-sensory awareness of the on-air light, so they just know when to stay out of the studio and even to keep quiet in the hallway. Melissa never got the hang of that, so she never graduated from her initial assignment."

That fit with the chatty woman Helen had known. Melissa would have wanted to be on air, spouting her own opinions. Sam seemed to take his work seriously, although she had a hard time envisioning him in a murderous rage. Sam turned the corner, and a door marked Studio A had its on-air light glowing. Across from it was another door marked Studio B, and that light was off. He jangled a key ring that weighed more than he did and opened the door to the dark studio. He turned on the ceiling light, revealing a cramped space, crowded with computer monitors and less easily identifiable electronic equipment. He ran a loving hand over the tabletop's electronics. "This is where I do my shows."

It was still a long shot, Helen thought, but she could imagine him engaging in a physical defense of his beloved electronics. "Melissa wasn't the sort of person to accept limitations. Did she ever sneak into the studios?"

A brief flicker of horror passed over his thin face at the idea that she might have touched his electronics, but no flash of anger. "Not as far as I know."

"I guess she was happy enough just listening to your show," Helen said. "You're a news station, right? Where are the reporters?"

"We do talk shows," Sam said in a defensive tone. "Mostly national issues, not local stuff. Nothing for us to actually investigate."

"You don't do any local news at all?"

"It's not like we're ignorant of what's happening. I do read a dozen newspapers every day, and that information gets passed along in my shows." He brightened. "Plus, we've got Geoff Loring. He does a weekly show about local stories. Sunday afternoons."

"I heard he'd been injured," Helen said. "Will he still be able to do his show?"

"He should be," Sam said. "We can give him some help with the controls until his wrist heals."

"He isn't afraid to come back to work? I heard he'd been told not to talk about some big story he was working on. How can he do his show if he's not going to talk about his big story?"

"I don't know anything about any big story. I just need him to fill an hour of otherwise dead air on Sunday afternoons."

"But if he had a big story, and he's abandoning it, wouldn't it be a great opportunity for you to take over and get the scoop?"

"I'm just the manager and the news announcer," Sam said. "No one here is a reporter. At best, they're on-air personalities. I read from the syndicated feeds we subscribe to, and press releases from the town departments. But that's not what anyone really wants to hear. If we want to stay in business, we need to stick to what people really want to hear."

"Which is uninformed people throwing sound bites at other uninformed people?"

He shrugged. "We just give the audience what it wants. They'd love to hear from you. Someone who has an insider's view of the governor's mansion."

"It's not all that interesting," Helen said. "They'd probably rather hear from people who *don't* know what it was like. The stories I've read about my life were always more interesting than the reality."

"See?" Sam said. "That's exactly the sort of comment that would make you such an interesting addition to our line-up. We could try it for a few weeks, and see what the response is before we make any long-term commitments."

"No, thanks," Helen said. "I like my privacy too much to risk becoming a 'personality.'"

"It may be too late for that," Sam said. "Wharton is a small town, and people are already talking about you."

"It's not my fault that Melissa got killed," Helen said. "And my attorney would insist on my adding that I didn't kill her. Just in case you were wondering."

Sam chuckled like the trained radio announcer he was. "No one thinks you killed Melissa. And that's not what they're talking about. It's the way you talked back to Judge Nolan, in open court. We're all amazed she didn't have you tossed into a cell for contempt."

"I didn't back-talk her," Helen said. "I just asked her a question."

"Same thing, in her court," Sam said. "I'm not saying she's a bad judge. She does a lot of good for this community, on and off the bench. But she's been a judge for two decades now, and she might be just a little too used to getting her own way all the time."

"Sounds like a good topic for one of your station's call-in shows."

"That would be one heck of a show. The ratings would probably be worth the cost of the lawyer we'd have to hire to defend against the judge's defamation suit," he said. "Are you volunteering to moderate it?"

"Still not interested." Even if she did want the job, she couldn't take it now, not while the judge held Jack's fate in her hands and might blame him for Helen's actions. "I'd just as soon let my notoriety fade away."

"Yeah," he said. "That's how everyone feels after they've dealt with Judge Nolan. But if you change your mind, just give me a call."

That wasn't going to happen, but she didn't want to antagonize anyone else in town, at least without provocation. Sam Johnson might not be a reporter, but he obviously knew a good deal about the behind-the-scenes working of the town. He'd be a good addition to her Rolodex.

"I'll get one of your business cards on the way out," she promised.

CHAPTER SEVENTEEN

———

Helen glanced out the window of the taxi as it turned onto her street, trying to concentrate on what she'd learned at the radio station, but all she could think was how much she missed having Jack in the driver's seat.

The current cab driver was everything he was supposed to be—polite, careful, efficient—but he wasn't Jack.

It was annoying to realize just how much she'd come to depend on him. Not just the transportation around town, which the taxi company had adequately replaced, but Jack himself.

If Lily were here she'd be saying, "I told you so. Everyone could use a little help."

Fortunately, her niece didn't need to know about this little epiphany, if Helen could just get Jack out of jail and make sure the real killer got put there instead.

Except that to get Jack out of jail, she needed him to already be out of jail, and giving her feedback on her impressions of the radio station employees. As far as she could tell, no one there had cared enough about Melissa, positively or negatively, to have a motive to kill her. No one was obviously in mourning, and no one was obviously gloating over her demise. But Jack knew the community better than she did, and he might have had some deeper insight into the station's employees that would have given her a reason to doubt them.

The taxi turned smoothly into Helen's driveway and bumped along the gravel surface. Once the vehicle had stopped, the driver hopped out and held the rear door for Helen while she struggled to climb out. He offered his hand, the way Jack would have known not to do, and Helen ignored it to struggle out on her own.

It was only after she'd handed the taxi driver his fare and tip, that she noticed another vehicle was parked in front of the garage. An expensive car, the sort she associated with her ex-husband's cronies. It didn't belong to Tate, who would never waste that much money on a second car when he could have spent it on wood. So who else might be visiting her uninvited?

She turned to ask the taxi driver to wait a minute in case the newcomer was someone Helen wanted to avoid by leaving again, but the taxi was already halfway to the end of the driveway. Jack wouldn't have left without saying anything, and he'd have known she might want to make a fast getaway.

Helen dug in her pocket for her cell phone, in case she needed to call 911, and headed for the cottage, hoping to get inside before the unannounced visitor could come out from wherever he was hiding.

She had only taken a couple steps before a woman—it took a moment for Helen to recognize Judge Nolan in a classic beige skirt suit instead of the formal black robes—came around the far corner of the garage. Her beige pumps were getting grass stains, and the heels that narrowed to a tiny point were sinking into the spring-rain-softened ground.

"Oh, there you are," Judge Nolan said. "I thought maybe you'd be out in the back yard somewhere on such a lovely spring day."

"I went for a drive instead." Helen dropped her phone back into her pocket and waited at the foot of her front steps. "What can I do for you?"

"I didn't get a chance to talk to you at the funeral home," Judge Nolan said as she approached. "I wanted to tell you how sorry I am for what you went through. You must have been traumatized by finding Melissa's body."

Not as traumatized as I'd been by the living Melissa.

But that was old business, and, while the judge's face didn't reveal any emotion, her presence indicated that she was truly upset about the consequence of her decision. From what the radio station manager had said, it wasn't common for the judge to admit to a mistake, and here she was, not just admitting it to herself but saying it out loud. Not in writing, of course, and there were no witnesses to her admission, but still it had to have been difficult for the judge to say the words. Helen wasn't sure she, herself, would have had the courage to do it.

In any event, Melissa's death hadn't been the judge's fault, and there was no need to make the woman feel any worse than she obviously did. Plus, she needed to keep on the judge's good side as long as Jack was the prime suspect. "I appreciate your concern. I'm fine now."

"If only…" Judge Nolan looked away.

Helen finished the thought: if only the judge had issued the restraining order, Melissa might still be alive. Of course, the restraining order might not have changed anything. Melissa might well have ignored the court order, the way she'd ignored everything else she hadn't wanted to hear.

Judge Nolan smiled ruefully. "Judges aren't supposed to admit to any regrets. We all have them, though. It doesn't make any difference now, but I thought you'd want to know how sorry I am. I hope this whole business doesn't scare you away from Wharton. It's really quite a nice little town."

"I'm not going anywhere. You won't get rid of me that easily."

Judge Nolan laughed. "I'm glad. Strong women are always good for a community."

"You're the only person around who thinks I'm strong." Helen tapped her cane on the walkway beside her. "The police took one look at this thing and assumed I was a doddering old fool. Even when they were here, having to admit they got the wrong murder weapon and searching for the right one, they couldn't acknowledge that they might be wrong about other things in this case."

"Did they find what they were looking for?"

Helen nodded. "They originally thought the murder weapon was a branch, but it turned out to be a cane. My cane. The one I had before this one. They were here with a search warrant this morning, and they found it out there." She used her cane to point toward the woods across from the back deck.

"I signed the warrant, but I didn't realize the police had been here already," the judge said, glancing in the direction Helen had pointed. "They don't usually act this fast on nonemergencies. They're understaffed like police departments everywhere."

"All municipal departments are struggling, I'm told," Helen said. "I heard that there have been some cutbacks at the town's nursing home."

Judge Nolan shook her head irritably. "I don't know why people keep saying that. The nursing home is in solid financial shape. Fully staffed and no problems paying them what they deserve. I'm on the board of directors, you know, and my mother lives there. I wouldn't let anything happen to that place or its residents."

"That's good to know," Helen said. "I've met some nice people there, and I've read too many newspaper stories about people taking advantage of the elderly and the frail."

"Good thing we're both strong women," Judge Nolan said. "No one will ever take advantage of us."

"Right," Helen agreed.

As the judge got into her car and drove away, Helen couldn't help thinking that Melissa had been a strong woman too. Stronger, at least physically, than either Judge Nolan or Helen. And yet, Melissa was dead.

* * *

After the judge left, Helen wandered from her built-in desk to her recliner to the kitchen island and then around the room again, unable to settle anywhere while trying to think of who else might want to kill Melissa. Even without Jack's input, she was fairly sure that no one at the radio station was even worth adding to her spreadsheet of possible suspects, and Betty and Josie were still being held incommunicado in their rooms at the nursing home.

Eventually she heard Tate's car coming to a stop outside the garage, followed a few minutes later by the sound of his lathe. She'd thought he'd left for the day, but he'd apparently just taken a late lunch. It was tempting to go out and see if he agreed with her about the unlikeliness of the radio station employees as suspects, but Tate deserved a little uninterrupted time to do his woodworking. Better to save her interruptions for when she had a solid lead to discuss with him.

As Helen went past the kitchen island one more time intending to make a cup of tea, a movement out on the back deck caught the corner of her eye. She blinked and looked again, and there was Jack, waving to her through the glass door.

What was he doing out of jail?

Helen limped over to the door and let him in. "Are you all right?"

"I'm fine." Jack scurried over to the kitchen island where he'd be out of the line of sight for anyone who might be looking in through the glass doors. "The court-appointed attorney got me out on bail. She said they don't have enough evidence to hold me on the murder charge, and the judge agreed. But I'm supposed to stay in Wharton where they can find me if the situation changes."

"I'm afraid it is going to change," Helen said, returning to the sink to fill the kettle with enough water for a whole pot of tea. "They found the real murder weapon this morning, and it's probably got your fingerprints on it."

"That's not possible," Jack said from his seat on the far side of the kitchen island. "I didn't do it. You know I didn't do it."

"I've been telling everyone that you didn't do it, but they aren't listening to me," Helen said as she set a mug in front of Jack. "The problem is that the murder weapon was actually my other cane, and I'm pretty sure you held it for me a few times. Unless they can affix a timeframe to the fingerprints and compare it to the time of the murder, it won't look good for you. I'm so sorry you got involved in this."

"It isn't your fault," Jack said, slumping deeper in his seat until he was barely visible over the island's top. "I should never have stolen all those remote controls. They wouldn't suspect me otherwise."

"I still feel responsible. I was the one who figured out you'd stolen them."

"But you didn't rat me out. It had to have been Tate." He sounded resigned, rather than angry.

Helen shook her head. "Tate wouldn't do that. It's against the rules for lawyers, I think. Even if it weren't, he's too busy with his woodworking to bother turning you in as long as he didn't think you were going to commit any other crimes."

"I've completely given up burglary," Jack said, straightening a little for emphasis. "Trust me, there's no way I'm risking jail again. Some friends of my cousins—the ones who didn't hire Tate—have done time in state prisons, and they said it wasn't so bad, but I'm pretty sure now that they were lying. The holding cell was bad enough, and I'm absolutely sure prison is worse. They wouldn't even let me have my smartphone so I could play games on it."

Helen poured the boiling water into the teapot. "I'll do what I can to make sure you don't do any time for the burglaries."

"I'm not so worried about that," Jack said. "My attorney said I should be able to get a plea bargain that's nothing more than probation and restitution. Probably a fine too, but no jail time. It's a whole 'nother story if they charge me with Melissa's murder."

"I'm working on that. Tate is too." The sound of the lathe in the garage contradicted her. "The woodworking helps him to think."

The lathe stopped, and Jack glanced in the direction of the garage. "Are you sure he didn't turn me in?"

"I'm sure."

The garage door opened, and Tate walked out into the yard carrying a four-foot length of wood toward the front of the cottage.

"I'd better go," Jack said, sliding out of his chair but remaining crouched down low, as if that made him less visible. "I'm not actually supposed to be here. Condition of my bail: stay away from you and the scene of the crime. All the crime scenes. But I couldn't stay away from here. I had to be sure you didn't think I'd killed Melissa. I wouldn't hurt anyone."

"I know," Helen said. "And I'm glad you're here. Before you leave, I need to know everything you can tell me about the people who work at the local radio station. Anyone there who has a history of violence or any motive for killing Melissa."

Jack was silent as he slunk over to the glass doors. When he reached them he shook his head. "I can't think of anyone who's ever been in trouble. They talk big, but it's just words. They'd never *do* anything."

"That's good to know." Helen saw Tate approaching the front steps. "Don't worry about anything. Just take care of yourself. And stay away from here until we get everything cleared up. Tate is here most of the daytime, and he'd probably have to report you if he knows you're not supposed to be here."

Jack hesitated with his hand on the back door. "How are you going to get around town without me?"

"I'll manage," Helen said, pushing him back out onto the deck. "Just until you return to work, I promise, and then I'll be calling you again. Now go."

Jack had just disappeared into the woods on the other side of the cottage from where the murder weapon had been found when Tate knocked on the front door of the cottage. Helen moved as quickly as she could, hoping to convince Tate to come inside, where there was no chance of him catching a glimpse of Jack. Otherwise, Tate might feel obliged to turn Jack in for violating the terms of his bail.

"Come in, come in," Helen said.

Tate's eyebrows rose. "What's wrong?"

"Nothing's wrong," Helen said. "Why would you think something was wrong?"

"You answered the door the first time I knocked," he said. "You hate unannounced visitors."

"Ignoring people isn't working." Helen stealthily peeked outside, reassuring herself that wherever Jack had gone, he wasn't easily spotted from the cottage. She closed the door behind Tate. "I figured I'd try a new strategy. Maybe if I'm nice to visitors, they won't feel the urge to pester me so often."

"Are you going to offer me a drink next?" he asked, with obvious suspicion. "Like the little old ladies in *Arsenic and Old Lace*?"

"I'm not old," Helen reminded him. "I don't need to poison anyone. I'm still strong enough to thwap my victims on the head with my cane. Which I'm going to do to you if you don't tell me what you're doing here and then go away so I can figure out who killed Melissa."

"I knew the 'nice' wouldn't last." Tate held up the piece of wood. "I'm making you a new walking cane to replace the missing one. I just need to get a rough idea of how long it should be."

"You don't need to do that," Helen said. She was indebted to him enough already. "I've got another cane."

"I'm not really doing it for you." He held the wood against her side and made a pencil mark at a point even with her waist. "I needed a new challenge."

"You could help me solve Melissa's murder."

He shook his head. "Not that kind of challenge. That's too much like work."

Fat lot of good it did her, having him around. He wouldn't help her investigate, and he wasn't much of a security guard, especially when he was running the lathe with his ear protection on. If Jack were really a killer she'd be dead by now.

"You've got the measurement you needed," Helen said, "so don't let me keep you from your workshop."

"There's no rush," he said. "I've got time to hear about what Jack was doing here and how he got out of jail."

"You saw him?"

Tate shook his head and then pointed the soon-to-be-cane toward a jacket on the kitchen chair Jack had just vacated. "He left his coat behind."

CHAPTER EIGHTEEN

———

Tate accepted her explanation for Jack's visit without either calling the cops or having a change of heart with respect to helping her find additional suspects for Melissa's murder. After he left, she checked with the nursing home only to find that Betty and Josie were still confined to their rooms. For their own good, was the implicit explanation, but Helen had the distinct feeling that Betty and Josie wouldn't have agreed.

First thing the next morning, though, she got an email from Betty that they'd been released to join the other ambulatory patients in the activity room for the morning, and they were looking forward to a visit.

When Helen arrived Betty and Josie were seated in their usual spot in front of the unlit fireplace, working on their knitting and crochet. They weren't entirely free of restrictions, though. A petite young woman in pastel scrubs and a suspicious expression was leaning against Josie's chair, apparently charged with making sure the women didn't exhaust themselves again. Her nametag identified her as a CNA, but she was acting more like a bodyguard, vetting anyone who came too near her clients. Why wouldn't the woman be happy that Betty and Josie had a visitor? Unless she had something to hide from those visitors. Could she have been involved with the big story Geoff Loring had been pursuing? Or was it something about Helen's investigation into Melissa's death that made the CNA anxious? Had she ever worked with Melissa?

Betty and Josie would know, but she didn't want to get them into trouble. She'd have to wait to do her questioning until they were alone. It shouldn't be too difficult to convince the CNA that Helen offered no risk to her patients, since most people started out with the assumption that Helen was powerless, but she resented having to encourage an impression she usually worked so hard to dispel. Still, she owed it to Jack to do whatever it took to keep him from going to prison for a murder he hadn't done.

"Thanks for making time to help me," she told Betty and Josie. "I'm ready to learn how to crochet now."

Josie looked surprised and said, "But didn't you—"

Betty interrupted, saying "We never turn away new volunteers," and tossing a skein of yarn that landed with a surprisingly solid thump in Josie's lap.

The two women exchanged a look, with Betty flicking a glance at the hovering CNA, and then Josie said, "Right. We can use this yarn that Betty so kindly gave me to start your lessons. Pull up a chair."

The hovering CNA said, "I'll get it."

While she was gone Betty leaned forward and whispered, "Don't trust anyone. Wait until she's gone."

Helen nodded, and Josie began digging through her Hello Kitty bag for a spare crochet hook.

The CNA returned with a chair for Helen just as Josie raised a triumphant fist holding a crochet hook. "I knew there was one in here. We'll have you making hats in no time at all. I used to be a teacher, you know. High school science. Lots more complicated than crochet, but my students all did great."

Helen accepted the crochet hook and watched Josie's demonstrations as if she hadn't seen them before. Helen could tell the woman had been a good teacher, but unfortunately that didn't mean she herself was a good student. She didn't have to pretend to act like she'd never seen the demonstrations before. The movements that seemed so obvious in Josie's hands remained awkward for Helen, bordering on painful. At least her incompetence was useful for convincing the suspicious CNA that Helen truly was a rank beginner at crochet, and nothing more stressful than a few dropped stitches was likely to be discussed.

After about ten minutes of Josie's instructions and Helen's incompetent but determined attempts to follow them, the CNA finally grew bored enough to wander away and find a new person to impose her supervision on.

Josie immediately asked, "So, have you figured out who killed Melissa yet?"

"Not quite," Helen said, dropping her yarn and needle into her lap. "I've run out of suspects. I was hoping you two might have some leads for me. Tell me everything you know about Melissa."

"That would take for*ever*," Josie said. "We might not live long enough to tell you everything we know about her."

"Speak for yourself. I plan to live until I've knit a cap in every imaginable color and pattern, and that could take fifty years." Betty turned to Helen. "Josie is right, though, that it would take a while to go over everything we've ever heard about Melissa. We know everything that goes on here. The staff assumes that everyone here has short-term memory issues, so they don't watch what they say in front of us."

"Let's start with what the staff are saying about Melissa."

After a brief silence Betty said, "They thought it was odd that Pierce offered her a job."

"I always figured she had some leverage she could use against him," Josie said. "Something she'd learned from a patient. But we couldn't figure out what it could have been. He's practically the only person in town who hasn't had a relative staying here at some point during Melissa's tenure here."

"Maybe he made a blanket job offer to all the nurses here, and Melissa was the only one interested in it."

"None of the other nurses were offered jobs, though," Betty said. "Just Melissa. I doubt any of them would have accepted, but they were all a little irritated that they hadn't at least been asked."

That was odd, Helen thought. "Why would Pierce have singled her out? Was she that much better than all the other nurses?"

"We couldn't ever figure that out. He couldn't have wanted her for her medical knowledge," Josie said. "And she wasn't any good at all with the geriatric patients here. Mostly, we just want someone to listen to us, and she wouldn't. She was like an old-fashioned schoolmarm, like you used to read about, with rulers to rap your knuckles. Except she didn't do anything physical to her patients, because that would have left evidence and gotten her fired. Instead, she used to play mind games, terrifying the patients into obeying her."

Betty nodded. "One of her favorite tricks was to steal the patient's walker if they didn't do what she told them to. Without it, they couldn't leave the room, and she wouldn't give it back until they promised to obey her. One time, she had a particularly stubborn patient, and somehow she convinced the management that the patient had thrown it out his window, where it was run over by an arriving ambulance. It turned out the walker had some sort of special customization, so the patient was bedridden for over a week until a replacement could be obtained."

Helen wondered how many of the recommendations in Melissa's files had been written under threat of the patient's walker being confiscated. Still, none of the recommendations had been anything more than adequate, not the sort of thing that would have prospective employers chasing after Melissa. "If Pierce didn't want her for her knowledge or her bedside manner, then what did he want her for?"

Betty glanced around the room until she found the CNA trying to coax a scruffy old man out of the far corner of the room. Even with the CNA occupied and a good distance away, Betty leaned forward and whispered, "Insider information."

Josie copied Betty's actions, checking on the location of the CNA before adding, "Pierce has contracts with the nursing home to provide some of the services here, and he does a crummy job of it. We think he used Melissa's knowledge of the nursing home to get really favorable terms in his contracts. He knew all the right buttons to push when he was pitching to the board of directors, so they didn't look at the contracts all that carefully."

"Some people think he's been using her inside knowledge to run an insurance scam," Betty said. "You hear about that sort of thing in the news all the time. Billing for services never provided. There have been a lot of complaints about cancelled physical therapy sessions lately, ever since that work was subcontracted to his agency. It would be easier to do that sort of thing if you had an employee who could identify good targets, the ones who don't pay any attention to their medical records and who don't have family members keeping an eye on them."

"Someone from the nursing home's administration must be keeping an eye on him," Helen said.

"Not really," Betty said. "The administrative staff here has enough to do with all the paperwork and all the rules and regulations they need to follow, and they don't get involved in individual patients' issues unless someone complains repeatedly, and most of us don't have enough energy to do that."

"What about their board of directors?"

"Everyone on the board is a volunteer," Betty said. "Most of them have a relative living here, and that's why they're on the board, to make sure that family member is taken care of. As long as their family members are happy, the board members aren't interested in hearing about anyone else's complaints."

"Someone had to have noticed if there was widespread fraud," Helen said. "Detective Peterson spends time here, and his job is investigating crimes. And I know Geoff Loring spends a lot of time here. If there's widespread fraud, wouldn't he have heard about it?"

"He's as bad as the board of directors," Josie said. "He's got a cousin living here, so as long as the cousin seems reasonably happy, Geoff doesn't want to notice the little, annoying problems., "

"What about his big story? The one he kept talking about? "That was just Geoff, always trying to sound important. He didn't have anything," Betty said. "Ironic really, since someone apparently thought he was onto something and assaulted him for it."

"Maybe there really is a big story, even if he didn't actually know it." Helen had a sudden thought. "Do you know if he did a story on Melissa leaving the nursing home for her new job?"

"I can't remember," Josie said, looking at Betty, who shook her head.

"What if he interviewed her, and someone thought she had told him something controversial about one of her patients, something that person didn't want investigated. Then Geoff starts talking about his big story, and the person thinks that killing

Melissa will stop the investigation, but it doesn't, so then the person goes after Geoff too."

"It's possible," Betty said. "But Melissa's seen an awful lot of patients over the years, and there's far too much gossip flying around here to even begin to figure out who might have been desperate enough to commit murder to keep something quiet. Everyone's got something to be embarrassed about."

Still, Helen thought, at least now she had a lead of sorts. She just had to narrow down the possibilities a bit. "How many people are there in the nursing home?"

"Including just the patients and staff? Without their visitors?" Betty said. "A couple hundred. Double that, if you include the family members who visit regularly.

"That makes four hundred people who might have wanted Melissa dead." So much for thinking she was making progress. It would have been a stretch for the local police department to interview and background-check that many people; it was completely impossible for Helen to do it alone, even armed with a spreadsheet and search engines. "That's almost as big a list as the people who've threatened my ex-husband."

"I wish we could be more help. With both the investigation and your crochet skills." Josie pointed to the mess in Helen's lap. "You've missed a few stitches in that last row."

Helen pulled out the row she'd just completed. "I'm as bad at this as I am at helping Jack prove he didn't kill Melissa."

"Jack Clary can take care of himself," Betty said. "He's been in all sorts of scrapes over the years from what I've heard, and he never ended up in jail."

"Until now," Josie said.

"At least he's out on bail," Helen said.

"Probably not for long, though," Josie said. "Detective Peterson was here visiting his father earlier today, and we heard him talking about the case. He said Jack had called them with some wild story about being afraid for his life because someone had mugged him on his way home last night and told him to leave town. Everyone at the police station thought it was funny, that he was making it up as some sort of publicity stunt to convince them he was innocent."

"He *is* innocent, and Jack wasn't making it up," Helen said, stuffing her yarn and needle into her too-small purse. Two muggings in this little town, both with ties to Melissa, and the police couldn't see that something was seriously wrong. Maybe Tate could do something about getting Jack some police protection. "I've got to go. Call me if you think of anything that might help narrow down the suspects."

* * *

When Helen arrived back at her cottage, Tate was sitting on the front porch steps. He was up and across the front yard, opening the taxi's back door for her before the driver could do it.

"I don't like this," Tate said as the taxi was leaving.

"What did I do now?" Helen said. "You waylaid me, not the other way around."

"Adam called to tell me that Jack was mugged," he said. "I don't like it. Things are escalating, and you're in the middle of it."

"I'm not in the middle of anything except a bunch of trees," Helen said, on her way to the front door. "No one takes me seriously."

"I do," Tate said, following. "Okay, I didn't at first, but I do now. We don't get random muggings in Wharton. Not like what happened to Jack. I've had to listen to almost as many arraignments as Judge Nolan has, while waiting for my clients' cases to be called. In pretty much all the assault cases I've ever observed, the assailant and the victim knew each other, and more often than not they were under the influence of something. Alcohol, drugs, hormones. That sort of thing. But according to Jack, his assailant came out of nowhere, knocked him down, and told him to leave town before he got what was coming to him."

"I bet the police think one of his burglary victims came after him." Helen unlocked her front door.

"That's what I thought at first, and it's definitely the simplest explanation." Tate followed her inside, and wandered around the great room, checking out her bookshelves and inspecting the construction of her built-in desk cabinetry.

"But not the only explanation." Helen left her cane at the front door and went over to the kitchen. The spring air wasn't particularly warm today, and Tate had probably gotten chilled while outside waiting for her. "What if Melissa's killer tried to scare him into running?"

"I'm listening." Tate dropped onto one of the stools at the kitchen island. "Convince me it was the killer."

Of course now when she wanted to be wrong, Tate had to go and believe her. Or at least not disbelieve her. "For one thing, Jack's victims were low-level jerks. Not violent. And it would take some work to have found him. Plus, they'd have to have a certain mindset to attack him physically. It's not like Jack hurt anyone, so why escalate to assault instead of just accepting compensation for the things he took?"

"Crime isn't entirely rational."

"Okay, but Jack isn't the only person who was assaulted and warned off." Helen opened a can of chicken noodle soup and dumped it into a small tureen with a pouring spout. "The reporter, Geoff Loring, was too. Someone beat him up, broke his wrist, and told him to stop investigating the nursing home. Like you said, Wharton is a small town, and two muggings like this with a common thread are more likely to be related than not."

"What's the common thread?"

"Melissa. She used to work at the nursing home before she joined the agency that assigned her to me." Helen placed the soup bowl in the microwave and slammed the door shut. "Melissa's death and Geoff's nursing home story could be related. Betty and Josie think Melissa might have been involved in insurance fraud while working for Pierce's agency. She could have been killed to cover up the fraud, and then Jack became a convenient scapegoat."

"That's assuming facts not in evidence, that there was a fraud scheme and she was involved with it."

"But it would be so perfect if it was true," Helen said. "I can't think of anyone I'd rather see behind bars than Pierce, and if his agency was committing fraud, I doubt their contracts would be enforceable, so you wouldn't have to waste any more of your retirement time helping your nephew get my contract cancelled."

"Just because he's a convenient scapegoat doesn't make him guilty. Jack is a convenient scapegoat too, according to the police," Tate said. "A lot of assaults are just a matter of being in the wrong place at the wrong time. The police could be right that Melissa was killed by a burglar, even if it wasn't Jack. Wharton isn't too small to have more than one burglar, even if it doesn't have multiple muggers. You're a wealthy woman, living in an out-of-the-way house, an appealing target for thieves."

"I'm tougher than I look." Helen tried not to disprove her words as she carried the steaming bowl of soup to the kitchen island. "If you're right about what happened, then the not-Jack burglar is casing the joint, Melissa shows up, confronts him, and he kills her. It's possible I suppose, but it just doesn't feel right. For one thing, where'd he get the murder weapon? Melissa was killed outside, not in here where the cane would have been at hand waiting for him to grab it. And if he managed to break into the cottage, there are more valuable things for him to steal, so why would he only take the cane."

"Melissa must have had it with her." Tate frowned as he came around the island to rummage through her drawers for soup spoons. "You're right. That doesn't make sense."

Helen paused in the act of reaching for soup bowls. "Actually, maybe it does. Betty and Josie told me that Melissa used to take the patients' walkers as a sort of hostage until they did what she wanted them to. I bet she took my cane and let me think I'd lost it, so I'd feel indebted to her when she found it. Or so I'd be desperate to negotiate with her to get it back."

Tate took the bowls from her and placed them next to the tureen. "That would explain why she was here the morning she was killed. She came to return the cane, and instead she stumbled across a burglary."

"I'm still not buying it," Helen said. "Melissa would never have confronted a burglar directly. I'm sure she's performed heroic life-saving procedures like CPR as part of her job, but much as I hate to admit it, she wasn't stupid. If she'd seen someone suspicious in the yard, she'd have done the sensible thing: picked up her cell phone and called the cops. She wouldn't have tried to stop him herself."

"Let's say it wasn't any kind of burglar who killed her, then," Tate said. "Why would someone want to kill Melissa?"

"Because she was annoying."

"You think everyone is annoying."

"They are. But she was even worse than most. She never stopped talking."

"About what?"

Helen poured the soup into the individual bowls and gestured for Tate to eat while she tried to recreate the monologues she'd worked so hard to ignore when they were actually happening. "Melissa went on and on about how much she loved nursing, and all the years she'd worked at the nursing home, and how many people she'd cared for there."

"Maybe someone thought she knew something she shouldn't, and that she'd spill their secrets. Something that wasn't a problem as long as she was just talking to nursing home residents but could be a problem if someone outside found out about it."

Helen thought about the things Melissa had told her about her patients. "I have to admit, Melissa really wasn't a malicious gossip. All her stories were about how nice her clients were and how much they loved her."

"Still, she might have said something that wasn't meant to be widely known. In which case, you might have heard whatever it was that Melissa knew," Tate said between mouthfuls of soup. "And whoever silenced her would have a motive to come after you so you wouldn't tell anyone else."

"But I don't talk to anyone," Helen said. "Everyone knows that."

"You talk to me."

"Lawyer-client privilege," she said. "You can't tell anyone about anything I say, so it wouldn't become public knowledge. We're both safe."

"It's a little more complicated than that," Tate said, but he had the good sense not to go into any of the details her husband would have shared with her in the same circumstances. It was one of the things she didn't dislike about Tate.

"What I said about Melissa being annoying is complicated too. She was supposed to be helping me, but most of the time she made things more difficult. She tripped me once, and another time she managed to spill water all over my most critical pills, completely ruining them."

Tate shook his head ruefully. "Why do clients always leave out the most important facts and then wonder why I can't help them?"

"Melissa's clumsiness isn't important," Helen said, reluctant to discuss her frailties with someone who looked like he'd never had a frail moment in his life. "I hardly even remember the incidents."

"What if they weren't accidents?"

"They had to be," Helen said automatically, even as the possibility settled over her, causing her to shiver in a way that the hot soup couldn't fix. "She'd have been fired if anyone found out she was intentionally endangering me. Why would she risk it?"

"Either she didn't think you'd tell on her, or she had some reason to think she couldn't be fired from her current job." Tate helped himself to the last of the soup. "She had to know you weren't the type to keep quiet, so she must have thought her job was secure, no matter what she did."

"Maybe Pierce was desperate for employees."

"No one's desperate enough to keep an employee who's committing blatant malpractice."

"Unless the employee is more of a partner in crime than an employee," Helen said. "What if Betty and Josie are right, that Pierce hired Melissa specifically to help him scam the nursing home patients?"

"Then why was she endangering you? You're not in the nursing home."

"Not for want of everyone trying to make me go there. Melissa and Pierce could have been trying to convince me that I really did need full-time residential care. Then once I was in the nursing home, they could bill my insurer for all sorts of things that I don't really need, which would only make it seem more reasonable that I needed to be there, and also make it harder for me to get out again."

"Insurance fraud would explain a lot," Tate said. "Co-conspirators have a falling out, tempers are frayed, violence ensues, and a head is bashed."

"Just another boring case, in legal terms," Helen said. "It shouldn't be all that difficult for you to prove, and then Jack will be out of danger."

"I'm doing this for you, not for Jack." Tate took his empty bowl and hers over to the sink. "I'm acquainted with some members of the nursing home's board of directors. I doubt they'll say anything about such a sensitive topic over the phone, but they might talk to me in person. I'll go see if any of them have become suspicious about anything going on at the nursing home."

He wasn't the only one with contacts. It was time to unpack her Rolodex. "I know some people in the Attorney General's office. While you're gone, I'll check with them."

CHAPTER NINETEEN

———

Helen's contacts in the Attorney's General claimed to be unaware of any investigation into insurance fraud at the nursing home, and they'd sounded sincere, but they could have just been telling her the official story, keeping it secret until they had enough evidence for some indictments. In any event, if there really wasn't an ongoing investigation, she had a feeling they'd be starting one now. The local police might not take her seriously, but these contacts knew her from the days when she wasn't just a decrepit old private citizen but was the person in charge of the governor's mansion. She'd even gotten a promise that if there was an investigation and if it did find any wrongdoing, they'd give Geoff Loring some of the credit, maybe even give him a couple hours' advance notice before the official announcement. He deserved something for flushing out the story, even if it had been inadvertent.

Helen had just tucked her Rolodex back into the cabinet when she heard a car in the gravel driveway. She hoped it was Tate reporting back with whatever he'd found out. Her hip was bothering her, and she just wanted to get this whole thing straightened out, so she could take a painkiller and relax in front of the television. She didn't take the pills very often because they tended to make her so sleepy she couldn't do anything at all, but after the last few days the idea of dozing in her recliner was appealing.

Helen absently picked up her cane from where it leaned against the front door so she could let Tate inside. Too late, she realized it was Pierce standing on the front porch, rapidly scrolling through messages on his smartphone. Today's cravat was more somber than usual with white dots on a black background.

"Go away," she told him. "I'm sure Rebecca is a very good nurse, but I don't need her services."

"Rebecca quit."

Good for her. The woman did have some gumption after all. Helen just hoped she also had a new job. If not, maybe a recommendation from the governor's ex-wife would help. She'd have Tate's nephew check it out.

"Don't worry." Pierce gave the door a sudden push, jerking it out of Helen's control, and slamming it all the way open. He picked up the messenger bag at his feet and brushed past her into the cottage before turning around to face her again. "I've found you a new nurse. I just need you to sign the revised contract."

"I'm not signing anything," Helen said. "You need to talk to my lawyer."

"No time for that." Pierce grabbed her by the elbow with his free hand, and pulled her toward the kitchen island, leaving the front door wide open.

What would Pierce do if she refused to sign his contract? He wouldn't kill her, because then the contract would be worthless. Still, it might be better to just sign the damned thing and let Tate get it voided on the grounds that it was signed under duress. Now that Pierce had dragged her across the room, she was perfectly willing to swear in court that she was afraid of Pierce in a way that she'd never been afraid of Melissa.

Helen couldn't count on the court to do the right thing, though. Just because Judge Nolan felt guilty about what had happened to Melissa didn't necessarily mean she'd rule in Helen's favor on another issue. If she could avoid signing Pierce's papers just until Tate returned, it would save everyone a lot of trouble later. Tate should be back any minute, and as soon as he saw the front door open, even before he climbed out of his car, he'd know something was wrong. He'd do what she'd said a sane person would do when he saw something suspicious: call the police. And they'd listen to him.

All she had to do was to delay signing anything and keep Pierce from closing the front door. Helen stumbled, fumbling with her cane as if she couldn't move without assistance, so Pierce would be unable to let her go while he closed the door.

He pushed her into the first seat at the kitchen island, which freed him to take a step toward the front door. She needed to get his attention back on her, and that meant dropping her pretense of incompetence. She didn't care if he thought she was crazy. She just needed to provoke him. True or not, being accused of fraud ought to do it.

"You're wasting valuable time with me, when you should be packing up and leaving town," she said. "Everyone knows about the insurance fraud. Including the Attorney General's office."

Mentioning the Attorney General was what finally got him to forget about the door. He turned around, his falsely solicitous expression firmly in place. "You shouldn't say such things. Someone might take you seriously."

"They already did," she said. "Tate is at the police station now, arranging for your arrest."

"I know that you've been under a great deal of stress." Pierce's voice remained calm and condescending, but he brought his messenger bag up to his chest, hugging it like a security blanket. His fingers were turning white from the tension of his grip on the bag. "Even so, you can't go around slandering people. I understand, of course, but not everyone would, and you could get into a great deal of legal trouble."

"Don't patronize me," Helen said. "I know what you did. The only thing I don't understand is why you killed Melissa."

He didn't even blink. He just shook his head sadly. "Melissa was right. You're senile. I'm sure that when you've had the time to think about it, you'll realize I didn't kill anyone."

"There's no point in lying now," Helen said. "It's just you and me, and no one ever listens to me."

"You know, I hadn't planned to kill you, but it's starting to sound like a good idea." He tossed his bag on the kitchen island top and flipped it open. "It doesn't have to be that way, though. All I really want is for you to sign a few things. Like you say, no one will pay any attention when you claim I forced you to sign them."

Tate would pay attention, Helen thought. And he'd make sure others listened too. No point in pushing Pierce too far. Besides, she was curious just what he was planning. Maybe the papers in his bag were just what she needed to prove that Pierce was committing fraud.

"What do you want signed?"

"Oh, nothing much," he said, waving a stack of papers at her. "Durable power of attorney, health care proxy, that sort of thing."

He really was committing fraud, she thought, fighting down the urge to slip off her chair and dance around the room in triumph. Not that she'd be able to take more than a step or two without falling down. Being dragged and tossed into this chair hadn't done her hip any good.

But she'd been right. Or mostly right. Pierce wasn't just after her medical insurance; he was after everything she had. With those documents, he could have her put in the nursing home against her will. Not only would everyone ignore her wishes like they were already inclined to do but they'd actually be legally required to ignore them. Pierce could take his time, generating bills for expensive medical services she neither needed nor received, and, if that wasn't enough, he'd simultaneously be looting her personal financial assets.

"Forget it, Pierce." Helen's exuberance was evaporating, and she understood how Tate felt when a promising legal case turned into a routine matter. The sheer incompetence of Pierce's plan made Melissa's death seem even worse; no one, not even Melissa, deserved to die in furtherance of such an inept crime.

Helen didn't have to fake the fatigue in her voice as she explained, "Everything I own is in a trust. I can't sign it over to you, even if I wanted to. Besides, I already have a health care proxy filed with my doctor, who's a family friend. He'd be suspicious if I changed it from my niece to someone I'd only met recently."

Pierce let the papers slip from his hands to scatter across the kitchen island. He leaned over to lay his forearms on the island's top and then clutched his head between his hands. When he spoke again, his voice was too muffled to tell whether he was as distraught as he looked, or if this was just another act. "This is all Melissa's fault. She said you'd be an easy target, and if we pulled it off, we might even get our hooks into some of your Boston contacts as well. I knew we should have stuck to what was working instead of branching out."

"Greed does lead people to take unnecessary risks." Helen finally heard the familiar—and just this once, eagerly anticipated—sound of a car coming up the far end of her gravel driveway. She pushed herself to her feet and thumped her cane more loudly than necessary, to keep Pierce's attention on her and away from the sound of the approaching vehicle. "How long had you been scamming the nursing home patients before Melissa joined you?"

"A couple years," he said, straightening slowly and running his hands down his face. A finger snagged on his cravat and undid its neat folds, leaving it a wrinkled lump. "I was so careful not to take much from any one patient. Until Melissa came along. She knew which patients would know immediately if the billing was excessive, so we had to remain cautious with them, but she also knew which patients never looked at the billing or had anyone else do it for them, and there was practically no limit to the padding we could do there. Even after her cut, I made more in the six short months with Melissa than I'd made in the entire two years before that."

"So that's why you killed Melissa," Helen said. "Geoff Loring started nosing around, asking about Melissa and talking about a big story. You thought he'd figured out what you and Melissa were up to. You blamed Melissa for not covering her tracks better, so you killed her, hoping that would be the end of it."

"I didn't kill Melissa." He sounded genuinely surprised by the accusation.

"Yes, you did." She'd seen him lie often enough that she wasn't willing to give him the benefit of the doubt. "And then later, when Geoff kept poking around at the nursing home, following up on his suspicions about you and Melissa, you assaulted him to get him to drop the story. You even threatened Jack so he'd run away too, and everyone would think it was proof of his guilt, and they'd close the case without looking into anyone else's motive."

"Geoff Loring was a problem, and I took care of it. I didn't need to kill Melissa. Or do anything about Jack. He was doing a pretty good job all by himself of convincing the police of his guilt."

The tell-tale thunk of Tate's car door slamming startled Pierce. "Who's that?"

"No one."

He glanced frantically around the cottage, as if looking for a place to hide. "Melissa didn't say anything about a silent alarm."

"I just had it installed," she said, omitting the fact that it hadn't gone live yet. "Marty Reed designed it."

Pierce looked at the door, and then apparently deciding he'd never get there in time to escape, he took up a position on her left side, with his arm around her shoulder. It would look like he was just being friendly and supportive, but it also had the effect of preventing her from getting up and running—or at least hobbling—away from his control.

"You're going to tell the responders that everything is okay," he said. "Tell them that you tripped the alarm by mistake and we couldn't figure out how to disarm it."

"Then what?"

"It depends on you. Sign the papers, and keep quiet, and everything will be fine."

She didn't have to see his face to know he was lying. She could feel it in the grip he had on her shoulder, the tension of his body beside her. If she sent Tate away, Pierce would kill her, like he'd killed Melissa, and if that weren't bad enough, he'd probably find a way to implicate Jack. She'd have to be as much of a fool as he obviously thought she was to believe otherwise.

"I am *not* an incompetent fool." Her cane was in her right hand, out of Pierce's line of sight. She adjusted her grip on her cane, sliding her hand down the shaft until she could hold it like a baseball bat.

"What?"

"I am not a fool, and I am not an easy victim." She flipped the cane up to thwap Pierce's hand on her right shoulder. When he let go of her, she was able to get a few inches' distance from him. She knew she couldn't outrun him, not once he got over the surprise, so she had to find some way to slow him down. The cane wasn't strong enough to do any damage to his legs, but it might be enough to give him a bit of a concussion.

She reinforced her grip on the cane with her left hand, and, with a moment's regret that she hadn't taken her husband up on his frequent offers to teach her to play golf, she swung the cane at Pierce's head.

Even as she dropped the cane, Pierce fell back against the island, obviously dazed. She didn't know how long it would take for him to recover, and she was going to need reinforcements before that happened. She knew she was being a little foolish, but she couldn't quite make herself call out for help, not in front of the man who'd banked on her vulnerability. Still, she wasn't foolish enough to risk the possibility that Tate wouldn't have noticed the open front door. Pierce thought there were people responding to an alarm out there, so she just needed to foster that impression. She limped toward the front door, shouting "We're in here!" as she went.

Tate was just outside, phone in hand, to catch her as she almost tumbled down the front steps.

"Pierce is inside," she said. "He killed Melissa. Don't let him get away."

She didn't know whether Tate believed her, but at least he didn't try to tell her she was crazy. He just said, "The police are on the way," and offered his arm to lean on as they walked over to his car. He opened the passenger side door so she'd have a safe place to wait.

She settled into the seat while Tate kept an eye on the cottage to make sure Pierce didn't leave. Helen almost hoped Pierce would try to run; it would make her story more credible.

A few anxious minutes later, two police cruisers screeched to a stop behind Tate's car. She told them that Pierce had threatened her and had been defrauding the nursing home patients. They might not have believed her if Tate hadn't been standing beside her. He didn't say anything, but his presence seemed to be enough to convince the officers to go inside the cottage, at least to find out his side of the story.

Apparently Pierce was even less credible than Helen was, because it wasn't long before the officers escorted him out of the cottage and toward the police cruiser. One of the officers was studying the papers that Pierce had tried to force Helen to sign, and judging by the officer's face they were every bit as bad as she'd believed.

A trickle of blood ran down Pierce's ear, and he seemed dazed, either by the blow to his head or the shock that the victim he'd thought was such an easy target had actually fought back. Helen didn't regret having hit him, but she did regret having done it before she'd been able to get him to confess to Melissa's murder. His confession to her might not have been enough to convict him, since it would have been her word against Pierce's, but her testimony should at least have been enough to establish reasonable doubt at Jack's trial.

Pierce's hands were cuffed behind him, holding his cravat, which he'd apparently used to sop up some of the blood from his ear. As he passed Helen, he said plaintively, "Why'd you have to hit me?"

"You were in my cottage, trying to hurt me, and you wouldn't let me leave," Helen said. "Why wouldn't I hit you?"

Pierce glanced to his left and then to his right, at the officers flanking him. "You're delusional. I would never hurt one of my clients."

"Save it for the judge." Helen said, and then she had an idea. There were all sorts of reliable witnesses to anything he said now, and he was a bit off-kilter from the blow to his head. If she could just keep him talking, he might say something incriminating about the murder. "It's ironic, really. I hit you the same way you hit Melissa, in a disagreement over your fraud, and even with the same type of weapon. Except you killed her, and I only gave you a bump on the head."

"You're crazy. I didn't kill Melissa," he grumbled, but he didn't get a chance to say anything more before the officers stuffed him into the back of one of the cruisers. One of the officers climbed into the cruiser and left with Pierce, while the other one remained just long enough to let Helen know they were planning to charge him with assault immediately, but that the fraud claims would have to wait until they could be investigated by someone in the detective division.

As the second cruiser was leaving, Tate said, "Don't feel bad that you couldn't get Pierce to confess to Melissa's murder. It was a long shot at best. Confessions don't happen very often, and in the few cases when you get them, they're not always admissible at trial."

"Even if the confession didn't hold up in court," Helen said, "Detective Peterson would hear about it, and he wouldn't be able to ignore me any longer. I'd have at least had a chance to convince him not to pursue the case against Jack."

"Once Detective Peterson gets a look at the papers the officers confiscated, you won't have any trouble convincing him to listen to you," Tate said. "According to the nursing home board members I spoke to, they were just starting to think something was wrong with Pierce's agency, but they hadn't realized quite how bad it was. Yours won't be the only voice calling for an investigation."

"The state is probably looking into it too," Helen said. "But I'm not sure the fraud investigation will help Jack as long as Pierce is denying he killed Melissa."

"At least now his attorney has an alternative suspect to offer the jury," Tate said. "If it will keep you from doing anything crazy, now that you're no longer a suspect I might consider taking Jack's case. It's probably the easiest way to get our lives back to normal. If you're not worried about him, you can go back to living all alone in your cottage, and I can get back to my woodworking."

That was exactly what Helen had wanted originally, but the last few days had made her realize that she didn't just want to be left alone. She wanted to find something to do with her solitude. She wanted something that wasn't just a hobby, but was an avocation, a calling, something she could be as passionate about as Tate was with his woodworking and Betty and Josie were with their chemo cap knitting.

The only thing she'd felt passionate about recently was getting rid of Melissa and then figuring out who had actually gotten rid of Melissa. Unfortunately, she couldn't count on people dying just to give her something interesting to do.

CHAPTER TWENTY

———

After the police and Tate left, Helen considered calling her nieces to let them know that Melissa's killer had been caught, but then they'd have wanted to know about how Pierce had been caught, and that explanation was going to upset them. Helen was too tired to deal with it tonight. She'd call them first thing in the morning before the reporters got hold of the story. Tonight, all she wanted to do was go to bed early.

She was too wired and sore to sleep right away, so she took the painkiller that she'd postponed earlier. While she waited for it to make her sleepy enough to rest, she puttered around the cottage, putting away her notes on Melissa's murder. The police had Pierce in custody, and Jack would be cleared soon enough now that Tate was representing him.

It still bothered her that Pierce hadn't confessed to the murder, even after conceding the fraud. She understood why he hadn't said anything incriminating when the police were there to overhear it, but why hadn't he confessed when they were alone? He had clearly thought no one would listen to her about the fraud, so why think anyone would listen if she'd started claiming that he'd killed Melissa? Detective Peterson would have patted her on the head and told her not to worry about such things. Tate might have believed her, but he also would have told her that she needed more proof. Betty and Josie might have believed her too, but they also believed that Elvis had been seen at the nursing home two weeks ago, and if they became too agitated in their defense of Helen, the staff would likely send them to their rooms until they calmed down.

The ache in her hip wasn't going away with the first pill, and she couldn't relax until the pain receded. Reluctantly, she took a second dose of the painkiller and a moment later heard a car coming up the gravel driveway. As far as she knew, Tate hadn't planned to return this evening, Jack was still under court order to stay away from her, and her nieces didn't have any reason for an unannounced visit. Maybe Geoff Loring had heard from the police about Pierce's arrest and had figured out that Pierce was the one who'd attacked him, so it was safe to venture out to do his job.

Between the pills she'd taken and the effort it had taken to get away from Pierce, she was exhausted and more irritable than usual. Whoever was outside, answering the door would not be a good idea. She'd bashed one person's head today, and it wouldn't take much to tempt her to do it again. The police might start to wonder if maybe she was as crazy as Pierce claimed if she thumped all of her unannounced visitors with her cane.

Helen ignored the knocking at the door, until finally a woman's voice spoke. "Helen? Tate told me you were home. I need to talk to you about Pierce and the nursing home fraud."

She recognized the voice. Judge Nolan.

It figured, Helen thought. Now that the judge wanted to listen, Helen didn't feel like talking, and considering the two painkillers she'd taken, she wasn't even sure how much longer she'd be able to string together a coherent sentence.

"It's late," Helen said through the closed door. "I'll stop by the courthouse tomorrow. Just tell me when would be a good time."

"I'll be tied up all day. I've got a major trial starting in the morning," the judge said. "It's embarrassing enough that there was fraud at the nursing home while I was on the board of directors. I'd like to be able to show that as soon as I realized what was going on I took quick action."

Helen was feeling a little lightheaded from the first painkiller, but it should be another half hour or so before the second one really kicked in. She could tell the judge what little she knew before then.

Helen opened the door. As the judge came inside, Helen noticed that she was wearing sneakers. A haute-couture suit, trendy necklace and sneakers. She'd been wearing designer pumps in her previous visit to the cottage, even when she'd been walking around the yard. Why was she wearing sneakers?

The sound of the door closing and the deadbolt turning brought her back to the present. Her mind was wandering, she realized. She didn't have time for anything except telling the judge about Pierce.

"Come on over to the kitchen island and have a seat. All my guests sit there. I prefer the recliner, unless I'm working at my desk. I've been making spreadsheets recently. You can learn a lot from spreadsheets."

Helen glanced at the judge, to make sure the woman was following her across the room. The judge was right beside her, but there was something wrong about the judge. More likely, Helen thought, there was something wrong with herself, and she was projecting onto her visitor.

For one thing, Helen realized her words had been rambling. She didn't normally chatter about nothing. Probably the painkillers messing with her head. She forced herself to stop talking, except it didn't stop her thoughts. The judge wanted to know about Pierce. Who had admitted to the fraud but had refused to confess to killing Melissa. It was almost as if he hadn't actually done it. Which meant someone else had killed the nurse.

Helen slowed and then stopped in the middle of the room, vaguely aware that she'd lost her train of thought. She was supposed to be talking about Pierce. The police had him. He wasn't bothering her any longer. The judge was here now. Wearing sneakers. Ugly, beat-up sneakers that should have been thrown out a long time ago. They were so old, they really were sneakers and not running shoes. Everything else the judge wore was new and fancy. Designer suit. Silk blouse. Necklace that was as much expensive art as jewelry. All pristine. Except the sneakers.

Before Helen could bring her wandering thoughts back under control, the judge said, "You don't look so good. Why don't you have a seat? I'll get you a glass of water."

Helen was closer to the recliner than the kitchen, and she really didn't think she could stand much longer. She barely had enough energy to drop onto the chair. The pills seemed to magnify her usual lupus fatigue, sapping her strength.

The judge crossed the room to the kitchen and used a dish towel to open the cabinet under the sink. "I understand

Pierce confessed to his involvement with insurance fraud. What, exactly, did he tell you?"

Pierce. Right. That was why the judge was here. Helen needed to explain everything she knew about Pierce, and then the judge would leave.

"The fraud started two years ago, but Melissa didn't get involved until later. That's why he killed her. Except he didn't kill her." Wait. That wasn't right. Pierce had to have killed Melissa. Why would Helen even doubt it? Stupid painkillers. They were confusing her. She needed to explain Pierce's actions more clearly. "Pierce used Melissa to ramp up the fraud. She had the inside information that made the billing seem legit."

"That's what I thought." Judge Nolan had pulled on a pair of yellow latex dishwashing gloves, and was now systematically investigating the contents of the kitchen cabinets. In the second one, she found the beverage glasses. She took one down and began filling it from the faucet. "There's a good chance that neither Jack nor Pierce will be convicted for Melissa's death. Someone needs to be punished."

"Exactly. Otherwise, the police will do a better investigation, and they'll identify the real killer." Her brain finally caught up to itself, but her body wasn't fast enough to do anything but sit where she was. "They'll identify *you*."

"You're not as silly as you look." The judge kept poking through Helen's cabinets, seemingly unconcerned about having been accused of murder.

Helen tried to concentrate, but her head was spinning. Maybe she was actually asleep, and this was all just a weird dream. The idea of the judge having killed Melissa was as surreal as the methodical way the judge was investigating Helen's cabinets.

What on earth did the judge want? Helen clearly remembered the woman saying she'd come here to talk about the nursing home fraud. Except no one official knew about the fraud yet. The police had taken Pierce away for assault, not for the fraud.

Helen knew she should keep her mouth shut, but apparently the painkillers were in charge of her actions now. "How'd you find out about the fraud, anyway?"

"My mother told me." The judge paused in her search of the cabinets to turn and face Helen. "Can you believe it? I only volunteered for the board so I could be sure my mother was in a good place, and my being there didn't help at all. Pierce was still cheating Mom, right under my nose. He'd been billing for physical therapy she never received, and she didn't tell me for months, because she didn't want to worry me."

"Family can be like that," Helen said. "I'd have been furious if someone had been taking advantage of my nieces. It wouldn't be enough just to have her arrested. I'd want to confront her directly. Like you did with Melissa."

Judge Nolan nodded and went back to opening and closing cabinet doors. "It wasn't going to be easy for anyone, once the police were involved and the story hit the news and the grapevine. I was going to get a lot of criticism for not preventing the fraud. I needed to know the truth. Beyond a reasonable doubt."

Helen's nod of agreement turned into a whole series of nods. She had to hold her head to make it stop bobbing. "You tried to convince Melissa to turn herself in, and when she refused you got angry and murdered her."

"Not murder," the judge corrected sharply. It was self-defense."

"Either way," Helen said, "Melissa still ended up dead."

"It matters to me," the judge said, seeming distracted by whatever she'd just found in a drawer. "You need to understand that I didn't mean to kill her. It wasn't my fault. I was on the way to her house, and we would have passed each other on the road, except her car had broken down, and she was waiting for the tow truck. I stopped and offered her a ride, so we could talk about the fraud."

"She asked you to bring her here?"

"Said she had found your walking cane and wanted to return it to you."

"She was lying," Helen said.

"I'm not surprised." The judge paused in her search of the drawer in front of her. "She lied about everything, didn't she? She certainly denied that she and Pierce had done anything wrong. I've been on the bench long enough that I've seen much better liars than she was. Eventually, they'll trip themselves up."

"Literally?" Helen said. "Melissa tripped and hit her head? But there wasn't anything near her body that could have done that much damage."

"It would have been so much better if that's what happened," the judge said wistfully. "Melissa did kill herself, in a sense, but not by tripping. She just kept lying about what she and Pierce had done and why she was at the cottage. When her key didn't work on your front door, I thought she'd break down and admit everything, but she came up with another story. I've learned to be patient, so I pretended to believe her. She wanted us to go around to the back deck, where she said there was a hidden spare key. I kept trying to reason with her, telling her she had to admit what she'd done and turn herself in and cooperate with the case against Pierce. And that's when she spun around with your cane raised to hit me. She missed, and it must have surprised her, because she hesitated just long enough for me to grab it away from her."

"You must have been pretty certain you were right about her at that point," Helen said. "Why didn't you just leave then?"

"I tried. I was already a few feet away from her when she screamed and started running at me. She was wearing her nursing clogs, much better suited for your lawn, and I was in my pumps. There was no way I could outrun her, not without more of a head start. So I spun around, intending to shove her to the ground just to slow her down. I'd forgotten about the cane, but my subconscious hadn't, and the next thing I knew she was on the ground, dead, with her blood all over the cane and my suit."

"Why didn't you just call the police and tell them what happened?"

"I meant to," Judge Nolan said. "But I needed to clear some things up at my office first, so I changed into a spare suit that I always keep in the car for emergencies, bagged up the bloody clothes, and went to the courthouse. Then I lost track of time until one of the court officers came into my chambers to tell me that Melissa's body had been found, and the police suspected it was the work of the Remote Control Burglar. I thought it might be best if they continued to think that. After all, it was self-defense, so I hadn't committed murder, but if everyone knew that I'd killed someone, it would have made it more difficult to do my job, presiding over criminal trials."

The judge seemed to feel the need to justify her actions, much like Helen's ex had never been able to accept blame for any problems in their personal lives, without first trying to split legal hairs to prove he was right, even when he knew he was wrong. Especially when he knew he was wrong. The habit had always annoyed her, but it might actually come in handy right now. As the judge laid out the detailed argument in her defense, the fog in Helen's head was beginning to dissipate. Not enough, but it might lift enough for her to escape if she could just keep the judge explaining her motives. "So you were the one who tipped the police to Jack's role in the remote control burglaries."

"I saw him with you at the nursing home, and getting him arrested seemed like a good way to distract you from investigating Melissa's death. His family has quite a reputation here in town, so the police were more than happy to follow up on the tip."

"You'd let an innocent man go to jail for you?"

"I'm telling you, I didn't do anything wrong, and everything would have worked out just fine if you hadn't meddled. I never thought Jack was really the Remote Control Burglar. I figured the real one wasn't stupid enough to stick around and get caught after all these years," she said. "Whatever game he'd been playing might have had its rewards up until recently, but it couldn't possibly have been worth the risk of being implicated in a murder. If he'd had any sense at all, he would have destroyed any evidence that could connect him to the burglaries and left town for good measure, starting fresh somewhere else, and the police would have had to let Jack go eventually for lack of evidence But no. The burglar had to be a Clary, and Clarys never leave Wharton for more than a few hours at a time. Compared to Jack's cousins, he's practically a world traveler, since he drives all the way to the airport on a regular basis, but even he would never completely relocate."

"You can still turn yourself in now."

"No, I can't." She had one of Helen's prescription bottles in her hand. The one containing narcotic painkillers. Judge Nolan poured all of them into her palm and stared at them.

Helen didn't know for sure how many would constitute a lethal dose, but she'd only taken four or five, including the two this evening, since filling the prescription. There had to be more than enough left for the judge to kill herself with. The only question was how quickly the pills would act. Would there be time to get help after the judge took the pills and passed out? She couldn't take the chance that it would be too late then.

Could she knock the pills out of the judge's hand? Helen wasn't even sure she could stand up. She tried, as she spoke. "You don't need to do this. Everyone respects you. They'll understand that it was self-defense."

"They couldn't have impeached me for anything I did in self-defense, but they could get me now for the cover-up. I'm not ready to retire, and I probably never will be. Melissa and I had that much in common, our dedication to our jobs. Except I do important and useful work, while she was hurting people." She closed her hand around the pills and looked up, resolute once again. "The citizens of Wharton need me."

"They do need you," Helen said as she finally managed to push herself onto her feet to stand somewhat unsteadily. "You can't take those pills."

"The pills aren't for me," Judge Nolan said, advancing on Helen. "They're for you."

CHAPTER TWENTY-ONE

———

"I don't need any more painkillers right now."

The judge smiled. "You already took some? Good. That should confuse the autopsy blood work sufficiently that they won't know the exact time of the overdose. I doubt anyone would think to question me about your death, but if they do, I was in the courtroom most of the last few hours. I have at least a dozen witnesses to my being there whenever you took the first pills."

Helen looked for her cane. It had stopped Pierce, and it would stop the judge. Except it wasn't where it should be, next to the front door. Then she remembered she'd taken it into the bathroom to clean off the blood and had left it there. It was too late to retrieve it now, with the judge between Helen and the hallway.

Helen took an involuntary step backwards and bumped against the recliner. It was enough to knock her off balance, and she fell into the chair. There was no time to gather her strength to try standing again. She reached surreptitiously for the cell phone in her pocket.

The judge leaned over her. "Just relax and take your pills like a good little patient."

Helen clamped her mouth shut and shook her head.

"Don't be difficult," Judge Nolan said. "I've done this a time or two before, you know."

Helen's eyes widened.

"Oh, don't look so horrified," Judge Nolan said. "I didn't kill anyone. Except Melissa, of course, and that was an accident. I just meant that I've given pills to a reluctant patient before. My mother's been resisting her heart medications for the last few months, on the bad days when she can't remember who I am."

The judge pinched Helen's nose, not hard enough to leave a bruise, but enough to make it impossible to breathe without opening her mouth. Helen resisted the automatic urge to do just that. If she was going to use her phone, though, she had to do it now while the judge's hands were both occupied. Helen hadn't had this particular model of phone for long enough to dial it without looking, so she raised it just enough to be able to glance down at the numbers.

She only managed to hit the 9 before the judge released Helen's nose to grab the phone. Judge Nolan erased the number and then tossed the phone across the room. "What a pity you dropped your phone and broke it before you took the pills. If you'd had it, you might have been able to call for help when you realized you'd overdosed."

"No one who knows me will believe I overdosed," Helen said before the judge leaned over her again.

"But that's the beauty of the situation," Judge Nolan said. "The people who know you won't be directly involved in the investigation. And no one here knows you. Not like they know me. I'm sure I can drop a few hints about your instability, and no one will question anything. Now, open wide."

Helen clamped her mouth shut, and the judge pinched Helen's nose again.

Helen tried to push up out of the chair, but the judge just used the fist holding the pills to press down on Helen's shoulder, keeping her in place. Frustrated, and feeling a little faint from lack of oxygen, Helen struck out with her hands, pushing at the judge, who grunted in surprise but didn't move more than an inch or so.

Helen needed to do something more decisive than pushing the judge back inch by inch; she needed to incapacitate her, at least briefly. Otherwise, it would be nothing more than a back-and-forth shoving match that Helen couldn't win. She had to aim for a more sensitive spot, one that would hurt enough to give the woman pause. The face or ears, perhaps.

Helen struck out again, this time aiming for the woman's head, but, seated as she was in the depths of the recliner with Judge Nolan leaning over her, she couldn't reach that high. Her fingers brushed the chunky stones of the judge's necklace.

How strong was that necklace, anyway? Helen had read once about a woman who was inadvertently strangled by her own necklace, although that one had been made of leather. The judge's necklace wasn't that heavy, but its stones were strung on a thick silk cord, which looked more than capable of serving as a garrote. The weakest element might be where the two ends connected, but usually one of the hallmarks of pricey jewelry was the strength of its clasp. It was certainly worth a try if the judge really intended to kill her.

The judge had the advantage of having been able to breathe freely for the last few seconds, so Helen had to get at least a little more air into her lungs before she made her move. She kept her teeth clenched but opened her lips in a grimace to let in whatever air she could, without giving the judge access to her mouth.

"That's a good girl," the judge said. "Just a little wider, please, opening the jaw too. Although really, this will do. All I have to do is put the pills inside your cheeks and wait for them to dissolve. It will take a bit longer that way, but I'm a patient person. It's one of the traits that make me a good judge."

Helen tried to ignore the image of herself sitting here, unable to breathe properly, while the lethal pills dissolved in her mouth and the judge waited patiently for the end. It was a little too easy to picture, which only renewed her determination not to give in. It was bad enough that people insisted on helping her against her will when she knew the help actually benefited her; she was not going to sit still for someone helping her to die, which definitely didn't benefit her.

Helen's irritation gave her a spurt of adrenaline, and she used it to grab the judge's necklace and twist the cord around a finger, making it into a tourniquet. For a moment, she thought it might break, and she forced herself to slow down, tightening it gradually so as not to put any sudden pressure on the cord or the clasp.

"Cut it out." The judge pulled back, trying to get Helen to release her without, in turn, releasing Helen's nose. "You're going to break it, and I don't have time to waste on getting it fixed."

Helen tugged carefully on the necklace and decided that no, the cord was not going to break. She was growing lightheaded, though, so she didn't have time to gloat.

The necklace was going to hold, and the judge needed to choose between freeing herself and feeding Helen the lethal dose of painkillers. The only question was whether the judge would pass out before Helen did. Helen had the advantage that she could get some air, even if it wasn't anywhere near what her panicked lungs were demanding. The judge's air, as well as the blood supply to her brain was going to be completely cut off in another twist of the necklace.

Helen twisted, aware that the blood supply to her fingers was also being cut off, and the pain was beyond even the power of the painkillers in her system to deal with. Still, it was better than dying.

The judge's lips were turning blue around the edges of her lipstick, and her eyes were going wide in anger, but she remained determined to hold onto Helen's nose. She even began dropping pills onto Helen's mouth, pushing them between her teeth and her cheeks.

They were going to kill each other, Helen thought. Just like in the movies, when the hero and the villain manage to shoot each other in the final showdown. The villain would be stopped, but only at the cost of the hero's death.

Better than dying without taking the judge with her, Helen decided, and twisted the necklace one more time.

The judge made a strangled sound, dropped the remaining pills all over Helen's face, and using the one free hand to grab for the necklace, tried to slip her fingers underneath the thick silk cord. It was too tight, and her only escape would have been to jerk away from Helen, but she couldn't do that without releasing Helen's nose.

The judge gave her head a tiny shake, a show of defiance, and stared at Helen, a wordless challenge.

What was she doing? Why didn't she just give up and save herself? Helen had a belated realization that the judge, given her experience with criminal trials, probably knew just how long it took to pass out from pressure on her neck compared to how long it would take Helen to pass out from lack of oxygen, and had calculated that Helen was going to go first, and then she wouldn't be able to resist the pills.

And then it dawned on Helen's painkiller-fogged, oxygen-starved brain, that the judge had dropped all the pills, scattering them all over the chair and the floor. Helen could open her mouth to breathe and even spit out the pills already in her cheek long before the judge could possibly retrieve the ones she'd dropped.

Helen's grimace became a smile of triumph as she unclenched her jaw and sucked in as much air as she could. She could breathe, and Judge Nolan couldn't. Even before her breathing normalized, the judge's eyes fluttered closed and she dropped to the floor.

Helen waited a moment to make sure the judge wasn't faking it before releasing the necklace, hoping that she hadn't held it too long. She didn't want to kill the judge, just give herself enough time to escape.

Helen unwound the cord, massaged the feeling back into her fingers, and checked the woman's pulse, which was still beating. Then she limped over to her bedroom, and just in case the judge regained consciousness before the police and ambulance arrived, she locked herself inside. As she dug out one of her spare cell phones, she couldn't help thinking that if it hadn't been for Melissa, Helen wouldn't have had hidden extra phones all around the house, and she'd have had to scramble out of the cottage and through the woods to the neighbors' house again. She refused to feel grateful, though, as she dialed the emergency number. If it hadn't been for Melissa, Helen also wouldn't have been the target of a murderer.

CHAPTER TWENTY-TWO

———

"I'm fine," Helen told the paramedic twenty minutes later.

For once, Helen didn't mind that her nieces were hovering over her, tidying up the cottage and fluffing her pillows while she sat in the recliner. They could stay, but the paramedic had to leave now. He should be outside with his partner, helping to take care of the judge who was out in the ambulance. Detective Peterson hadn't been willing to handcuff Judge Nolan to the gurney, but he did have a couple uniformed officers watching her.

"Aunt Helen is *not* fine," Lily told the paramedic. "If you knew her you'd know that the fact that she's letting us fuss over her means that she doesn't feel strong enough to chase us away. That's not good."

Laura stood behind the recliner with her hands on Helen's shoulders, patting them anxiously. "Maybe you should go to the hospital, just to be checked over."

"No." Helen looked at the paramedic, a pleasant but persistent young man who was crouched down to be at her eye level. "I've already told you the date, the address here, and the president's name. I'm a little sleepy from the original doses of painkiller, but I'm fully oriented, I'm breathing normally, and I'm not bleeding. You took my pulse and blood pressure, and they're fine, considering someone just tried to kill me. I really don't need your help."

"Never mind," Lily said. "I know that look. She's not going anywhere. At least not while she's conscious. If she passes out, we'll drag her to the hospital."

"You'll keep an eye on her?" the paramedic said. "She shouldn't be alone for the next few hours."

Oh, great. Helen wouldn't mind someone staying here overnight, but Lily was probably already calculating how many hours there were in a whole week, and considering whether she could argue that it counted as the medically recommended *few.* If Helen wasn't careful, the nieces would be using the paramedic's advice to justify a full-time, live-in nurse for the rest of her life.

"Could you be more specific about that?" Helen asked the paramedic. "Exactly how many hours do I need to be watched?"

The paramedic laughed as he packed away his blood pressure cuff. "No one's ever asked me that before. Somewhere between twelve and twenty-four hours. If you're going to have any problems, they should manifest by tomorrow morning."

"I can stay with her overnight," Lily said.

Satisfied, the paramedic picked up his equipment and headed for the door.

"Just the one night," Helen said. "I can take care of myself after that."

"You haven't done so well at it recently," Lily said. "You've been associating with an infamous burglar, you were assaulted in your own home by a con man, and then you opened your door to a murderer."

Helen decided not to ask how she knew about Pierce. Adam had probably passed along the news, and the nieces had jumped into the car to check on her without calling first. Bringing it up would only remind Lily that Helen hadn't been the one to tell her nieces about the incident. She'd save that conversation for another day. "Jack wouldn't hurt me, and I dealt with the other two all by myself. No security system, no nurse, no bodyguard. Not bad for a decrepit old woman."

"A decrepit *lucky* woman," Lily said.

On the paramedic's way out he held the front door for Detective Peterson to come in.

The detective loomed over the recliner. "I just need to go over your story once more. Are you absolutely sure the judge killed Melissa?"

"I'm sure," Helen said. "She confessed to me. And you saw the pills she tried to make me swallow."

"It's just that, well, you thought it was Pierce before, from what I'm told," Peterson said. "And, well, we're talking about *the judge*."

She heard the unspoken words: Judge Nolan was someone he'd known and respected for years. All of his life, probably. And he didn't know Helen at all. Not in any good way at least.

She knew it was a lot for the detective to absorb. She wasn't sure she'd absorbed it yet herself. But the detective was listening to her, really listening, which was a big improvement over his previous attitude. She didn't have enough energy to get out of her chair and do a proper *I told you so* dance right now anyway, so she didn't demand an apology for his earlier dismissal of her input.

"I know it's difficult to believe," Helen said. "I couldn't imagine it at first myself, or I wouldn't have let her into the cottage. I would have caught on faster if I'd remembered that the judge had been here right after you took away the murder weapon. I think she was hoping to find it before you did. She probably hadn't been too worried when you had the wrong murder weapon, and there was no reason to suspect her. But once you knew about the cane, there was a risk that her fingerprints were on it, just waiting for some time in the future when the judge's fingerprints might end up in some database. As long as I kept questioning the theory that the Remote Control Burglar had killed Melissa, she would never have been completely safe from exposure."

Detective Peterson obviously wished Helen was wrong, but he couldn't simply ignore her this time. "The forensics team did lift some prints from the cane. I'll make sure they're compared to the judge's."

"There's probably some evidence in her car too," Helen said. "The judge gave Melissa a ride to my house the morning she was killed, so there might be something to confirm that they were together then."

"Did she tell you anything else we should know?"

"There's a bag with the judge's blood-covered suit somewhere. Maybe still in her car," Helen said. "Call me if you think of anything else." Detective Peterson left the cottage, appearing as anxious to leave as Helen was to have him leave.

She could hear voices just outside her front door, although she couldn't make out the actual words as Detective Peterson chatted with Tate and his nephew.

A couple minutes later, the two attorneys let themselves inside. Adam looked past Helen at Lily, an infatuated look on his face, confirming her guess about how the nieces had found out about the situation so quickly. Adam had ratted her out. She was about to lecture Lily on the unfairness of using her feminine wiles on poor, defenseless attorneys, when she noticed that for the first time ever Lily looked equally infatuated with one of her admirers.

No wonder Lily had been so quick to volunteer to stay here overnight. She'd be closer to Adam. Next thing, Lily would be volunteering to move to Wharton. At least this way she'd want her own space without an aunt serving as an inconvenient chaperone.

"Lily," Helen said. "Would you and Adam please go outside and see if there are still police and rescue vehicles blocking the driveway? I bet Laura would like to be able to go home to Howie, and I'd like to talk to Tate for a minute."

Lily herded Laura and Adam outside, and Tate dropped into the sofa across from her. "I knew you were going to be trouble. Strangling a judge into unconsciousness. How do you think the replacement judge is going to feel about that?"

"That justice was served?"

"I doubt it. Judges take a real dim view of their colleagues being attacked, even if it was more than justified. They might even blame the attacker's attorney." He looked more energized by the challenge than his words suggested. "You won't have to work with Judge Nolan's replacement, but I probably will, since you won't let me retire from the practice of law."

"You did say you liked a challenge," she said. "And you've got to admit that I lived up to my promise that any murder case I got involved with wouldn't be an ordinary one."

"I appreciate that, but I didn't expect you to get yourself assaulted just to keep me entertained."

"It won't happen again," Helen said. "I'll leave you to find your own entertainments, all alone out in the garage, as soon as you make sure that the murder charges against Jack are dismissed."

"About the garage," he said. "Now that you don't need my legal advice any longer, are you going to evict me?"

"I hadn't planned to." Tate was never intrusive the way Melissa had been, and his presence would keep her nieces from worrying or trying to impose someone else on her. "Not as long as you don't pester me the way everyone else does."

"You're the one who keeps interrupting me."

"It won't happen again," Helen said. "Now that Melissa's murder is solved, I can take care of myself. I won't be pestering you for any more advice on criminal matters."

Still, it was kind of nice to know that while she didn't need help most of the time, on those few occasions when she did she would have someone nearby to call on. She could rely on him to wait until she asked for help, and to never, ever be cheerful when he was helping her.

ABOUT THE AUTHOR

Gin Jones is a lawyer who specializes in ghost-writing for other lawyers. She prefers to write fiction, though, since she doesn't have to worry that her sense of humor might get her thrown into jail for contempt of court. In her spare time, Gin makes quilts, grows garlic and serves on the board of directors for the XLH Network.

To learn more about Gin Jones, visit her online at:
https://thewritegin.blogspot.com

Enjoyed this book? Check out these other fun reads available in print now from
Gemma Halliday Publishing:

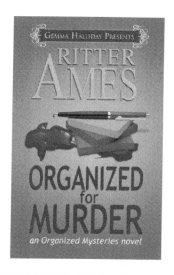

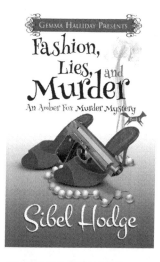

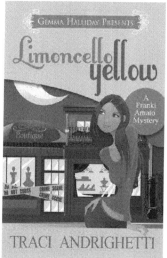

www.GemmaHalliday.com/Halliday_Publishing

Made in the USA
Charleston, SC
15 June 2014